E

EarthZoo

P.R. SHEPHERDSON

Published by Rusty Penny Books

A CIP catalogue record for this book is available from the British Library.

ISBN 978-0-9930053-0-5

Book design & layout by Clare Brayshaw

Prepared and printed by:

York Publishing Services Ltd
64 Hallfield Road
Layerthorpe
York YO31 7ZQ

Tel: 01904 431213

Website: www.yps-publishing.co.uk

Contents

CHAPTER ONE

Doorstep World

Doorsteps come in all shapes and sizes and York's Micklegate has its fair share. My favourite one is half way up, or half way down this street, depending on your viewpoint. After a good or a bad night out it's my final resting place.

Tonight, or perhaps more accurately 2am early morning was a deviation to this rule. This doorstep felt familiar yet it was further up the street than my usual. Although cold and wet (it had been raining) vital things were missing. I should be totally drunk as normal at this time and the inclination of the cobbled road (it's on a hill) should be swaying pleasantly so that I have to hang on to the doorway. Now however I have never felt so level headed; practically buzzing. The last time I felt like this was after my divorce five years ago! It was to be short lived of course with mother dying and then losing my job, all within two months of each other. The road accident was the final straw. I realised now that this had been no excuse to go to pieces and turn myself into an alcoholic. I had hit rock bottom and then discovered there was a basement attached to it.

Fragmented thoughts filled my mind. My previous recollection was last night in my living room. There was a gap between that memory and now, but this morning painful thoughts had taken on a fresh perspective and had become more soft focussed and manageable. I had become a new dynamic person squatting within this No 84 doorway; there was a purpose in my life – if only I could remember it!

Plainly focused within my right hand was an empty whisky bottle. The equation – alcohol plus mouth – should equal oblivion? Another vital point was my clothes: they were as dry as parchment yet outside my doorway the rain was pelting down. The final thing that spooked me was on my feet. I was wearing carpet slippers. Now I know that occasionally I am forgetful but tonight coupled with all the other irregularities that took the final straw. I began to shake and it wasn't with the cold. Something nuzzled against my left thigh. Looking up at me with shiny red eyes was a rat the size of a small cat. We gazed at each other with curiosity and silence. The rat had wet black fur, slender delicate paws and shimmering whiskers. It began to wash itself vigorously. "Don't forget behind your ears," I whispered.

Down the far end of the street the echo of footsteps sharp upon the dawn air began to hold dominion. Fearing that it might be the police, I cowered within the doorway: being arrested for vagrancy was all I needed. A figure abruptly appeared. All black glasses, white overcoat and black hair he scrutinised me closely. "There you are Ross. How are you feeling?"

"I am fine thank you – just taking a rest." I scrutinised him closely. "Do I know you?"

"Don't worry; it will take some time to adjust to your new surroundings."

He took off up the street and I watched transfixed at this retreating form. The rat too then scurried off into the advancing dish water sunrise. I stood up to go home. An abrupt thought trickled into my mind. I am in love with Stella, if only I could find out where or more importantly: who she is.

CHAPTER TWO

The Forever Present

At Time Loop Purple

A silent scream fills my head and stays there like a congealing wound. I am rigid with pain that sears from my throat and down my upper body. My face is covered preventing me from seeing anything but a dull blackness. Occasionally I smell a cold waft of ozone, and it reminds me of an electric train set I had when I was a boy. The breeze dances over my body and I know that I must be naked. If only I could see. As if in answer my sight is restored and I gaze up into a masked face bathed in a red glow.

"Am I in hospital?"

Abruptly the masked face descends until it hovers inches away. An illusion of peace claws my senses and I am flying through soft woolly clouds. I fight against this drugged state of mind and regain consciousness but the penalty is the return of agony. Once more he is back inside my mind sifting and scattering my thoughts like confetti. I can hear the whirr of a helicopter, the smell of aviation fumes and then Auster's worried face swims into view. Pointing straight at me is a gun. There's a sound like a branch snapping and instantly I double up in pain. In stark contrast, close up, there is a woman's bloodied face looking concerned at me.

"Stella?" My voice sounds dull and far away. With tremendous effort I snarl. "These are my private emotions and not for sharing. Love, hate, can't you feel the difference?"

My body convulses as if a lightning bolt had skewered it. Around me are three swan-like necks bearing down upon my throat; red needle-points of light spit from each; they look like lasers. A sound like a faint swarm of bees hypnotise my senses.

"Who are you?" I gasp.

The figure totally ignores me; his entire concentration and hand movement are focused around my throat and upper body. I began to realise that this is no hospital because I am totally reclined within a dentist chair. Above my head, beyond the face beyond the smell, and beyond my pain I can see an oval shaped window. Through that I swim into a whirlpool of stars. Abruptly my friendly clouds return.

I have no concept of time but hours must surely have passed before I regain consciousness again. My attention is drawn towards a focused beam of light that spills from a huge porthole in the domed ceiling and onto the floor. The room itself is small and circular with a dank musty smell giving it a cavern like impression. The single light beam was too weak to reveal my surroundings with any clarity. What I do see however fills me with dread. Against the far wall are three stainless steel cabinets that look like water fountains. Protruding from each are thin swan-like necks. I glance down and see that I am wearing a single piece of white clothing that looks oriental in design and texture. The flat slab upon which I am lying appears like white rock – but is soft to the touch.

Close by I become aware of a strange swishing sound and then a subtle fragrance of cinnamon wafts into my nostrils.

"Are you rested?"

That whispered voice fills my head. I sit bolt upright frantically trying to locate its source but there is no one there. "Where are you?" I exclaim.

"It is of no matter. Tell me, can you remember where you live?" I suddenly feel a sense of loss; of being homesick.

"I live in the City of York," I murmur.

"Do you know it well?"

"I thought I did but your viewpoint can change."

"You mean your friend David Austerfield?"

"How do you know so much about me?"

The voice is urgent, almost demanding now. "He has stolen something of ours?"

"I know nothing about it."

"But you do."

"How come?"

"You must find him for us"

"I haven't seen Austerfield!"

"You will. A new beginning awaits you. Now sleep and forget everything you have learnt here."

"I most definitely will not! Who are you?"

"I am merely a figment of your imagination. For you, I simply do not exist."

"I know you exist."

"Not for long."

"What are you going to do?"

"Relax. There is nothing to fear. You reside here in the 'Forever Present' and are safe."

"Safe? I don't think so."

"Relax. Now tell me more about your City of York?"

CHAPTER THREE

Dark Undercurrents

Time Loop Purple

"I thought I knew the City of York with its Roman Walls, and museums – you know, from the tourist viewpoint of things. It holds an easy pace and charm; a place to relax and unwind. Of course I don't believe that now."

"Why is that?"

"Beneath the surface of this city lie dark undercurrents of extortion, petty criminals and murder. There's easy money to be made and that can attract amateurs down on their luck. The lucky ones get arrested – whilst the others? The river Ouse holds council on many a grisly secret."

"You are one of the lucky ones."

"Why do you say that?"

CHAPTER FOUR

Cardboard Passport

Time Loop Red

Bad dreams come in all shapes and sizes, mine just happened to involve poverty. Early one morning with the sun struggling to fight through the rain, I awoke distracted by thoughts. Something important was going to happen today, but what it was, totally escaped me. I staggered downstairs and gazed around at the practical realities of life.

One was to wash the dishes; my second was to tidy up the living room until it looked more like its name. I picked up a full whisky bottle from beneath my room table with feelings of disgust. How had I allowed myself to sink so low? Abruptly however, that all familiar desire arrived again: I badly needed a drink. The cork top was pulled out. It was a tussle between emptying the contents down my throat or life. I paused and marvelled at its dark yellow colour; its clarity of nature; its distinct rich aroma. Close up and personal the aroma was very overpowering. Compulsion and anger created an imbalance; I paused at this crossroads to destiny. "Get thee behind me!" I shouted which instantly caused me to giggle. With deftness the top was twisted back on and this Devil was hidden within the confines of the fridge next to the milk.

A glance at my 'Yunphuk' made 'Rolkex' informed me that it was Wednesday. It also said 4am but I was confident only the day was correct. This was a new experience for me: being focussed and coherent before midday. I made my way towards the bathroom via the hallway. The same heap of letters that lay upon the doormat since yesterday greeted me like an old friend. I reached down to fumble through my post, and one caught my eye. It was from the Job Centre. Experience had taught me that Second Class meant that I hadn't been selected for interview. This postage was First Class and thus promising. Cautiously I peeled open the envelope and peeked inside. An interview! The bad news was, it was for 11 am. So what was the correct time? In a frantic state I rushed into the living room and looked at my Grandfather clock. 9.00 am. I would have to hurry.

My wardrobe revealed a suit that needed dry cleaning, mowing, re seeding or throwing out. There was only one man who could help me out of my dilemma and he was called David Austerfield.

If you had impressionable daughters, then keep them well away from him. If you had money to burn and were slightly gullible, ignore his latest scam of a moneymaking opportunity. If you had suffered a recent redundancy; no money or a demolished ego, then he could be your friend for life. However that came at a cost. Honesty was a dirty word in his vocabulary. He bought and sold anything that turned a quick profit; no questions asked. One took a risk of course: it didn't do to examine his merchandise too closely. I glanced down at one of his bargains on my wrist and reset it. I considered how I could explain to him (not too desperately of course) of my immediate need for a decent looking suit.

At this time of the morning, Auster might still be at Christ Church. To catch him, it would mean a stiff walk into York. I hesitated at my front door and turned back to collect a document that the Job Centre insisted I bring with me. It was an unusual requirement for the interview and it unnerved me a little.

Situated between Colliergate and the Shambles is the little building of Christ Church. Commonly called Butchers Church because of its association with the local traders, it is a small quaint little place. With its oblong length and watchtower, the building looked more like it was made from Lego. As the Minster chimed the hour I walked through the church door and headed towards the altar. When I drew closer I noticed fresh red roses and a single glowing candle, the wick fresh and lively. I must have only missed him by minutes. Every Wednesday between ten and eleven he would be here with flowers, lighting a candle and praying over the once, real love of his life.

His wife's sudden death was a tremendous shock and I don't think he ever recovered from it. After a particular drunken night out Auster confided to me that he would never re-marry.

As I turned to leave I saw next to the altar rail, a rolled up bundle. It was a thick wad of twenty-pound notes bound with two red rubber bands; Auster's, trademark.

A new suit sprang to mind.

I held firmly onto my find and hastened towards the sunlit porch. At the doorway within a halo of light, a fresh-faced Vicar smiled towards me. With a tugging conscience I mentally informed him that I would repay this debt to Auster later, much later.

The Job Centre was a non-descript building looking half way between a warehouse and a fast food outlet. I gulped hard and entered.

"Can I have your name please and your Reference number?" Her matter-of-fact stare and bored voice made me wish I could turn and run away.

As she brushed back her curly brown hair, I caught sight of dynamic blue eyes that matched her suit. My confidence like my grubby suit struggled to regain a former glory.

"RF457. The name's Ross."

"Is that for the researcher vacancy?"

I felt a lump in my throat. "Yes that's right,"I croaked.

There was a questioning tilt to her head now. "It's a phone number, I'll ring shall I?"

The phone connected and she said something I didn't quite catch. The receiver was handed over to me but I scarcely had time to speak, when a simpering male voice suggested an interview to be arranged at twelve noon today at the Station Hotel. His squeaky voice unnerved me but what can a poor peasant do: bills have to be paid. He claimed I was one of several that day; I didn't believe him. Even over the phone, the glib sales patter irritated me. And what Company of any status held interviews in a hotel foyer? So why was I here? I tried to kid myself that money had nothing to do with it. In my back pocket was a thick wad of notes, yet I was honestly broke. I must be the richest dole seeker she had interviewed.

Leaving behind the tolling bell of Great Peter, I walked into the lounge of the Hotel and tried to identify my potential boss. At one end appeared to be a desk which looked like the Reception. At my approach a short cropped brunette looked up at me; her elfin face beamed like a toothpaste commercial. I paused for a minute and stroked my lip in contemplation. She had the power to make or break my day.

"I have an interview with Mr Smythe from Eboracum Television."

She cast her gaze down the hotel's family bible before giving me her apologetic reply. "Sorry. There is no Company of that name here. Smith did you say?"

"No! It's Smythe. That's with an 'E'." Slowly she shook her head and perused the register again. "Not here I'm afraid."

I stared wild-eyed at her. "He said he was staying here for a couple of nights."

Her glance was sharp, like off cheese. "Have you got the right day?"

My immediate response was to ask her to recheck, but impatient breathing upon my neck dampened my resolution and so I merely shrugged my reply.

With great reluctance, I turned to walk away and immediately collided with a man behind me. All black glasses, black limp hair and gaunt face, he appeared clearly embarrassed.

I walked over to where a huge rubber plant was attempting to mate with the stair's ironwork banister and carefully looked around. There were four tables that held four possibilities.

One had a male and female arguing, no doubt that they were husband and wife! On the second, another story was being played out: a couple sitting so close you couldn't see the join. They seemed to exist for each precious moment. She looked married but he didn't. And at the third was the man I had somehow bumped into earlier; he was busy fussing with his shoelaces, but where had I seen him before?

It was then that I saw a man in deep conversation with a youth. They sat almost touching. Nervously clutching his rucksack, the young lad appeared clearly intimidated. The interviewer – all bald head like a wrinkled walnut – wore a baggy almost crumpled black suit that put me instantly on my guard. Presently the youth left. From the seclusion of my rubber plant I observed the man's next intention. He looked around, almost like a snake seeking prey.

With a confident air, I walked towards him. "Mr Smythe I presume?" Taken somewhat aback he eyed me up and down before replying. Abruptly we were both distracted by angry voices coming from the direction of Reception. An American tourist, all five-gallon hat and swishing waistcoat, clearly was expressing dissatisfaction over his hotel bill. Eventually the matter was finally settled and he was ushered to the entrance. Silence brought a moment of reverence.

"Who wants to know?"

I turned to look towards Smythe. From beneath those shifty eyes, what was he hiding? I looked at him with grave politeness. "The name's Ross."

His worry lines reminded me of a ploughed field and his voice, crisp as Walkers. His face softened. "Of course: the noon appointment! Please let me apologise but I have to be careful you know, competition is fierce in this game." He motioned me over towards the table where I had seen the youth vacate earlier.

As he lit a cigarette and sprawled down over a chair I gave him a studious look. Extremely thin with bulbous eyes and small narrow lips, he reminded me of a tarantula. The job he described was a pretty simple affair, nothing elaborate. All the competent researcher had to do was collect names and addresses from the general public about their preferred TV programmes. It was too simple, but there was a catch. "Can you start right away? I need an answer within, let's say..." He paused clawing the air. "Let's say by the end of today?"

I heard myself saying casually. "I would like to think about it," whilst my fingernails bit into the chair arm.

Smythe leant forward and I caught the whiff of sweaty aftershave. His response had now acquired the same texture. "I have got other candidates to consider you know. However I am very pleased with you and I feel that we could work well together. A man of your calibre should know when he is offered such a prestigious position?"

I allowed my ego to glow awhile, but then confirmed my statement with an attempted smile.

His reply was cold and caught me off guard. "Don't leave it too long. Oh! Have you got your passport with you? Did they tell you it was one of the requirements for the vacancy?"

As I retrieved the document and handed it over, my thoughts returned back to this morning. How I wished now that I had stayed safe in bed. His cursory glance made me nervous and I felt intimidated by the way he tucked the passport back inside my pocket. Abruptly he got up and gave me a limp handshake. It was an unpleasant cold sweaty experience and I was pleased when he let go.

"I will let you know," he said briskly, and without waiting for any reply he left. I watched bewildered at this retreating form until the revolving doors swallowed him up.

At home I pondered his offer. After much soul and bill searching I finally rang his number. There was no reply. A feeling of unease overcame me. It was then that I realised that my passport was missing. A neat touch: from inside my coat all I found was a piece of cardboard.

That night, my diary related a depressing account. I fell into restless, faltering sleep. The next day I reported my theft to the Police. Their matter-of-fact methods made me feel inadequate.

Time Loop Purple

"Hush now. It's time to forget."

CHAPTER FIVE

A Missing Church

Time Loop Blue

"Where has Christ Church disappeared to?"

The man to my left, all duffel coat, acne and bushy eyebrows looked at me perplexed. "There's a church around the corner in Goodramgate pal, but this is King's Square and there's no church here." He then scurried away. I watched his diminishing form and somehow felt relieved when he entered the Shambles. At least that medieval street still existed. Somehow, that felt comforting.

King's Square comprised of stone slab flooring and dotted with wooden benches. Upon these sat a multitude of tourists busily immersing their faces inside fish and chip trays.

"Careful! Watch what you're doing."

I must have sat down rather abruptly upon a nearby bench. Adjacent to my right sat a rather plump woman, her face indignant. She shuffled along allowing me room for my left buttock.

"Sorry, I didn't see you there" My apologetic voice seemed far off and detached, as if someone else had spoken. It had done the trick however because she ignored me then, and returned to demolish her fish and chips. I focused upon her stubby ringed fingers that were blathered with grease and batter. It was the only normal thing I could relate to, within this insane world.

Walking around this Square, I noticed that branching off were streets with familiar names like: Goodramgate, Church Street and Colliergate. Close to an ice cream cart there was a black stoned plaque on the pavement. Inscribed it read:-

'Holy Trinity Church commonly called Christ Church stood on this site in Kings Court for over seven centuries until 1937'.

For some considerable time I stood there, closing my mind to everything but that plaque. An entire church that had existed for centuries suddenly had vanished! I was baffled. Perhaps Auster somehow had played a very cruel trick on me, but he really had excelled himself this time.

This had been a nightmare morning for me already. To find myself in the early hours, slumped inside a Micklegate doorway with no idea how I had got there, and then there was that cloying comatose sleep, which abruptly ended with the letterbox being demolished by the postman. I concluded it was all a nightmare and resolved not to eat cheese at bedtime.

In my pocket was a letter from the Job Centre.

Should I go?

Would it even be there?

In my mind a thought trickled through: it might be useful to keep a record of this: if only to prove my own sanity!

"Please give me your name and Reference number?" Her voice was as soft as snow and complexion to match. I wished I had the nerve to ask her for a date.

I took out my recently acquired diary. "RF457. Oh, the name's Ross."

Her brown eyes caressed mine as she scrutinised her display screen. "That will be the Researcher vacancy?"

I nodded and allowed my attention to wander over her brown suit that was as well cut as her figure. She wore a *brown* suit? From deep within, a memory stirred.

"It's a phone number," she purred."I'll ring shall I?" The phone connected and she said something I didn't quite catch. The phone was handed over to me. I scarcely had time to speak, when a simpering male voice suggested an interview to be arranged at twelve today. His squeaky sales pitch unnerved me and after much soul and bill searching, I thought: "Sod it! I am not that desperate."

I gave her my best smile reserved for such occasions. "Have you anything else on offer?"

She looked shocked. "With your abilities and skills you would be a fool to turn down such a job opportunity Mr Ross. It does seem to be a very reputable Company."

"Have you met the man?"

"Yes I have. Mr Smythe and his partner came into the Job Centre yesterday and so I had the chance to vet them properly. They were both very charming I can assure you of that fact."

"He had a partner?"

"Yes." She looked thoughtful. "He was a tall looking man; nice smile."

"What was he called?"

"I don't recollect the name; does it matter?"

I painted on a smile for her benefit. "Call it premonition, but I've got bad vibes about that interview."

There was an icy touch to her voice now. "What do you mean Mr Ross?"

"He sounded too pushy and after all, I spent eight years in my last job behind the camera, not in front of it."

The way she looked, I felt the temperature plummet. "It is merely for a Researcher; not too difficult for most candidates to accomplish."

I felt myself stand tall and with a proud nod I turned and walked away. At the door I paused. All of this had happened to me before: like a re-run of a movie.

"Mr Ross?"

I turned and even from this distance, her eyes had regained their sensuality.

"Oh go on, give it a try?"

My hand lingered upon the door handle.

CHAPTER SIX

A Personal Goodbye

Time Loop Purple

There was only one Watcher on that fateful shift – the day planet Earth died. Upon the Transit Station he was the latest galactic intelligence (TRINITY) recruit and represented his home planet Tengaluma. If he had known he would be witness to such a catastrophic event he might have done things completely different. Fate though, sometimes loads the dice and there is no chance to alter its outcome. However this game was yet to be played out as he sat huddled at the observation desk nervously caressing his latest Earth toy: a Rubik's cube.

He briefly observed his Watcher Team pack up for their shift end. They never spoke to each other or to him during the duty rosters. Even both their names were unknown to him. They were slip shod in missing out vital detail in their intelligence reports (INTELS). Once more he watched them enter the Transit Alcove; there was no farewell as the transport beam engulfed them taking them home to Gropeni.

The Gropie species were a recent and unknown addition to TRINITY and that caused him great worry. Their sloppiness which often placed field agents at risk annoyed him to the point which made him think it was deliberate.

Haunted with suspicion he scrutinised their Teleport log. Gropeni was their destination yet Earth coordinates had been sloppily input by one of them. "Typical!" he screamed as he corrected the log entry for Gropeni. He shuffled the cube again and shuddered. A brief acknowledgment, even a cursory nod would have made all the difference to these long vigils.

He banged his fist on the desk. "Where could she be?" His brow became covered with sweat. He took deep breaths until he felt more at ease again. This was a career move he would not have chosen through choice. Even the apparatus he used unnerved him with its unnatural angles.

The observation desk was triangular in design and with tripod legs of uneven length at each corner. The top was not flat but had a steep inclined 'V' shape, which held a shoebox like structure. The whole contraption should have fallen over, but enigmatically it did not. It puzzled him a great deal. On top of the box was a crystal lens and his face glowed with an ashen blue light as images danced before his eyes. It drew him in.

The display was the recorded history of a recently discovered planet called Earth. This new planet had experienced a turbulent past of near extinction events. As eons swept by an entire species of creatures had abruptly been wiped out by an asteroid collision. He recoiled back in horror at being witness to this awesome brutality. The scene changed again and with some trepidation he leant forward towards the crystal display. The image now revealed a new species referred to as Homo sapiens. They had now taken precedence on this evolutionary scale. However this species were extremely volatile and dangerous to one another and it wasn't expected that they could survive very long. His face grimaced as he witnessed further bloodshed and carnage but his overall concern was for the Tengalese Watcher teams who were down on the surface. Their job was to observe and catalogue Earth's history. Many had just made it back up to Transit, nearly becoming casualties themselves within this whirlwind of violence. With this in mind he had perhaps been over protective with his daughter Stella. She of course rebelled against his wishes and had volunteered for a field mission on Earth. Then she went missing – the main reason why he had created extra duty rosters for himself to search for her.

Briefly he noted a distress call triangulated from within Earth's stratosphere but the Watcher on that duty roster had only recorded it as an anomaly. Reading the report he realised why: the distress came from a Tengalese spaceship and since even in that century of recording – some sixty Earth years ago – these craft had become obsolete. Furthermore Earth was strictly off limits. Obviously then the Watcher had catalogued it as a local ballistic missile abort signal; however it niggled him and he flagged it up for more detailed classification later. He felt he had just cause: the Watcher in question was one of the Gropie species.

His hand shook as he rotated a dial back to present Earth time. "Where are my teams?" he lamented as he gazed at a blank display. Once more his fist hit the table. "Of all the rosters she could have chosen, why did she have to disappear on one of mine?" He inhaled slowly becoming aware of his rapid heartbeats.

His first duty on the Station had been to create his own field agents who were now below but their *accurate*

INTELS – like their forebears – were also not encouraging. Some indicated that an extraterrestrial presence could have contributed to the lack of Earth's development. The Watcher code was clear regarding non intervention of evolving species by external aliens; The Forum would have to be notified; swift justice would follow.

As evidence was being gathered – which added substance to this scenario – the first deaths began. It began with a young agent who had been involved in a motor vehicle accident. How could that have happened? She had never driven before but her body was discovered at the steering wheel of a car which was all wrapped around a tree like clinging ivy. She had only just got married and he had gone to the wedding. He breathed heavily and shook his head trying to work out this riddle of senseless death. Only one Earth week later more sinister things happened, when it was recorded that a further two had been strangled.

"Where is my errant daughter?" he screamed this time willing the display to feed him with good news for a change. A glance down at the Rubik's cube greatly puzzled him. He wiped his sweaty palms. His shift would soon be over, but he had failed again. Some ill omen was going to happen on this shift – he knew it. Could he endure any more of this torment? He gazed with incredulity at the cube again. All the colours had been correctly aligned and it couldn't have been by his hand. He looked suspiciously around as he jumbled up the sides again.

Abruptly the display suddenly jerked into indiscrete flashes and then a blinding light engulfed the planet.

"Oh no!" he exclaimed. "They have finally annihilated each other." As fast as his hands could work the Teleport controls he attempted to extract all of his Watcher teams. He had been assured that the transport system could not fail because of a built in safety feature called Time Loop Purple. The Transit Station was also bathed securely within it. Well it had failed and for all his attempts, his transport signal couldn't locate any of his teams.

Tears welled up and he wrung his hands. "My poor daughter," he cried. "Where is my poor daughter."

More composed he recorded the Earth end segment and began the routine autopsy on yet another world that failed the evolutionary path towards a stable civilisation.

He looked puzzled at the autopsy results. This should have revealed atomic fallout and biological warfare decay, typical of an all out attack by their species upon each other. What he found however were traces of Tachyon wavelike decay which indicated something totally unexpected. That might also explain the transport problem. Deep in thought he reached for the audio connection to speak to his Control who was back at the (TRINITY) Command Centre.

"Sir we have a problem with planet Earth: it has been totally destroyed." He paused whilst the information was being transmitted but then supplemented his report with what he thought was conclusive evidence. "There has been an unexpected complication which I suggest might need further correlation." He nodded quietly to himself. After all these findings were important so he wanted thinking time at the other end. The reply when it eventually came back was terse and objective and he was not happy with Control's, 'yes I am aware of the facts. Now proceed with the report', command.

"Sir, with respect: please re-evaluate the data I am transmitting to you. I have found traces of Tachyon wavelike decay which may indicate that perhaps..." he paused hoping to emphasise his next statement, "the destruction was assisted by illegal alien interference."

There was a pregnant silence that put his nerves on edge before the reply came back. "Message received and understood. Yes, you are quite right with your concerns regarding this matter. Already I have initiated Protocol 174. As you are new to our organisation, I will assist you with finalising that procedure. When that has been completed, then a detailed forensic analysis can be undertaken. "

His body quivered with emotion as the display now revealed command codes that he had to input. Tears threatened to blind him as he stared. "Protocol 174 – that was the message you want me to complete – cocoon this planet forever within a Red Time Loop?"

"And also close down the Transit Station. Is there a problem with that command?"

"Yes sir! There most certainly is a problem." He imagined the final intense moments leading to his daughter's death and her agony as she was engulfed by an intense fireball of light and heat.

This train of thought was cut short by activity coming from the Transit Alcove. A figure abruptly materialised from within a cocoon of light followed by an acrid smell of burnt wood which permeated the room.

"Boss – thank goodness it's you on duty tonight; there's all hell on down there. A nuclear war's brewing; Stella's been located – and..." His voice tailed off as his body dematerialised leaving a buzz of static. Hastily he attempted at retrieving the transport carrier signal but this proved futile.

Miraculously his team were somehow alive. He gave up caution. As long as he remained cautious he could lose his Watcher Teams forever. He tried to remain analytical and aloof however because Control only responded to pure logic.

"With respect sir, my teams are alive. Transport has picked them up." He could feel his hands shake. "If they are still alive, please let me try to retrieve them. I have personal reasons for doing this," he paused to compose himself. "One agent is in fact...," he felt his voice quiver. "One agent is my daughter."

The reply was swift and uncompromising. "It is too late. I am sorry but finalise Protocol 174. That is my command."

"Please let me at least say goodbye?"

"Cage that planet. That is an order!"

"And turn Earth into a zoo; a deathly Earth zoo that we can scrutinise in cold seclusion – is that it?"

"An Earth zoo scenario?" There was a pregnant silence and he could almost sense Control's brain cells whirring with cold logical analysis. "Now that is an interesting analogy. Re-classify this as: – Operation EarthZoo – now proceed!" The communication abruptly ceased.

He thought quickly. Compassion clearly was not a virtue but perhaps cold facts were. Faithfully the command codes were input, but he gave himself a brief timed interval to do one last thing.

Just before Operation EarthZoo was implemented, he stepped into the Transit Alcove and at the final countdown, transported himself down to the surface.

If they were still alive his mission was twofold: there was a daughter to hug for one last time and then an illegal alien to kill. His life rested on this simple hunch. If he was right then the Earth had survived. But not knowing whether his daughter was alive or dead was too much to bear. He couldn't face that again.

If the Teleport placed him down onto a radioactive toxic planet then in his final moments at least he would know he had tried.

Goodbye is a personal thing – best said face to face.

CHAPTER SEVEN

First Beginnings

Time Loop Red

Teleport had set him down within Pump Court in Newgate, which was situated at the end of the Shambles in York England. The area was busy with a small group walking down the street carrying, 'Ban the Bomb' and 'Better Red than Dead' placards, but he had arrived unnoticed; drifting through the Court's metal gates before materialising.

"Phew! I am alive," he shouted but still no one noticed or challenged him. Perhaps Yorkies are used to ghosts arriving unexpectedly?

He allowed a few minutes to adjust to these new surroundings. After all, only an eye blink ago he was on Transit and now he had to once more think as the natives do. There was a fresh smell of coffee lingering on the air which blended nicely with the wintery sun trying its best to fight the gloom of autumn. A secret smile was stifled; he loved York with its Roman walls, museums and river walks, but he could also compare it favourably with his own city of Yashum Commune Tengaluma. Strange how two alien cultures could create familiar architectural similarities? However this was a foreign land full of people who could wish him harm. Luckily he was not a conspicuous figure. He caught his reflection in a shop window and smiled. Perhaps he was not quite as good looking as his wall poster hero but his figure was perfect for blending in with the tourist flotilla of York.

Now he had to focus up. There was urgency in completing his mission and with this in mind he turned left towards Christ Church and into Colliergate; his main objective was to make contact with his Watcher Teams and importantly – his errant daughter. What made him leap quickly into a shop doorway was seeing someone he definitely wanted to avoid. Clutching a bouquet of red roses was a business colleague called David Austerfield, the man who ran Apple Pie Antiques. From the safety of the doorway he watched him walk deftly into the entrance of Christ Church. Breathing a sigh of relief he resumed his journey. Turning off into a side road he approached a bland white multi-storey building and scrutinising the copper plated name plates he selected the third one down and pressed the intercom button; it buzzed away happily.

"Can I help you?" The voice through the intercom was a female Scottish accent and unfamiliar to him.

"I sincerely hope so: I want to speak with your travel consultant from Global Train Journeys?"

A door release buzzed into life and he was inside the building. Once within the lift he pressed the button to take him up to the third floor. He alighted into a brightly lit office full of neatly arranged computer screens and fresh faced employees busily typing at keyboards and speaking into headphones. From a side office a curly red haired young woman approached; she didn't shake hands but looked concerned.

"Mr Ben Gallagher I presume?"

He nodded more in politeness than anything else.

"My name is Elizabeth Ross. We were expecting you."

Gallagher registered surprise. "We?"

"Our new Managing Director will answer all your questions regarding your daughter's disappearance."

"What! There is news regarding my daughter?"

She beckoned him into his office without further comment. Once inside he quickly realised something was badly wrong. Even Humphrey Bogart, his wall poster, seemed to dryly sympathise with this dilemma. Sitting at his highly polished mahogany desk was a familiar but totally unexpected face.

"Control – how... *why* are you here?"

Across the desk and perched in a deep red leather chair, Control beamed impishly back at him as he indicated to a vacant leather bound arm chair. In his hands was a Rubik's cube and he was busily placing the coloured layers in order. Almost casually he threw it onto the desk; it rolled and propped itself alongside two white folders. Gallagher noted a long measured breath. The accent when he decided to speak was an educated one and stern. "Sit down."

He stood his ground. "This is a surprise."

Control lay back within his chair and gave him a measured stare. "I approve of your Service name of Major Ben Gallagher; a nice homely touch. Now please sit down. "

Ben Gallagher relaxed and sat down obediently. "You seem to know the whereabouts of my daughter?"

Control merely shrugged. "This affair will eventually become apparent to you – but this is an active investigation. The legality will have to be negotiated with TRINITY Legal – It's an extremely delicate matter." He paused. "Welcome to the search!"

"What search?"

"Your surmise may well prove quite correct and your brave daughter has risked her life to prove it."

"What surmise?"

"That this planet and its inhabitants have been liquidated by an exo-terrestrial presence." He looked expectantly at him. "And now – what's your excuse to be here?"

Gallagher's face crimsoned. "My daughter should not have been posted to Earth; I tried my hardest to block her entry into TRINITY." He looked up into eyes that scrutinised him impassively. "Her disappearance has devastated my life. I have spent many agonising years trying to locate her. Now I discover she has been found!"

"I sympathise."

"And now, since I am trapped here, my last wish is to hug her goodbye and," he looked stony faced at him, "also seek revenge."

Control closed his eyes and let out a deep sigh. "We live in dangerous times Mr Gallagher. First Contact is always a risky endeavour. And that is why I'm taking over." He raised his hand at Gallagher's protestation. "You came here against all my wishes and sanity which dictated otherwise; I deduced this illogical outcome of yours," His face revealed a smile. "Revenge: you surprise me!" He picked up the Rubik's cube and idly played with it. He looked up sharply. "TRINITY rules would condemn you! However you have just cause. All the facts point towards a Viral Quantum bomb which has destroyed this planet. Few civilisations possess that type of technology. Earth definitely does not. The Gropeni species yes – but then so have your Tengalese species." He scrutinised Gallagher to observe reaction before continuing.

"However, I have now quarantined this planet within a zoo like cage." He waved his right hand around the room. "And that's why we can all exist here at present – albeit only temporarily. I have also rescued your daughter – she is quite safe for the present."

"Where is Stella – I have searched everywhere on the recordings?"

Control threw the cube across to Gallagher. "See that Rubik's cube and then marvel at the genius behind it. Here is a man far ahead of his time. You have seen this Earth toy before – have you not?"

Gallagher nodded. "It happens to be mine," he lamented.

"Ah yes. You had left it at the Station in your haste to get here. The Earth has now been caged within this Time Loop Red." He indicated the red side of the cube. "As we try and find who has destroyed the Earth, we and all those we interact with will create multi dimensions – many alternative histories if you like." Here he swivelled the cube until it became multiple colours. "Just like that cube with all the sides jumbled up." The cube was swivelled to become its separate colours again. "Unravel this mystery by finding the VQ bomb should give proof of your Gropie interference theory – *when* presented as positive evidence to the Forum. Now do you follow?"

Gallagher swivelled the Rubik's cube until it became a maze of multi colours again. "I'm trying to," he lamented.

Control stood up. "Oh you will do more than that." He pointed to each of the red sides. "Unfortunately your daughter and you have – and will, become lost amongst these multi loops until we both can fulfil our missions." He leant across. "Now there are important things to remember.

My Service name here is Michael Tombs; we meet only when necessary; any questions?"

Ben Gallagher gazed up into the face of Control and thought carefully before replying; he fiddled with the Rubik's cube again; the colours refused to re-align. "My world of Tengaluma – until joining the Community, had primitive spaceships that could just travel a few hundred light-years; the measure of our development and culture. Yet through joining TRINITY my knowledge has become exponential in depth. Remote-viewing and trans-galactic travel is the norm for your species using these Purple Time Loops – what you refer to as Purple TLs." He paused. "It is hard for me to grasp your reasoning because they are so high tech. For example: The Earth has been totally destroyed – yet it's safe; how can these TLs affect Earth's history?"

Control glanced across with an air of reproach. "Possibly Earth is safe. However I cannot tell you or show you how this may be. Our species learn by trial and error; you haven't the luxury to do likewise – but you will have to try." He picked up a pair of black glasses from the table and rubbed the lens with his dark blue shirt sleeve. Carefully they were placed onto his face. His look was stern. "Operation EarthZoo is now activated; your mission here was to find your daughter." His voice raised into a shout. "Elizabeth: you can bring her in now."

Gallagher heard the office door swish open; a familiar fragrance filled the air. "Hello dad; nice of you to drop by and see me! I gather we are going to work together?"

Gallagher stood up open mouthed as he saw her. "Stella – but this cannot be! You haven't aged since last time I saw you?"

She smiled impishly. "Control explained it as a result of TLs. Time and space travel is so exciting – you'll soon get used to it."

"Agent Stella Hunnybun; please give an explanation to both of us regarding your conduct here on Earth?"

They both looked towards Control who now held a benign expression. Gallagher knew this spelt trouble. Inwardly Stella trembled; she sat down heavily upon the offered chair. "It's all there in my INTELS sir," her finger pointed to a white folder on the desk. "It's all there; if you care to read it."

Control raised an eyebrow smile. "Video et taceo Stella; Video et taceo!" he observed her frown. "I am intrigued as to your motives in disobeying that simple code of conduct."

Gallagher brightened. "That is Earth Latin meaning..."

"Let Agent Hunnybun enlighten us."

Stella wriggled uncomfortably in her chair. "It means 'see and keep silent' sir; I have failed you; I am so sorry."

"You can never fail me Stella: success is failure turned upon its head."

"What's going on?" declared Gallagher. "Please give the girl a chance to explain herself."

Control nodded. "Ben will you please double check that the door is firmly locked." He reached over and retrieved two white folders. He put one aside. The first one was opened and it revealed blank A4 paper vellum sheets held with a simple purple plastic paperclip. Holding that between finger and thumb he depressed it twice and abruptly the room filled with a holographic display of a space ship cockpit.

The viewpoint was slightly behind and above the two occupants who were seated. In front of them was a glowing control panel. A woman's voice spoke. "Why are you hiding within a Tele-Presence suit; who are you?"

Control depressed the paperclip and the view freeze framed. His voice was softer now. "What do you recall next Agent Stella?"

"Absolutely nothing sir – it is as if my mind went completely blank."

Control sighed. "A Tele-Presence suit and now mind control – both Gropeni charms and so quaint! What was your next memory?"

"I was fighting for my life above planet Earth sir."

Ben looked puzzled. "Mind control I can understand but what is a 'Tele-Presence' suit?"

Stella grasped both hands firmly to cover up the fact she was still trembling. "It is the latest Gropeni technology. Why travel vast interstellar distances when you can remain at home and use these suits remotely."

Control gazed deep into her eyes. "Now you shall relax. There is nothing to fear. You will now go back to that time you were fighting for your life above planet Earth."

CHAPTER EIGHT

Armageddon Delivery

The blue planet called Earth filled her scout craft window. The re-entry angle was dangerously far too steep and she switched to manual to correct for it. Abruptly her hands felt an electric shock and involuntarily they gripped hard which burnt her fingers until she could smell burning flesh. Reluctantly but in great pain she relinquished control.

"It would be far safer if you would let me handle the controls!"

A male robotic voice said. "You are perfectly safe in my hands; I do so want this craft to land safely with its special load." The voice was low and menacing.

"A twenty six degree re-entry angle is far too steep for this planet. It would be far safer if..."

"Safer? Don't fret child; I certainly wouldn't have managed it without your cooperation and excellent piloting skills to evade detection. And it was your brilliant idea to use this primitive craft which is invisible to TRINITY detection systems. But you knew rather too much, didn't you? Don't bother to answer: I have known for a long time that you are a spy working for them."

She turned towards the co-pilot to her left. His body and face were merely a bio-mechanised entity; the eyes, nose and mouth were grotesquely misshaped within a shrivelled hide-like skin. This species called the Gropie were detestable even without their remote controlled 'Tele-Presence' suits. Her body shook and words became difficult to utter. "Who are you and why have you tricked me in coming here?"

"Don't fret child. And please no denials: your Galactic Intelligence Service – is not that secret"

She glared. "If you continue with this descent, your precious cargo will burn up."

"I do think you are right!" His manner was now condescending. "Since this trajectory is typical of an Inter-ballistic missile, Earth will be on full alert by now and more likely to start retaliation. This craft will be destroyed either by them or by the re-entry. Don't fret my child; the cargo is cryogenically sealed and thus safe." His huge lips opened and thick yellow green saliva dribbled down his chin. "You Tengalese women are so beautiful; what a pity to have to let you die in such a painful fashion but you have made an excellent choice. Your planet or this planet; the Viral Quantum bomb is no respecter of worlds. It is a pity to destroy your homeland, when this Earth is of no consequence even to the Forum Community."

"Your cargo is a VQ Bomb?" Stella gasped and then grabbed again at the controls but the electric shocks once more burnt her hands. "You scoundrel! Violation of quarantined planets will give you a hefty prison sentence." She took a deep intake of breath and stared directly at him. "In fact it is me who has fooled you: I have arranged for your arrest as soon as we land."

A sickly grin permeated his face. "Your communication signals with your TRINITY masters were all blocked, but I do so admire your pluck. Anyway they don't hold much hope that this planet will survive for long; in fact its Head almost suggested I hasten Earth's tumble into destruction. An atomic war or VQ extinction; does it make a difference?"

"This is madness."

"Your act of martyrdom is therefore most commendable. It was a difficult decision for you to make," his face leered towards her, "but you really had no choice." He dribbled again but more profusely. "My profit margin for planet salvage is still the same. Your Tengaluma planet, I assure you will be safe in my hands."

"You unfeeling scoundrel," she cried defiantly. "Do you think I believe that?"

A cruel grin widened his lower face. "Believe what you like. I do so like these little chats of ours and would like to stay around, but things are going to get hot around here and so reluctantly – I must be going."

The figure suddenly slumped forward into the seat totally bereft of life.

Abruptly the controls became more manageable as they were released from this unseen hand. Quickly she switched back to manual and grabbed hold of the controls; pain engulfed her entire body and mind but she increased the angle until the craft violently shook and glowed with intense plasma of the ionised atmosphere and craft metal which now glowed incandescent. Inside the heat became unbearable; there was a smell of burnt electrics and a low roar assailed her ears. Her plan had worked: the craft now had become shielded within the Ionosphere; the controls totally free from remote control. "How I love ionised plasma," she screamed. "Now I want to live." With renewed determination she pulled back on the controls with all her strength. This resulted in a sharp upward parabolic arc of the craft and she watched a twelve G force warning upon the monitor; luckily the inertial dampers shielded her from blacking out from this extreme pressure upon her body. Beyond the atmosphere, the craft tumbled out of control through lack of pitch and yaw control. She observed through the window white smoke flowing past her. It bathed the glowing craft nose causing it to rapidly cool. "Cryogenic fluid, how I love you!" she shouted in relief. This rapid release of fluid gas would temporarily disable the VQ bomb and give her the chance to win through.

Her hands reached for the emergency call sign. She hoped that TRINITY could now be able to monitor her craft through their interstellar Com's link. Their assumed opinion that this was an Inter-ballistic missile flight path from Earth would now be changed. Her erratic change would alert them to the fact that an alien craft had violated the 'hands off' protocol of fledgling planets like Earth. Her mind focused on staying alive. Deftly she pumped the last remaining fuel to the thrusters and stabilised the craft as it re-entered the dense atmosphere. Her roughly formulated plan was to send it into a parabolic descent pattern. On Tengaluma it was great fun to glide without power until touch down, but Earth, although similar to her home planet, had an entirely different gravity and atmospheric pressure. However she felt optimistic because her descent pattern was going well and far better than she had hoped for. From her window she observed the glowing shockwave which shielded the craft from incineration. She sighed deeply.

Far below were thick clouds that looked like there was a thunderstorm brewing. There were lights twinkling through which suggested a township of some kind. Abruptly the controls were once more snatched from her grasp forcing a steep terminal dive. She fought the pain shooting through her hands, and wrestled the controls until the craft became engulfed in thick rain. Miraculously this released back the controls to her and she managed to lessen the descent. The crash land when it came was a violent one and she was knocked unconscious.

When her senses returned she found herself outside the craft which appeared completely wrecked; her thoughts of trying to escape therefore were quickly dismissed. The 'Tele-Presence' suit looked grotesquely mangled beside her. Her own spacesuit hadn't fared much better. With tremendous effort from the heavier gravity, she managed to crawl some way from the stricken craft and onto a little hillock. A desert plain surrounded by hills, reminded her of home but she was in no doubt that there would be many differences too.

Tengaluma had only recently been accepted to join the Forum Community and TRINITY was used as Probation Overseers. When it was then discovered that Tengaluma and Earth were almost twin planets with similar cultural development, her government became enthusiastic about making contact with this new species.

She had read up as much as she could to familiarise herself with this strange and exciting Earth planet. Romantic fiction was her favourite; she had just finished 'The Scarlet Pimpernel' and adored the costume extravagance. Tengalese clothes by contrast, were more functional. She was extremely disappointed when her application to join TRINITY had been initially rejected at the second interview. The Board had not been impressed with her. She had lacked experience they had said in their: 'Tell me about yourself' and 'Give me an account of when you succeeded in a certain situation', type of appraisals. What had never been taken into account at these simplistic interviews were her strong survival instincts and willingness to quickly adapt. Mysteriously however someone far higher up in TRINITY had overturned the Board's decision and she had been finally accepted. This was her first mission and now she had screwed up very badly.

In the distance she heard a motorised vehicle approaching, its lights splitting the desert sky. Close up she saw that it was a white pickup truck; the driver had a mean and hungry look but his charming feature was the enormous hat pulled well down over his ears. She took a deep breath and racked her brain for an explanation for being here. From Earth fashion books, her silver metallic spacesuit, although torn, could be interpreted as evening wear that women here wore at nightclubs.

The man wound down his truck window. "Little missie are you alright?"

His gravel peppered voice unnerved her. "Thank you, kind sir. I saw this strange craft crash down from over there and the blast must have fair stunned me!"

The man climbed out of his vehicle, took off his hat and wiped the back of his neck in a thoughtful manner. "Darn it, you're from England," he exclaimed as he looked across at the craft which now began to hiss violently and vent streams of plasma. Then he caught sight of the crumpled body lying next to it. Taking a closer look he nearly vomited.

"If you are an alien you're a sure darn pretty one, but I don't think much to your boyfriend!"

She smiled prettily up at him and wiggled her hips hoping the close fitting space suit would look alluring. Her survival required quick thinking and a dialect re-adjustment. "He sure wouldn't win no beauty contest now would he?"

He laughed. "We are too close to an airbase and soon USAAF police will be crawling all over this." His face looked puzzled "How come you are so far out in this desert?"

She walked closer and felt relieved that he allowed her to take his hand. "I am totally lost and at the mercy of your dear kind self. Will you please take me home?"

He scratched the back of his head. "Nearest town is Roswell, and there's a storm brewing, so it wouldn't be natural to leave you here."

"That will do just fine."

She climbed inside the vehicle and waited for him to join her.

When he did so, there was a reluctant pause before he released the hand brake. "Please don't mention this to anyone; people gossip like crazy around these parts!"

"My lips are zipped."

He turned to give her a puzzled look."You English; so eccentric to a fault. I bet you're from Surrey?"

She nodded politely. "You must have read my mind."

"My aunt Betty is from Surrey."

"Well darn it: she's my neighbour!"

He clunked the gears and the truck rolled forward. "Marcel is my name; what's yours?"

"So nice to meet you Marcel." She thought quickly as she wriggled out of her suit and threw it in the back. The fashionable Tengalese clothes she wore underneath would look quaint but Earth like. She waved towards the silver paper thin suit. "That will give your town something to talk about."

"Shucks, this will be a tall story; I'm going to be a laughing stock all over town."

Her hand sought his and caressed it. "My name's Stella and I won't breathe a word about your encounter." She leant across and lightly kissed him. "Your close encounter with an alien space girl!"

As they approached his town, worried thoughts invaded her mind. A crashed spaceship might be interpreted by these aliens as hostile and she might be captured and tortured to reveal its design and purpose. Her main objective now would be to hide somewhere and await retrieval. If her distress call had been picked up then this should not be too long. Gazing upwards into the desert sky, realisation abruptly kicked in; she was 600 light-years from home and very, very alone. The thought of being stranded paralysed her. Tears flooded down her face and there was no attempt to stop them. Marcel had looked across at her once or twice during the journey but appeared too polite to comment; she felt relieved by that.

She was dropped just on the outskirts and stood for some time trying to put her plan of action into place. It was then she saw a figure enveloped by dust and swirling brushwood coming towards her from back along the road. Closer up she realized it was a male figure in a gabardine raincoat. So this was it; capture and slow torture. Could she face this type of death? Her body shook.

"You were hard to locate; I have come to take you home."

"I am Stella Hunnybun; a native of this town and ..." She gazed into hazel eyes that held an immediate intensity of scrutiny, "I am just out walking."

"Relax, there is nothing to fear: I am your TRINITY Control here on Earth."

Her eyes lit up. "If that's so, then I have just crash landed a space ship over there and against my wishes it contains a

VQ bomb. I am convinced that someone is behind a plot to…"

He nodded. "To deliver Armageddon to planet Earth – yes I know all about it; don't worry. All of this will be sorted out much later; but not now." He held out to grasp her hand. "You have done well by disabling the bomb – and against all odds to survive. Now I must take you away from here. There is one who also has risked death on this planet just to be with you and we must not be late to greet his arrival?"

Her whole world swirled into blackness, like water down a plug hole.

CHAPTER NINE

Watch Your Back

Time Loop Red

"Relax Stella: you are safely back."

"Phew!"

Control appeared quietly amused. "Your mission was merely to observe the Gropeni whilst they were on duty roster on the transit station. Please explain why you ended up in that situation?"

She cleared her throat. "I found the mission you had set me impossible to complete because they were such a close knitted group and abhorred strangers. No one talked to each other – never mind me. I noted certain peculiarities however. One particular male individual appeared to frequently transport to Earth and Gropeni. I checked to find that no proper tracking records had been logged by him. Armed with this information, I decided to follow his movements when he transported to his home planet. Once upon Gropeni however I found myself being shunned again. The Gropie there also consist of closely grouped communities suspicious of each other and doubly so of strangers; how they manage to trade with each other... Goodness knows!"

"But you did manage to trade and thus form a liaison with one or two trading groups; what did you uncover?"

"It wasn't clear at first but eventually I uncovered sufficient intelligence regarding a trading operation with a planet called Earth. Hence this was why I decided to advertise my spaceship for sale. I thought it would be excellent bait to entice the guilty parties out in the open. However my buyer used a 'Tele-Presence' suit to disguise his real identity."

"Although naive and dangerous I cannot fault your well meaning or logic." He raised his hand in contemplation. "I'm intrigued by your logic but it will further complicate our mission."

"How was I to know those input coordinates were Earth's?"

"No harm done Stella, it was to be expected."

She looked open mouthed at him. "What do you mean?"

Control sighed and raised a finger as if to say something. Instead he indicated to the other white folder on the desk. Once opened it revealed a single A4 white blank sheet fixed with a paper clip. It was gripped between finger and thumb. Abruptly a cold mustiness permeated the room.

Time Loop Purple-Red

The room had now become the hallowed confines of a small church. Their viewpoint was slightly from above an altar rail which was adorned with fresh red roses and a single glowing candle; the wick fresh and lively. The sound of the Minster chiming the hour was prelude to the arrival of a young tousle haired man. They watched open mouthed not daring to speak at his approach. Abruptly this peaceful scene was cut like a knife down the middle. It peeled open to reveal a busy square. Only the man remained transfixed at its centre.

Time Loop Purple-Blue

The man looked in anguish upwards and then to a duffle coated man to his left.

"Where has Christ Church disappeared to?" he lamented.

"There's a church around the corner in Goodramgate pal, but this is King's Square and there's no church here."

"They cannot see you," Control whispered.

Abruptly the scene became frozen in time and as quickly dissipated; they were back in their familiar room once more.

Time Loop Red

Control looked at them both and then bent down and opened a drawer of the desk. "I think you understand the grave situation that you have just observed. We have yet another TL to deal with and more importantly indicates instability." He sighed heavily. "We might not be able to save Earth after all."

Stella stared in astonishment. "What?"

Gallagher looked as if he would explode. "Control, how can you say that?"

He shrugged and retrieved three glasses and a bottle of Ouzo which were placed upon the top. The bottle top was cracked open and he poured out equal measures of the transparent spirit. Picking up two, he passed them around.

He paused to scrutinise each one in turn. "Have I said to give up? Success is failure turned upon its head." His glass lightly touched each one in turn. "It is an Earth custom to toast a new venture and ours certainly can be called that. Let us raise glasses to our mutual success!"

"Which is..?" Gallagher looked perplexed.

"Bring the Gropie to justice and yet remain alive," answered Stella. Her confidence returned. "Do we return back to Time Earth 1947 Roswell?"

Control revealed a knowing smile. "No – we most certainly do not. With your crashed spacecraft containing a lethal bomb and a planted body wearing a 'Tele-Presence' suit, I would then be forced to arrest *you* Stella. Both items appeared totally destroyed – yet here we are in this situation. You have no hard facts to support that Gropie theory of yours – however tangible it seems. Tengaluma would also be expelled from the Community in disgrace. Therefore categorically no! Your mission now is here in York finding vital evidence by witnessing Earth's history up to its destruction. We must catch and reveal our culprit's identity. Hard evidence will also reprieve Earth from the salvage operators – who I see from your Report to be the Gropeni! An irony to contemplate – but we need hard facts. I have previously traversed these TLs before you and believe me they are littered with hidden snares. But you have a good chance for fortune."

"So we've noticed," retorted Stella.

"Won't Earth scientists detect our presence here?" remarked Gallagher.

Control shook his head. "All their astronomers will discover is that the universe is accelerating away from them and on a personal note for you all to observe: there will be déjà view experiences; an unfortunate result of TL displacement. We must all take our chance – especially if one is all we may have."

Gallagher looked pensive. "May fortune favour the foolish!"

"I will go with that," Stella replied. Her hands shook once more. "I'm frightened."

Control looked concerned before he toasted both of them. "I shall further emphasise my point. We live in dangerous times. First Contact is always a risky endeavour and my aim is to get it correct so that the right calibre joins the Community Forum." He paused looking at each in turn. "Let the mission begin." He waited whilst they drank and then added, "since you cannot return, your first priority is to find someone who will provide lodgings and furniture for you both. And I know just the man!"

"You don't mean David Austerfield?" declared Ben nervously.

Control nodded and smiled benignly. "Yes but take care with your dealings with him. Watch your back or you'll find a knife imbedded in it with his fingerprints on the hilt." He sipped his drink thoughtfully. "Nice chap though!"

CHAPTER TEN

Sea of Smiles

Time Loop Red

Situated high up and overlooking the entire warehouse floor, the office of Apple Pie appeared vulnerable and exposed. If it was a small and cluttered room, David Austerfield barely noticed. If his denim shirt bulged in the wrong place and his trousers cut into his crutch – it was because his mind dwelt on higher things.

He closed and locked the door and prepared to count today's takings, spilling the coins and notes all over the antique desk in the process. An old rickety chair creaked under his weight as he sat down. He gazed upwards and mouthed. "Easy money? Where has that dream disappeared to?" Even without counting it, he knew today would be short. The heady days of thriving profits were long gone. These days the punter demanded a bargain for the piece of tat or bric-a-brac that he'd managed to convince them they so badly needed. Perhaps he had been rash in dishing out a shed full upon his other business venture: the fleet of bouncy castles. Initially it had earned him a stash that he could skyrocket, no questions asked, but then the summers became extensions of winters and it rained and rained and yet more rain. His head shook. "Why pick on me?"

He wasn't a superstitious man (or one that would own up to be) but on more than one occasion his mind had wandered along the lines of Divine Retribution. If only he could come up with something different. Something every kid would want to play. That would be a money earner. Kids like activity ventures like Dodgems and go-carts. Perhaps he could investigate the market; buy one or two to rent out at parties. Something simple that would capture a child's imagination.

He abruptly froze. From far away he heard an indistinct noise. He strained his ears to breaking point, hardly breathing trying to determine its source. Finally he heard a faint creak, followed by 'swish – swish'.

Austerfield racked his brain trying to remember where he'd heard it before. By straining his neck until he could peer through the office window, he scrutinised the scene below.

Directly beneath him, an old red pillar-box and an ancient red Scot's telephone box stood proud like Beefeaters on patrol either side of the central isle. Feeding off from either side of this, were layer upon layer of bedsteads, dining tables, bedroom furniture and finally upon the far wall at the back, a plethora of mirrors. He watched in amazement as the end wardrobe quivered. The mahogany door became visible as it swung open and then he heard that familiar 'creak', as the invisible partner opened too. Then there was a 'swish' as both doors closed. After a slight pause, a solitary dark figure came into view. Only his back was visible and he appeared to be finally admiring the mirrors.

Auster's initial response was to bang upon the window in anger at this unwanted customer: after all damn it, it was long past closing time. He hesitated however when that cold familiar fear crept up his spine. There was something about his unwanted customer that made him remember the kind of people he wished to avoid. Could he possibly think it: the Eastern European Mafia – here in England?

Call the police was his next thought. Auster reached for the phone, and then paused, his finger hovering over the digit nine before glancing once more at the scene below. He dialled and thought; he dialled and thought; he thought and allowed his finger to quiver over the final '9'. In his mind he was wrestling with his ghosts.

"Nah!" He was allowing his imagination to blur his judgement.

Was that a footstep upon the bottom step? He strained to listen. It was obvious now that someone was carefully shuffling up the stairs, their breathing, laboured and wheezing in the process. The stranger was outside his door now, closer than a heartbeat.

Tap – tap – tap.

Resolutely he dialled the last digit trying to force the ring to return back faster.

"Can I have a quiet word in your ear, David?"

Auster slammed down the phone and choked with relief: it was Ben! He leapt up, swung open the door and dragged him inside.

"Yer daft Gawpead. Prowling around like a thief. I nearly wet messen!"

Ben Gallagher gave him a disdained look before he brushed himself down and then carefully stepped across discarded groups of files until he found a vacant chair. He carefully flicked it with his gloved hand and then with deliberation, sat down. He wheezed.

All brown tweed, regimental tie and shoes that shone like chestnuts, he looked decidedly out of place. There was his brave smile now; was it just for his benefit?

"You've been rather hard to find lately. Any problems I need to know about... and talk proper English if you please!"

Auster hesitated before replying. He felt too proud to admit that over the last few days he had been scared. "Nothing that I can't handle Ben."

Gallagher brushed away traces of dust from his trousers. "Major to you, if you please!"

Auster scoffed. "That's for your hired help. Me – I'm a first-name person."

Gallagher huffed. "I was admiring your furniture out there. I'm looking for a wardrobe for my daughter's flat."

"How much are you willing t' pay?" he said leaning against his desk.

"That's not what I've come here for."

"I thought as much."

"How was Athens?"

That caught him off guard: what did he know? "You mean, how was Stella?" he ventured.

Gallagher merely raised an eyebrow. "Go on."

"She's a real pro I can tell you; soon brought me up to speed about the 'players'."

"Whose idea was it to infiltrate their organisation?" Gallagher's voice held an edge now.

"Stella told you then?"

"Amuse me Mr Austerfield. Amuse me."

Auster picked up a pen from his desk and fiddled nervously with it. "Listen will tha, before tha bites ma head off?"

"Your value to me is based upon your experience and connections. I do not tolerate maverick behaviour."

"I'm not your 'push me pull me' toy."

"Did Stella put you up to it?"

"Stella? No. She thought it would be a good idea to spend a few evenings at the Moulin Rouge nightclub. Pulling the girl was my idea!"

Gallagher growled at him. "Of course you knew who she was?"

He threw the pen on the table. "Well not reet then; later perhaps."

"Your 'pull' as you call her, is Anya Perraki. She is the leader of the terrorist group you were supposed to observe." He leant closer towards him until their noses touched. "Carefully!"

Auster leant back and puffed out his chest. "Ben – Major. Look at the advantages. I've found out more from the 'inside' than I could have done in months."

"Such as?"

"Who their chief courier is for one thing. Name of Manolis Paterakis," he shuffled in his chair. "They have never met him personally, but I know him very well."

"And why's that pray?"

Auster' cherub face beamed with pride. "He works for me, that's why... but that's all you're knowing!"

"I need a description?"

"Wears an earring and has a deep scar on the left side of his face. A banker did it just before he died."

"Died?"

"Manolis owed him money and didn't feel like paying up."

Gallagher scrutinised his fingernails carefully before replying. When he finally spoke it was in measured tones. "An interesting man I perceive. Anything else you can tell me?"

"There's something big coming into the country." Auster looked carefully at him. "It's something to do with a consignment of Red Mercury. Why have they turned to smuggling chemicals?"

"Red Mercury?" interjected Gallagher.

"Yes." Auster's eyes locked briefly with him.

Gallagher became suddenly distant, pensively rubbing his chin. "Are you sure it was called Red Mercury?"

"What's wrong with that?"

"Mercury is a silvery liquid and the only metal that is fluid at room temperature." He paused and raised an eyebrow. "The only red Mercury I am aware of is the oxide of Mercury, but I'm sure that's not it. What do you think?"

Auster ignored the question.

"Well?"

"There is something else I'm forgetting. That tart is involved with a Pagan Cult. She disappears for days with them in their hideaway somewhere up near Mount Olympus. I found out that its members are: Politicians, bankers, lawyers and shipping magnates. They even have a chocolate Managing Director from York. What's happening?"

Gallagher suddenly became very concerned and leant forward. "That's a clever way to distract official interest. Find out what you can... but watch your back."

"I can take care of messen 'av no fear on that account."

"Quite," nodded Gallagher, resuming his relaxed posture. He turned over to one side so that he could extract a packet of cigarettes from his trouser pocket. He threw them onto the table.

"No thanks, I don't smoke."

"On no account smoke those: they'll blow your head off! Notice the filter: triple red ring?"

"Oh," remarked a puzzled Auster. "They're a bit posh for me."

Gallagher's voice became stern. "For once, smoking these may well save your life. If at any time you feel in danger or you have to scrub one of your contacts with Stella, light one and carefully drop it. It'll warn her you're in trouble."

"Why light it?"

"They burn like slow fuses for up to an hour. It'll give her an indication of the time you were at that location."

Auster smiled ruefully. "Learning all this secret agent stuff is upper crass-crap to me."

"Think of it then as insurance. As long as you keep up the regular contacts with Stella and be extra vigilant this time – you'll survive. I hope I can count on you?"

Auster raised his hand in a mock salute. "Smugglers honour Gov'."

Gallagher shook his head. "I have a bad feeling about this and you're in far too deep to be pulled out. Remember just one thing will you: I believe that you have integrity and judgement. Apply it. If you think you can trick me in your pursuit of selfish aims, then think again!"

Auster rolled his eyes in mock horror. "Don't worry – Major."

"Don't worry?" Gallagher shifted uneasily in his chair. "You've, given me a lot of sleepless nights lately." He scrutinised him carefully before speaking again. "Why do you choose to travel under the assumed name of Ross?"

Auster sat bolt upright and wide-eyed. "How did you find that out?"

Gallagher slammed his fist down onto his lap. "Damn it man: I'm giving you a second chance. Can't you see that?"

"Anyone would think you don't trust me."

"Then prove me wrong?"

Auster gazed once more into that sea of smiles.

CHAPTER ELEVEN

Kalispera – Dear Friend

Time Loop Red

Auster put his feet up upon the dashboard and worried himself to death. Normally Robby would have paid him a visit before each trip, if only to re-assure his fat wallet that the next precious shipment was on the van. His other concern was Ross. He gazed across at his friend and hoped his fears were groundless. Suddenly there came an almighty crunch. He tried not to sound too condescending "Careful with those gears: third's a sod to find." There came an exchange of smiles that eased his mind.

He had watched him go downhill after his divorce and it was hard to look him in the eye during it all. His conscience wriggled like a worm inside: but there is no second chance in this life; what was done was done – he would make amends. Still, a Grand is fair wallop to the lad bah no mistake. It will put him on his feet and this trip should be less risky than the others. This time he was running only half illegal.

Auster looked across again and hoped that Ross' matching denim jacket and shirt would be ample against the cold of the Channel. His outfit was more practical: a white trench coat that was fully reversible, black on the inside and with more pockets than a poaching jacket.

A blaring horn jarred him temporarily from his thoughts. He caught the flash of headlights speeding into the night.

This journey seemed to drag by like lead weights around his ankles and he found himself counting the passing vehicles. How many more white vans like his were heading over to Calais partaking in this 'trade of gentlemen'? He was no villain however. He whispered quietly. "Drugs or illegal immigrants are far too complicated. I am a travelling salesman that's my style; merely dealing in trinkets." He held up a finger in turn as he murmured again to himself.

"One. Designer jeans that was OK as long as they weren't washed.

Two. Till register parts that fitted surprisingly well into high-tech computers.

Three. Deodorants full of an unfortunate amount of ozone depleting propellant. These items were better than owning a gold mine in some countries.

Four: His favourite line was the plastic Father Christmas's. The kiddies went wild-eyed when his van door opened and their smiling faces popped out. Even the Managing Director of the chocolate factory in York had bought one along with his stainless steel container delivery."

He fingered his chin in a pensive manner as he paused to look across at the package that Ben had given him. How innocent was that? He heard a snore and just managed to catch Ross before he rolled forward. "Careful Ross; have a care!"

"Uhh?" came back the reply.

"Just be careful!"

It was a lucrative little market and he had worked hard to build up a network of "go-betweens" and this safe route into and out of Russia via Greece. Anya's trading deals that he negotiated worried him – but it paid the bills. The lucrative Middle East too would be their next venture. This shipment was different. He picked up the brown paper parcel from the dash and felt it again just to make sure he wasn't dreaming. He was supposed to give it to Stella when he rendezvoused with her; it was safely tucked within the folds of his jacket. If all went well he would cut a good deal; if things went to plan, he could make another profitable transaction on top of that. This game was very risky, especially with the people he was working with and the clarity in knowing what the merchandise was. However he had organised that another courier would do the swap creating yet another layer of safety. All identities apart from their voices were unknown, so this meant no one could grass on anyone else.

The agreed meeting place for the exchange was Piraeus docks Athens. What made him nervous had been that mistimed phone call; the unfamiliar female voice and that unauthorised change of plan. The courier would now be waiting at Calais docks.

Risky or what? He was however promised fifty Grand for this one. Fifty Grand! That was a lot to skyrocket for something that small! He patted his pockets. Concealed within was an ace or two just in case those awkward little moments should arrive. A mental note was made to make Church next Sunday if this operation went smoothly.

"Please God. Please?"

In silence they made Dover as a pale sun blossomed. In silence he gazed across at the friend whom he had once betrayed. Now it was an agonising guilty silence that had to be endured – forever.

At last after what felt like a million eternities, there seemed a change in the throb of the engines and the ferry appeared to be rolling less. "Brandies and heaving ships are a witches potion bah no mistake," he muttered as he ventured up on deck to watch the Calais docks grow ever closer.

"Where are you Ross?"

Almost straddled over the bow rail he noticed a familiar figure, heaving for England. Auster however breathed in the French air that felt so warm and fresh after the stuffy confinement below. Over the bow in the scattered half light, Auster saw the black profiles of land and twinkling yellow window lights from distant houses. They sharply contrasted against the sickly sky.

It hadn't taken long before Auster's nerves were twanging like over-taut catgut again: something was wrong, but he couldn't place it. Had he overlooked anything?

Amongst the swirl of embarking cars, vans and passengers, Austerfield noticed a parked white van with its logo: 'Jacques Baguettes'. Upon closer inspection he noticed its silver earring driver looking with mechanical curiosity across at him. He turned towards Ross. "That's the van but I don't recognise the courier. I'm going to investigate."

Auster climbed out and headed over towards the parked van. Close up and Auster noticed the bulging lump beneath the black suit, which was as informative as any label. This premonition jump-started his heart again.

"Hi I'm Ross; I'm your contact. I've got the merchandise, have you got the....?"

Suddenly an overwhelming force knocked him to the ground, and Auster realised that Silver Earring must have had an accomplice. He looked up into the face of a gun barrel.

"David there's a change of plan," said a female voice; it was the voice on the phone that he had heard earlier.

Emerging from behind 'silver earring' was a gargoyle face. "You!" exclaimed Austerfield.

"I'll take that," growled Smythe as the parcel was whisked out of his hands. Suddenly Gendarmes swooped from both sides and engulfed the van. Caught amongst the swirling thrashing mass of officials and thugs, vans and scooters, he felt helpless. Abruptly invisible hands dragged him clear and he emerged some distance away. Looking around him his thudding heart slowly calmed. This entire scene felt so surreal like being on a film set. He could see the Gendarmes arrest his attackers but Smythe evaded capture by leaping into a nearby taxi. Ross was now outside on the pavement and looked entirely baffled. He had put up no resistance whatsoever whilst being handcuffed but had then looked around desperately searching. Their eyes met and guilt gnawed at Auster's soul. However he was safe: no one was taking any notice of him at all. It was about time that Ace card was played. With his coat turned inside out, false wig, moustache and sunglasses he headed for safety. His only regret was involving Ross, but that couldn't be helped now.

"Signomi," said a quiet voice from within the heaving mass of tourists.

"Kalispera."

The only witness to this little charade was Mr Michael Tombs who observed every minute detail.

Time Loop Blue

Auster was at last at Calais Docks. Travelling without his friend, he had at least managed to switch passports. It was a clever bit of forgery but it couldn't be helped. The Ross passport now held his face within it. This was a simple precaution in case things got rough at Customs: Ross had a clean record with the police – yet another safety layer. If anything went wrong of course his friend would be in the line of fire, but that couldn't be helped. Still, nothing should go wrong. And if Ross hadn't drunk so much that night he too would have enjoyed this trip.

Amongst the swirl of embarking cars, vans and passengers, he noticed a parked white van with its logo: 'Jacques Baguettes'. Abruptly he was seized by two custom officials; both were tall and athletic looking. Caution however was the better part of valour. His demeanour was relaxed and carefree as he took out his passport. "What appears to be the problem officers?"

"Are you David Austerfield?"

"No I am not!" He waved the passport under their noses. Behind them he spotted a complete stranger heading towards the white van. "My name is Ross. There's your man behind you."

They relaxed their grip to turn in the direction where he had pointed. He saw his chance of escape and broke free from them and ran for all his worth into the swirling mass of humanity.

CHAPTER TWELVE

Whisky Queen Checkmate

Time Loop Blue

The phone rang; the kettle boiled; the doorbell played Dixie. Nothing was going to entice me away from my bed or my headache. I heard a click from the kitchen, which placed coffee firmly in my mind. I therefore waited patiently. The phone stopped, the doorbell refused to comply.

"All right. All right, I'm coming."

In my haste, I put both feet into one trouser leg and promptly collapsed in a heap on the floor. The doorbell tinkled with amusement. With my dressing gown wrapped around me like Maypole ribbons, I leapt out of the bedroom and into the dowdy brown entrance hall. I inched open the door and was greeted by a man, medium height, well rounded and with a face that reminded me of a smiling Buddha. The next thing I noticed was that although the swirling rain beat upon my footpath, he appeared as dry as yesterday's sandwich.

"Hello?" I enquired.

"Mr. Ross?" His accent was a mild Scottish one; I judged it to be more Stirling than the gruff Glasgow dialect.

I grunted in my usual go away tone of growl, which had no apparent effect at all upon my sanguine caller.

"Good morning sir. My name is Major Gallagher. Can I have a quiet word with you?"

He opened the inside pocket of his black gabardine and produced an ID, which he promptly shoved under my nose. I tried to look suitably impressed at the black writing of the official kind scrawled all over it.

"Is it about my passport?"

"Can we discuss this inside sir?"

I nodded and beckoned him to follow me into my living room. He smiled as I offered a seat in my best armchair, the one with all the springs intact. He smiled at the idea of coffee. He smiled again at my perplexed look after I had re-emphasised concern over my stolen passport. In fact he kept smiling all the time, which I found annoying, especially first thing in the morning.

"How do you like your coffee?" I enquired.

"Ice cold frappé with three sugars, thank you."

My eyebrows raised in surprise. "That's an unusual request?"

He spread his hands in an expressive gesture. "I have it on good authority that it's a speciality of yours."

"Who would that be?" I enquired.

He was watching me very closely now. "That would be your friend David Austerfield."

It felt like an electric shock had rippled up and down my spine. "Auster can never be really called that!" I watched his mouth open and close like a pouting fish. "I'll go and make your drink for you,"

The correct way to make this drink is by using a little unsweetened evaporated milk and carefully whisking it with best coffee until a smooth thick consistency is formed. The final touch after adding cold water is the addition of ice cubes. I switched on the kettle again to re-heat the water for my coffee. As an afterthought I decided to add two pieces of Madeira on a side plate as a snack. My electric knife whirred into action, but unfortunately through haste, my left finger caught the gyrating blades. "Begger," I screamed sucking the blood before wrapping a Band Aid around it.

When I returned and handed him his coffee, with polite sarcasm I said, "I hope its cold enough for you?"

Open-mouthed and staring at my mutilated hand, he exclaimed. "Good God!" A troubled moment passed as we stared at each other and then another as he gave a suspicious glance into his coffee mug. His final scrutiny rested with the Madeira. When eventually he looked back at me, he appeared more composed.

I tried to sound deadpan. "Lucky for me it wasn't deep!"

He shifted uneasily in his chair. "Yes I suppose it was."

I excused myself to get dressed.

Upon my return I noticed that he was slumped back in the armchair with hands clutched around his mug. Major Gallagher appeared to have dozed, or perhaps he had choked upon my cake? Suddenly, bright as morning he announced. "Is it a good read?"

"What?"

He pointed to a blue leather book discarded at my feet. "'Highfield', by Maria Bronte," he read. "I'm intrigued."

"Well so was I when I discovered it was nestled amongst Tolkien and Dennis Wheatley. Austerfield probably sold me the book as a rare classic. He's always doing that. According to the jacket, she started writing crime fiction after surviving a near fatal illness as a child."

"How come?

"Being surrounded with all those medicines and leeches must have brought out the macabre in her."

"How intriguing," he said picking up the book to scrutinise it. "I am well aware of her other three sisters: – Anne, Charlotte and Emily – but now we have Maria," I saw a fleeting crafty smile as he placed it in my hands. "Please go on; what is the story all about?"

I looked uneasily at him and thought carefully before answering. "A seemingly innocent traffic accident turns out to be premeditated murder." I opened the book at the last page. "I particularly liked the unexpected twist at the end." I looked across and noticed his enquiring eyes. "Are you a book lover?"

He pointed towards my numerous bookcases delicately positioned around the room. "I can see you are". His face turned to look directly at me. "I believe that all the dreams and hopes of mankind are held within their pages."

It wasn't quite the answer I had expected and I must have appeared momentarily dumbfounded. "I'm sure you haven't come here to admire my books," I said at last as I placed 'Highfield' upon my chair arm.

"Quite!" He raised his mug and thoughtfully sipped his coffee. A slight wriggle in his chair held my attention. He abruptly sighed and then remarked. "I must say Mr Ross; this is the best coffee I have ever tasted. Is it a special make?"

"No," I replied casually. "It's merely the way you make it – even with your three sugars."

"Your friend surprisingly has some taste," he said quietly. "How come you know him?"

I expected him to answer but he didn't. The only sound came from the tick of my grandfather clock and the throbbing rain against the window. It seemed to intensify the warm smell of coffee that wafted up from my mug. I took another sip and allowed the liquid to scald my throat. He seemed fascinated now with my pictures and trophies above the fireplace. Abruptly he rose to his feet and wandered over to them and scrutinised each one in turn. "Judo Tournament; Diving First Class and Gun Sharpshooter Event; how impressive." He turned quickly and with a levelled stare, he said. "I must apologise for disturbing you from your sick bed."

"Sick? What makes you think that?"

"It is midday and yet still in your dressing gown? And now your clothes: they appear rather too big for you?"

I grunted and said nothing, but my eyes followed his around the room and saw a strange air of neglect. My chess set at the far end of the room, held an intruder. Peeping from behind a Rook and Queen stood proudly an empty whisky bottle. Had I drunk a whole bottle last night? Strewn beneath lay discarded lager cans, a pizza box and yet another bottle of whisky. This one was temptingly full. Through the open doorway to my left and towering above the kitchen sink were layers of an unwashed crockery mountain. A whisper of illumination dribbled through my greying mesh curtains. His final look was upon me. Those accusing eyes, expected, demanded an answer. My words struggled to get out. I hoped my lie would sound convincing. "I'm recovering from the flu," I stammered.

He leant across and he appeared quite moved as he grasped me firmly by the arm.

"You're now going to be just fine old boy; just fine." He then slumped back into his armchair. His coat slid open and I saw a deep green shirt, pale blue tie that contrasted interestingly with bright red socks. He took a long sip of coffee and in cold measured voice he said, "I have not come about your passport."

I glanced up sharply. "What have you come for then?"

"Will you help me find someone?"

I cocked an ear at that. "Who have you in mind?"

With meticulous slowness he sipped his coffee before replying. "Our mutual friend: David Austerfield."

I took out my diary. "Not much to say really. We had arranged to meet at Rik's..." I caught his enquiring eye. "It's a Bistro pub." It suddenly dawned on me that Auster was in trouble with the law and if I wasn't careful this could easily involve me. A mis-timed drop of sweat threatened to blind me in one eye and my voice wavered slightly. "He showed up late with some idea of dragging me off on a crazy goose chase of his."

He took another long deliberate drink and eyed me more carefully this time. "Do you know where he was going?"

"France, I think. I was dead against it." I instantly regretted my reply; it was always safer to play dumb when Auster was involved. "He wanted me to share the driving but I had too much to drink by then."

Gallagher shook his head slowly whilst muttering under his breath. "Drive to France, straight away and he hadn't arranged this beforehand."

This line of conversation was heading into murky waters and there was no 'Exit' light in view. "That's Auster for you, he can be very impulsive," I said adding, "he is the kind of person who is always full of surprises. I suppose that's one of his virtues: you never know what's coming next."

His voice sounded like a faulty sound recording. "Oh I see. Oh dear – dear- dear..."

I felt indignant. "Well what would you have done?"

He stared open mouthed. "Oh! I would have gone."

It was then I wanted him to leave. "Yes. I'm sorry I can't be more helpful. So if you could check again with the Job Centre about my passport?

Almost violently he leaned forward and grabbed my arm. "Will you help me find the man?"

I recoiled back and shook my head. "I wouldn't have a clue where to look,"

With a fleeting crafty smile he remarked. "I think that trip to France was more of a business proposition. Did you know he is an International smuggler; wanted by Interpol?"

I met his gaze defiantly then and it was almost like a battle of wits being played out. "I've known Auster for years."

He smiled indulgently. "You grew up together, went to the same school I believe?"

"That's right. And that's why I'm convinced he's no terrorist. Auster is more of an antiques dealer."

"Interpol doesn't think so. Terrorist connections they say." He leant over almost as if he was about to confide the most intimate secret. His voice, now in whisper was hard to catch. "I may agree with what you are saying – but that is why I have come here to ask you to find him before *they* do."

"They?" I felt suddenly short of breath. "Who are – *they*?"

"If I answered that one I would have to kill you!"

I momentarily flinched; my voice raised a pitch. "What do you expect me to…?"

He stifled a laugh. "Sorry for that – I watch far too many spy films for my own good!" The Major leant back heavily within his armchair and appeared more composed. "Give me an idea of his character. Happy family background was it?"

This line of his had unnerved me and I felt defensive. I tried to copy his posture and leant back; as he crossed his legs, so did I. Memories of the past struggled to find voice and surely minutes must have passed. Major Gallagher however was a patient man. When the endless tick of time was beginning to jar, I remarked in a caged voice. "My first recollection was when we had just started Secondary School and he was excused to attend his mother's funeral. After that he had a bust up with his father and finally he left home."

I was surprised to see the Major had tears in his eyes. "What caused the quarrel with his father?"

"His father wanted him to play violin in the school concert. Auster hated anything musical, but tried his best to please his dad."

"That's hardly something to leave home about?"

"Parents are alien when you're at that tender age; aren't they?"

He temporarily jolted; gave me an enquiring look and then slumped back into the armchair. To my surprise he appeared to have dosed off. The endless tick of seconds became minutes until it was interrupted by the striking hour. He jumped violently. "Goodness!" With extreme vigour he thumped the armchair, which released clouds of dust. "I must be going."

His next move caught me off guard, because striding over towards the chess table he retrieved the whisky bottle. This was firmly placed within my hands. "When you're working for me you won't need this anymore. And as for your chess play," he pointed to the chessboard. "You would have been checkmated on the next move with the Black Knight." I watched mesmerised as he grasped 'Highfield'. He caught my puzzled look. "I sincerely hope you didn't pay much for this priceless gem of yours because it's a fake. There can be no novelist called Maria Bronte, because she died of TB in childhood! You can look it up if you don't believe me."

I must have looked vacant as I replaced the bottle on the table. My next strategic move was into the kitchen; I needed space to think.

"Do you play?" I enquired whilst pouring hot water into the overcrowded washing up bowl. I heard a muffled reply. "What did you say?"

Upon hearing no answer I walked back into the room. He was not there! In disbelief I searched the entire house.

Perhaps he was hiding or had discreetly left? It was then I noticed that the front door was bolted and locked: exactly how I had left it. For a moment, sheer blind panic held me within its grip. He was no pink elephant; you're worth more than this I thought.

As I re-entered my living room, my gaze fell upon the chess set. Its pieces had been neatly re-arranged. Upon closer inspection I realised that only two moves had been made and that the whisky bottle had replaced the Queen in status, the most powerful piece in chess. Strategically placed, the White King was now at checkmate by it.

Mechanically I retrieved the bottle from the board and nursed it, hoping the cold warmth would allow me to retreat from this harsh reality. It was then I noticed another change: 'Highfield' had gone.

I tried to recall the entire visit with the Major and finally this left me with only one thing that I had to do. "Austerfield, you can go to hell," I screamed.

The next day the kettle boiled; the doorbell rang and then – silence.

Time Loop Purple

"You will go with Austerfield next time."

CHAPTER THIRTEEN

A Dead Body Cannot Talk

Time Loop Red

The hotel Principia in York held that past elegance associated with the British Empire. Queen Victoria herself could have strolled through the doors and blended perfectly with her surroundings.

It was Saturday evening and John (Willow) Wilson, Head barman, looked unhappily at the neatly stacked wicker chairs at the far end of the restaurant. His Victorian styled outfit and greased hair made him appear much older. There was a sense of achievement as his eyes flitted lovingly along the precisely stacked wine and lager glasses behind the bar but that suddenly changed as he looked finally upon his last solitary customer. He scowled at the dark suited man, propped upon the remaining barstool. As if in response the man promptly adjusted his black rimmed glasses and smiled back.

John was desperate to leave work and catch up with his girlfriend at the Grapes pub. She was celebrating her twentieth birthday and he must not be late. This time she had given him an ultimatum and her words still taunted him. "I'll stay until Ten o'clock, but just one minute after, and I'm gone. Then you can go and find yourself another doormat."

By his 'Albert watch', it was ten to ten. As long as he didn't change out of his work-clothes, he might just make it. Victorian costume or not, he was not going to be late. He swung the watch back into his waistcoat.

"Another drink sir?" he volunteered, hoping that it might precipitate a reaction: one of the leaving kind.

The man peered over his black glasses and was about to speak, when the gold barred Reception doors swished open and for the fifth time that hour, his gaze devoured whoever had passed through.

Nine minutes to go.

At five to ten Willow examined his manicured fingernails carefully.

'Swish'

They both responded to the noise this time. Twin anxious looks peered through the restaurant doors to yet another visitor that entered Reception. Willow began drumming his fingers upon the bar top to the obvious annoyance of Black Glasses. Their eyes briefly clashed. The visitor now appeared agitated by the way he looked furtively towards them as he entered the bar and then stood there as if his batteries had run out. Now he appeared captivated with the broad sweeping windows of the restaurant.

Three minutes.

Willow looked back at Black Glasses. Their invisible bond now however, was one of anxiety.

He dragged his eyes away and casually strolled over to the window again and fiddled with his 'Albert' chain. Below the ashen Moon sprinkled a magic carpet upon the river and in silhouette, two ducks bobbed.

Two minutes.

Both Willow and Black Glasses now approached the visitor who was trembling upon a bar stool.

"What will you have to drink?" questioned Willow in a non committal way.

Their visitor looked wild eyed at him and was about to speak but abruptly paused. Black Glasses addressed the man in soothing tones.

"You don't have to go through with this meeting upstairs. Come with me instead – and you will be safe – I can assure you of that."

"It's none of your business!" shrieked the visitor as he hurried into the foyer.

"No!" Black Glasses shouted as he rapidly followed him out of the bar.

There was no wasted time. With the apron hurled over a vacant chair, Willow was through both swing doors and into the flowing night of revellers.

It was later that evening that he stared through Yates window at the Principalis opposite; sipped his lager and pondered the same thought he'd nursed two pints ago. She hadn't even waited a minute. Not one tiny minute! It was in this foul mood that Willow noticed a black figure upon Ouse Bridge. He recognised it instantly; his third drink was rapidly swigged back; his bruised ego sought revenge.

The Principia hotel room which Malik Hamid had booked held a Victorian styled four poster and retro deco. His concept was a purely business venture and that was why he had taken this room. He heard his guest wheezing outside the door; there was a brief silence before a hesitant knock followed by a rasping cough. With the lift out of action (all it took was chewing gum and a spanner) he speculated that four flights of steps to climb could be a trial for some people to undertake. It was his simple enjoyment to hear them and much better than the radio. Quickly he opened the door and caught a momentary gasp of surprise from his guest as with both hands he heaved him inside. Small talk bored Malik.

The brown-coated man was made to sit in a vacant wicker chair opposite his own. A low coffee table separated them. There was an electric stainless steel coffee jug, and sachets in a raffia bowl, but they were ignored. From his jacket pocket Malik produced a fistful of peanuts and proceeded to shell and eat them. Occasionally his gold bracelet flopped around his wrist to the obvious enchantment of his guest. There was an air of cockiness bordering on contempt as he looked at his watch which now displayed 10:10pm.

He allowed the man's look of fascination to wander upon the oval shaped sepia-toned pictures that hung above the mahogany dresser and then linger at the flamboyant drapes before he unleashed his coiled anger.

"Why are you late, Mr Austerfield?"

The man grinned nervously showing his badly decayed teeth. "T... te...Ten minutes past ten wasn't it?"

"Ten o'clock was the time, and you know that perfectly well don't you Mr 'Bald' head."

Austerfield cringed before the omnipotence of the man and whimpered. "If you say so Mr Hamid; if you say so." He repeated the last sentence in a more condescending way hoping to ingratiate himself.

"Have you got the package?"

Austerfield straightened up at that; his head staring like a church gargoyle. He spoke with a rough accent."I've got that all right, have you got the money?"

Malik smiled carefully. There was a cruel glint in his eye as he slowly nodded. He noted that the dingy coat was warily opened and a brown parcel was withdrawn. As the man leant across to place it on the table, a black slim document also slipped out of his pocket and onto the floor. Malik leapt forward, picked it up and opened it.

"Do you always carry your passport around, little man?"

"Please call me David," he whimpered, rubbing his hands nervously.

Malik threw the passport into the man's lap and more leisurely grabbed the parcel. After careful scrutiny, he noted the clever way in which it had been re-sealed. It was a neat job but not good enough to fool him.

"What a clever little David you are." He sneered. "I suppose now, you'll want to be paid?" He noticed the man's greedy eyes brighten.

"£50,000 was the agreed price."

"Shut up!" Malik carefully climbed out of his chair and walked over towards the dresser, opened it and took out a leather strap.

As if he was wringing out a tea cloth, Malik swiftly wrapped it around the man's neck. Within seconds the man stopped wriggling. He then meticulously searched the man and found a wallet within his top pocket.

"So you're really called Smythe are you?" he muttered as the contents of the wallet were examined and then carefully returned: he was not a thief.

Next thing was to find something suitable to weigh the body down. His final intention was to throw the body over the balcony and let the freezing water finish the job off. What halted this process was a solitary man upon the bridge who appeared to be looking straight at him. A witness to his deed was a complication he could do without.

He therefore waited patiently. After all, he was in no hurry. A dead body cannot talk but witnesses can.

Willow crept up unnoticed to his prey until he was within an arm's length. "Has she stood you up then?"

The man in black glasses merely turned from gazing over the bridge parapet. "Huh?"

Willow suddenly felt the chill of the night and his resolution cooled. "I've been observing you all night: first at the bar and now here staring into the river."

"Ah yes. You are the barman at the Principia. I'm sorry to have disturbed your night." With that, he turned and gazed upward to one of the lit apartment windows of the hotel.

"That's an understatement," Willow shouted.

He briefly turned. "Mmn."

"Do you realise you've totally ruined my night. Can't you at least say sorry?"

Black Glasses ignored him.

"You really aren't 'a people's person' are you?"

Black Glasses swivelled around. "What would you do if a second chance was given to you?"

Willow was taken aback. "I've never had that sort of luck. With me it's always the painful end of the wooden spoon. Take tonight. My girlfriend has finished with me because she's fed up with my time keeping. I might have stood a chance if you had only left on time."

The man had resumed his upward gaze. "I'm sorry for your misfortune."

Willow followed his line of sight. "I begin to see it all now."

"Mmn?"

"Your woman is up there with that man at the bar, isn't she?"

Black glasses turned and smiled. Your logic is intriguing but no, it's nothing like that."

"Well, what, then?" He noticed that this question obviously caused embarrassment. "What is it then?"

Abruptly the man pointed along the bridge."There's a girl beckoning to you."

Willow swivelled round and then bellowed. "Maggie."

They walked slowly towards each other but as she increased speed so did he until their urgent passion was consummated in fused bodies. For several moments they became lost within each other's arms until Maggie commented. "Where's he gone?"

"Who?"

"The man you were talking to."

Willow followed her gaze along that naked bridge. From far below, there came an almighty splash. "He's done himself in!" he cried.

CHAPTER FOURTEEN

A Ragged Mile

Time Loop Red

The kettle boiled and the doorbell played Dixie. I had trained myself to ignore interruptions especially before twelve. I had paid dearly for this hangover, so why should I have my experience cut short? Life on hold, that's all I asked for. Eventually they ceased their irritation but then the phone rang. With reluctance I climbed out of bed, staggered downstairs and snatched the offending item.

"Hello?"

"Ross – is that you?"

That was a difficult question to contemplate, almost surreal and philosophical. I gave a knowledgeable grunt.

"It's Peter – from the astro club?"

"Uh?"

"Peter – you remember me don't you?"

I tried hard to place him from the sea of faces at the club I had recently joined. The one who belched a great deal? No. The one who was all computers and cheque books? No. The one with curly hair, a smile to match and had just missed out on the Sixties rock revolution, scored brownie points. "What can I do for you Peter?"

"You were... were... on the telly last night. Discovery channel's Mysterious World. It was about crop circles and you were eating a piece of bread made from the corn. The commentator agreed with your comment about "Not feeding this bread to the ducks".

I tweaked my brain into gear. "That film was made a long time ago Peter."

"Sorry for ringing you but I just had to make sure it was you."

"That's fine." I said "Feel free to ring anytime." I slammed the phone down but immediately it rang again. I began to feel really annoyed now. "What is it now Peter?"

"Mr Ross?" The voice, very authoritative and cultured was an unfamiliar one; I growled like a guard dog. "Who's this?"

There was a slight pause. "My name's Major Gallagher. I've called to give you some important news regarding your passport. Can you return to the station, in let's say," I heard a deep intake of breath. "Let us say – in one hour's time?"

In a mellow voice I said. "I'll be there."

There was a polite cough. "I'll give you directions to our new substation."

Dislike of police stations was beginning to show as I snarled out my name to the sergeant; he was polite in return. Feeling contrite I followed meekly behind as he directed me towards a door marked 'Interview Room'. I noticed a thick plastic portfolio in his hands, and decided this was not going to be a quick 'in and out' affair.

The room was bigger than a broom cupboard but not much more. Blue cold walls; blue cold doors; blue cold cups and the tea when it arrived, tepid.

The sergeant all tousle-hair and moustache had a dominant scar that ran down the left-hand side of his face. He must have a tough job.

He motioned me into the centre of the room where there were two chairs parked neatly under a table. I pulled one out and sat down expecting him to do likewise. He did nothing of the kind but stood over me whilst he placed the book upon the table and opened it. Every page held a multitude of photographs and one looked familiar. Mr Smythe, ex convict with a string of petty crimes involving extortion, was staring back at me in the 'Whose Who' in crime.

The sergeant jotting in his Report Book, made all the right noises in the correct order, but the resignation in his voice said it all: I could kiss goodbye to my passport.

"Sorry to keep you sir." His piggy eyes seemed convincing. "But if you can spare a few more minutes, Major Gallagher would like a quiet word with you." He then left the room and just as abruptly, another figure entered and sat down opposite.

As he shuffled his papers, I studied him cautiously. With his struggling wisps of black hair, a Buddha face, he looked familiar. As he leant back in his chair to study me, I held his gaze. With his Edwardian suit and dark velvet waistcoat equipped with a dangling gold watch chain I had reservations. He pulled out his watch, scrutinised it and then played with the chain like a Rosary. It was carefully returned. With meticulous care he swivelled around in his chair and leant back again to reveal bright red socks. That was the vital clue I needed.

"Have we met before?"

He shot me a glance that could have melted armour plate. With an accent that gave me my final clue he said, "all in good time." He glanced down and I noticed he was scrutinising a document that was to his left. Finally he removed a pen and black notepad from inside his left inside pocket. He looked business.

"I've found your written statements a little puzzling Mr Ross."

"Oh?"

He was scribbling frantically now and appeared to ignore me. Outside there was a crash of cups and abruptly the door opened and in walked the tea lady. Her rippled face managed a smile. "Do you want refreshing?"

I nodded, but already wizened nimble fingers uncovered a white cup and saucer and squirted steaming brown liquid from a black plastic jug, scooped up the blue empties and then as quickly; she was gone. Only a plastic tea aroma lingered. This time at least it was warm. With precision Major Gallagher closed his notebook.

"We have met before, haven't we?"

His smile quivered slightly. "No. I don't think so."

It seemed so real: watching him drink coffee all snug and cosy in my best armchair, but then I also remembered the shock of walking back into my empty room. I had to get a grip.

"Perhaps you've seen me in the Press?"

I half-nodded studying his next reaction. "Yes. That must be it."

He relaxed then, re-opened his notebook and started scribbling furiously. I put up with this for a while but then I started to get real annoyed. "You've not found my passport have you?"

The direct stare he gave was disquieting. "Please bear with me for the moment. I just want you to clarify a few things."

My pulse raced; sweat appeared hot upon my brow; I hesitated before speaking. "Was there something wrong with one of my statements?"

He carefully examined his fingernails and a long unnerving silence followed. I began to become conscious of the hum of traffic outside. Abruptly he leant forward. "Don't be alarmed – but I am puzzled over this." He opened the leather bound document and prodded it in my direction.

This was not about my passport. I leant back in my chair, brushed one sweaty palm along my right trouser leg and attempted to smile. "What's wrong with it?"

With a monotone deliverance Gallagher said: "I'll come back to that." The smile he gave me then was too crafty for my liking. "At the Job Centre, what vacancy had you applied for?"

"TV researcher,"

"Have you experience in that area?"

"My last, real job was in advertising and media."

"Aha," he said knowingly, "So this vacancy was tailor made for you then?"

I nodded without trying to be too enthusiastic. "I suppose you could look at it that way. Yes."

He stroked his chin and then scribbled frantically on his note pad. "Don't mind if I ask you a few personal questions do you?"

I searched his eyes for tell tale clues to where this was leading, but found none. "If it will help." I said at last.

"I take it you are still unemployed?" My hard chair suddenly became unbearable and I wanted to move but I felt welded to it. "I just haven't found the right employer yet."

He appeared unmoved; only his hand scribbled and quivered like a seismograph. He suddenly glanced up and gave me a curious look. "You appear to look rather flushed; can I open a window for you?"

I assured him there was no need.

"Your recent divorce; was it an amicable one?"

My fist clenched and this time I shifted my thigh and leant forward. "If you really must know, it wasn't."

Gallagher leant back and once more examined his fingernails, then eyed me very carefully this time. "Was there a 'third party' involved?"

Sweat trickled down my face now. "Hell no! She just wanted some time on her own, that's all."

Beyond a very slight elevation of his eyebrows, there appeared no trace of emotion. "Teenage marriages are always a gamble." There was a pause; a sharp intake of breath. "Rather drastic, getting a divorce wasn't it?"

"Listen here," I snapped. "You're being rather personal aren't you? What has this got to do with my stolen passport?"

He ignored me again, but his hand made 10 on the Richter scale as he furiously scribbled more notes. What seemed like an embarrassing silence later, he glanced up and gave me a far-away look. "Mmn? Oh sorry. Forgive my intrusion into what must be still very painful for you."

I shuffled in my seat and said nothing.

Outside a dog barked.

In a measured voice he said. "I want to know more details about your recent brush with the law. Focus upon Wednesday and Thursday of last week?" He tapped the document again; I smelt the whiff of leather. I began to feel more anxious this time but looking round the room however, vital things were missing.

"Are you interrogating me?" I ventured.

"What do you think?"

I shrugged my reply.

An impish smile appeared upon his face. His receding hairline appeared to abseil down the back of his head.

"I am going to tell you a story Ross". As he spoke his face inched forward until our noses almost touched. "Here is a man through no fault of his own becomes redundant. He looks for work and has no money."

An annoying drop of sweat trickled over my left eyebrow. I leant back in my chair and eventually composed myself. Outside a car horn sounded. "That sounds like a song by Bob Dylan?"

He smiled. "Hollis Brown perhaps?"

"You know your music!"

"We both do. I think you know where this is leading to." His face crystallised into a smile. "Tell me more about your friend – David Austerfield?

"Oh. You want me to finish this story?"

"Amuse me Ross. Amuse me. Hollis has friends; gives him a job, which involves a little drive to France. Unfortunately he is stopped by customs. The van appears to be full of hi-tech computer components which Hollis denied all knowledge of; claimed he was delivering till register parts." The Major's face twisted into a sarcastic smile. "What sort of till registers did *you* supply?"

"He was badly misinformed." I answered.

"They were bound for Albania, weren't they?" He nodded airily. "Oh! We know all about that."

My mouth fell open. "Huh?"

"I'm afraid it's the truth. Did it never occur to you how you and he never got prosecuted?"

"Being innocent and having a good solicitor, that's why." I said staring indignantly across the desk at him.

Gallagher laughed. "Oh really; are you that gullible?" he leant forward. "Even now you could be sent to prison!"

"The case was dropped," I pleaded.

"Posing as a hitch-hiker wasn't very smart and how small minded was your business partner to evade Customs by running away. The Prosecution would have had a field day with that one. No more games Ross. Didn't you stop to think for one moment how lucky you were to escape with merely a caution?"

The penny dropped then and at last I felt at ease. "It was you who suggested I go with Austerfield. I don't think you are the police or a Major. Who are you really...? MI5? SIX?"

He gave a coy smile. "Personally, I was never very good with numbers or letters. All points of a compass."

"How convenient for you," I said dryly. "I thought the case was closed; what more do you want, Mister Gallagher?"

It was his turn to shuffle in his seat and appeared to nod as he opened his jacket revealing a green shirt and blue tie. He retrieved a passport, which was airily thrown onto the desk. A photograph too was extracted and placed on top. "What do you think to this?"

The face was that of a dead man. The morgue slab was a dead giveaway. It was Smythe. My eyes seemed glued to the picture.

"We fished him out of the Ouse this morning." He studied me carefully. "That passport was on him."

"Is it mine?" I ventured.

"No. It belongs to your business partner, Austerfield. I am puzzled, my friend. Why should this passport be on him?"

I pondered his words carefully. "Is this where I request a solicitor?"

He laughed. "Relax. No one is going to be charged, at least not yet. I'll be brief Ross. You are out of a job. I'll give you one. I need to know where your friend has gone; who his friends are; his movements leading up to the disappearance. You are the only person who knew him well enough to find that out for me. Will you do it?"

I thought it over. For Queen and Country or personal gain – these thoughts conflicted with one another. "At what rate of payment?" I enquired at last.

He laughed. "I admire your cheek."

"It will be expensive tracking him down." I gave a wily smile. "And I've children to support!"

"I'll see what I can arrange," he said soberly.

At the thought of having an income again I began to feel euphoric but still looked deadpan before replying. "I can't promise anything; but I'll give it my best shot."

As I got up to go he unexpectedly grasped my hand firmly. His other hand held a passport. "Oh! And by the way, I prefer to be called Major Gallagher – if you don't mind?"

I released a beaming grin. "Whatever you say – Major!"

CHAPTER FIFTEEN

The Lady Dressed in Blue

Time Loop Red

It was early evening; I was walking in the Shambles and I hadn't gone looking for trouble. Major Gallagher's job seemed a dream come true.

The long golden shadows seemed to entwine the medieval houses in a tender embrace and the cobbled street appeared gaunt and lifeless. A cold shiver rippled up and down my spine. It was something I couldn't quite put my finger on, but something was wrong and out of place. It felt like I was intruding. Involuntarily I turned to look in a doorway and saw a young couple embracing. Momentarily I harmonised with their intense sexuality, but then the old feelings welled up inside me which brought back the anger and the hurt of that fateful night: my last wife's hug which was her way of saying goodbye forever.

It was history now, like rotting fish on the beach of the Ouse. I reminded myself that my energies must be directed on finding Auster. In truth I hadn't a clue where to look first. He had a girlfriend who worked at Kristos restaurant. Perhaps she could be my first port of call. It must have been a couple of weeks ago now, when he first introduced Suzy to me. Not one for splashing his money around he had taken me there for a meal. He forced me to wear a tie – I detest ties.

"Does tha think she'll like it?"

I put my fork down on the table and regarded him with renewed interest. "Presents? You've only just met her last night."

He erupted into a smile. "Wait 'til you see her. She's a fit lass; ample buxom and pert arse."

I moved forward so that I could inspect the gift in his hands. "Where on earth did you con the money to buy an engagement ring that size?"

He leant back in his chair and with an air of cockiness remarked. "Tha'as daft tha knows: you'd folla' balloons and think it a wedding wouldn't tha?" He then rolled up his sleeve to reveal an armful of Rolkex watches.

I looked suitably impressed, which was a mistake. Ten pounds exchanged hands as he attached a watch to my wrist. It was a 'Yunphuk', 'Rolkex'. "I thought they were Swiss made?" I lamented.

He ignored my anguish. "She is an out of work actress," he said preening his jacket for unseen fluff.

I shuffled a few chips into my mouth trying hard to disguise my mirth. Auster's females are usually hard faced and quickly find him an easy touch. "How intriguing." I said at last.

"I soon found her a nice little number in the cabaret business. Who needs RADA?" He noted my questioning look. "That's a school for actors."

I mumbled confirmation whilst trying to cram another forkful of chips down my throat. As I struggled with cutting the fish, I heard a deep sigh.

"My fish were crap."

"Nice chips though?" I offered a smile and tried to force

the vision out of my head of Auster wooing yet another woman with his pre-set routine. It usually started with presents; with romance; with over indulgent charm and finally with pleading as they backed off from his cloying advances. If it wasn't so funny I would think he was a secret stalker.

He had turned towards the entrance; I looked too and nearly choked upon my prime haddock. A fluffy blonde in black leather jacket and trousers that moulded like cling film, stood poised there. When this vision moved it was like watching a model on a catwalk. Close up, her eyes smouldered with ruthless ambition. She looked trashy and classy all at once.

"Hi," she said giving a slight pout of her lips towards me.

Abruptly I became aware that I was perspiring and mouthing, "hello."

Auster leapt up and offered his chair. "Sit down lass and I'll introduce you to ma best mate Ross." He hugged her passionately as his face beamed supernova. "This is Suzy."

His hand now was in his back trouser pocket and lovingly he produced a fat roll of money bound up with two rubber bands. I had never seen so many fifty pound notes snuggled up like sardines before in my life. He offered to buy more drinks but I shook my head.

"I must go," I said. "See you around."

"I've got a business trip lined up soon. There's money in it for you if you help out with the driving."

I merely nodded.

We arranged to meet at Rik's the following Wednesday. I began to have second thoughts about keeping that appointment.

I paused to look into a photographic shop window, and admired the laughing-eyed redhead there. I was brash enough to give her a sexy wink, but she couldn't return the compliment, even if she wanted to. Only her Kodachrome smile beckoned. I wished that I had been that photographer.

My instincts told me I wasn't alone. Within a shop doorway; amongst the shadows; a pair of petite boots peeked. It shouldn't have bothered me: after all this was normally a busy York street and I had just caught it resting awhile. The shadow moved and the effect upon my neck was electric; yet still I couldn't understand why. I dived through a narrow opening into the now deserted market place and instantly regretted it: there was nowhere to hide, but why should I? My instincts were playing havoc with my reason but raw fear had gripped my senses and flight was the resultant force.

I moved deftly across the market and into Parliament Street. This at least possessed a few tourists milling around searching for eating-places and my intention was to blend in with them. I made my way towards Coney Street.

Momentarily I glanced into a window and caught in its reflection; a flash of blue.

I increased my pace.

Coney Street is a long narrow street. I walked halfway down it, then smartly turned about and ventured back the way I had come. It was time to confront my ghost.

My pace increased. There were three people coming towards me. Two appeared together, wearing white overcoats with Texan hats, but behind them – all red hair and blue two-piece was an elfin-faced girl. She matched the reflection I had glimpsed earlier. Close-up, her perfume hit me like a sledgehammer. She appeared startled as I sped past her. I turned left at Woolworth into Market Street. My intention was to get to Parliament Street as quickly as I could and then disappear into one or two of York's famous snickleways. Those thoroughfares: Three Cranes and Mad Alice lane are an excellent means of discrete rapid travel and so I drifted like a ghost between the main streets. Eventually I doubled back towards Coney Street.

It worked. I had out-foxed the lady dressed in blue – or so I had thought.

CHAPTER SIXTEEN

Nervous PhD

Time Loop Blue

She was nervous. It didn't take a PhD to see that. He had noticed the rapid pacing around the room; the clenched agitated hands; the muttering under the breath.

"Relax; you'll ruin your mascara."

Beneath short red hair, eyes flashed in anger. "Dimitri, shut up! The courier should be here by now."

He rolled his brandy glass in his hands, leaned against the sliding doors that opened onto the balcony and in a measured response said, "he *will* arrive soon Anya – but I thought your intentions were to take me to bed."

Abruptly she smiled. "It's your turn to relax now. There's plenty of time for that afterwards."

The way her hands smoothed down her tight leather skirt caused his heart to pound.

"In that case I had better not drink too much of this brandy."

She pouted seductively at him. Her laughter, when it came, sounded like tinsel that rustled with no real substance. "Ooh! I can't wait Dimitri!"

He forced a smile and raised his brandy glass before taking a discrete mouthful. These last few days she had scared him with her moods: they had been up and down like shark's teeth. Action was required. The glass contents were gulped down; he straightened his suit and tie. He stood up and firmly opened the sliding doors, brushed aside the lace curtains and walked outside onto the balcony. What greeted him as he peered through the rubber plants and down to the street below was utter chaos. Athens was never a place to drive in safety at any time. New cars, old cars; the busy suburb held no respect. To see a brand new 'Rolo' covered in dents was a normal event. This particular variety: a white Cornice with a scraped right wing, held a fascination to him as it parked outside the apartment to a fanfare of angry horns. He turned towards her through the swirling lace. "The courier has arrived."

"Oh really," she cooed.

He watched fascinated as Anya walked over to the French dresser and opened the left-hand drawer. A gleam of sadistic pleasure momentarily flashed across her face. Through the flapping curtain he caught a glimpse of a gun that was pointing directly at him. In an idle surreal sort of way he recognised it was a small calibre Beretta with a silencer. Sharks teeth all over again; she could pull that trigger without a moment's thought.

Unaware of his gaze, she smiled and slowly replaced it back inside the drawer. However what really caused his heart to flutter was a small pen like device she next pulled out of the drawer. He noted her chilling smile. He must have gasped because she turned in his direction and then quickly replaced it back inside the drawer. It felt as if he was watching a small child caught with her hands in the cookie jar. Could she have known that he possessed a copy inside his left-hand pocket?

Unexpectedly the door opened and two men entered, one dressed all in black with a gold earring and the other, a gypsy looking man dressed in a shabby brown raincoat, his face part shielded by his lapels.

"Thank you Manolis, you can go now."

The gold earring man briefly smiled at Anya before he left the room.

"So glad you have eventually arrived Mr Ross." She turned briefly and Dimitri witnessed her secret smile. "We almost gave you up."

"I'm sorry; I got caught in the traffic."

"Oh yes." Anya was purring nicely now, "Athens is notorious for it. Please sit down." She indicated towards a white lace covered settee.

Ross meekly did as he was told, but didn't take his eyes off Anya. "Yes I would love that very much."

"Dimitri, stop hovering out there and show our guest some Greek hospitality by pouring a glass of our finest Five-Star Metaxa."

"Yes Anya."

The colour drained from the face of Ross at the sight of Dimitri. "You!" he exclaimed.

Dimitri blushed and headed towards the dresser. His back turned, he filled two glasses with Metaxa. "Do you know me?"

"I thought I did – from England – but that's impossible…."

"I've never been to England," retorted Dimitri as he gave him his drink. "You must be confusing me with someone else?"

Anya looked amused at each of them in turn. "Curious? And most interesting to observe."

Dimitri reclined in a vacant chair and shrugged. "I have encountered many doubles whilst here in Athens."

Anya gleamed with pleasure. "A mystery then?"

"Sorry for my mistake," Ross stammered, staring into his brandy glass.

"I most definitely hope so... Mr Ross!"

Ross gazed open mouthed at Dimitri's glare but said nothing.

Anya looked hard at Ross. "I hope your flight was a pleasant one with no mishaps?"

His eyes were searching the brandy glass again. "I had no problem with customs if that is what you mean."

She admired his directness but his shifty downward look intrigued her. "Have you brought the merchandise?"

Ross looked up briefly and reluctantly placed his glass upon the oak table at his feet. Reaching deep within his inside pocket, he revealed a small brown paper parcel. She walked over to where he was sitting and almost dragged it off him. After scrutinising the parcel she noted the clever way in which it had been re-sealed. It was a neat job but not neat enough.

"You have done well and you will be handsomely rewarded. It was a considerable risk you have undertaken in bringing this to us." She noticed his greedy eyes light up.

"When will I be paid?"

"Now if you like? Fifty thousand was the agreed price."

"In Sterling?" enquired Ross.

"Greek Drachmas may leave you a little short!" She noticed Dimitri trying hard to swallow a laugh. "A thousand to the English pound – I believe it is now. Correct me if I'm wrong Dimitri?"

Anya's stony face was prelude to trouble. He looked across at Ross calmly sipping brandy; the man who had nearly blown his cover. His voice became husky. "Something like that Anya."

"You don't seem yourself today; a little pale perhaps?"

Dimitri inwardly shivered: this was danger time; an urgent response was required. He got up but was immediately pushed down by Anya who stood over Ross and slammed the parcel into his lap, "Open it," she screamed.

Meekly he did as he was told to reveal a book bound in yellow leather. The spine had been torn and a silver pen – like instrument peeked from within.

"What is that?" she demanded.

"I don't know," he replied with surprise clearly held in his voice.

She walked over towards the drawer and carefully opened it, not daring to turn, not daring to give away the rapture in her face, and not daring to reveal what she now held. "Before I pay you, have you anything else to say to me? Anything at all?

He looked up nervously. "What else is there to say?"

"Oh nothing," she casually replied turning slowly opening her hands to reveal an identical pen like device. "I think you will find this is the real thing!"

Abruptly the air smelt of acrid flesh as a beam of intense blue light engulfed Ross. His face twisted and he screamed like a banshee as his entire body blackened as if set alight. Finally his body slumped back onto the chair; a shrunken mummified form.

Dimitri smelt acrid flesh and retched. "Good God! What have you done?"

She gave him a contemptuous look. "The less you know the better."

"You've killed him?"

Anya cackled. "It was purely a precaution after he failed to give the password. I gave him ample warning."

Dimitri wiped the back of his neck with his hand. "I assumed he forgot, after all one area of operations is not familiar with another's. That is how it must be for security reasons"

"He was not our courier, I am sure of that point. By the way, the parcel had been tampered with." She paused waiting for her words to sink in. "Why the fake device I wonder; it stinks of a double cross. Either way – he behaved as a rank amateur and as such, dangerous." She turned and spat in the direction of Ross.

Dimitri's finger quivered towards the instrument in her hand. "What devilish thing is that?"

Anya angrily waved it towards him and screamed. "No questions or else!"

"Whatever you say darling."

"Yes – obey me!"

He watched amazed as she calmly placed the pen like device upon the table then rolled the body onto the floor. She then carefully straightened out the chair covers. With indifference as if examining a dinner menu she leant over the body "Do you think he was the one that our English cell was investigating? Calmly her fingers sifted through the jacket pockets and produced a wallet and two passports. One was in the name of Ross, the other Smythe. Both had identical photos within.

Dimitri got up from his chair and peered over her shoulder. "Gawpead," he murmured under his breath. Whilst Anya was distracted he picked up the strange pen device from the table and swapped it for the one in his pocket. "Can we find out who he is?" he suggested.

She merely shrugged. "Who he was," she corrected primly giving him a chilling smile. "He appears quite a mystery." Her attention was drawn towards examining the wallet which produced a hotel bar receipt in the name of Smythe. "The Royal Hotel, York." she murmured. "Let us assume his name is this. "Kalanichta Mr Smythe."

Dimitri felt as if someone had walked over his grave. "Then who the hell is Ross?" he said as he regained his seat.

She walked over to a table where a white phone was situated and held up the receiver and dialled. "I seem to recollect that you *had* been to England?" Before Dimitri had time to answer, Anya spoke rapidly into the mouthpiece. Eventually she replaced the receiver. "I intend to go to York to deal with this matter personally. You know what to do here."

He nodded, and then stood up as if to go.

"Oh no you don't!" Her voice was low and seductive. "We have some unfinished business to deal with." Anya took him roughly by the arm and propelled him into the bedroom.

"It's pamper time," she drooled.

A dead body slumped in an armchair was not the world's best seduction line.

CHAPTER SEVENTEEN

Sledgehammer Perfume

Time Loop Red

Through the corner of one eye, I had seen her. That flash of blue against the black frontage of Little Betty's Café was a dead giveaway. I hung back inside Coffee Yard and with a great delicacy glanced once more into Stonegate. Clutching her handbag, she held the air of the tourist: peeking through this and that shop window.

I wasn't fooled.

Perched against the wall above my head, a carved red devil gave a wicked smile and I wondered whose misfortune he was contemplating.

Unexpectedly she stopped and appeared in deep thought. I felt as if I could read her mind. She turned first one way and then the next. There was something within the shop window that held her fascination now. Mesmerised I shifted my weight in an attempt to gain a clearer view only to realise that it was my reflection that she had seen. Meticulously she turned and stepped across the street. In sheer panic I hurled myself down Coffee Yard hoping it would swallow me up.

She must have entered now. I only had a couple of seconds before being discovered.

To my left, the courtyard stairway of Barley Hall beckoned me to be devoured within its shadows. I crouched low on the steps with my face to the wall. Her echoed footsteps seemed to pound and echo around the alleyway. I cowered and contemplated my fate.

She stopped. A simple left turn of her head and surely I would be discovered. This was a strange union; two minds focused upon the intensity of the night. Abruptly her footsteps resumed their rhythmic beat and as quickly, softened into oblivion. I followed at a discrete distance and just managed to dive into a shop doorway when she headed back upon herself, along Davygate, past Bettys and towards Kristos. In trepidation I waited five minutes and then tentatively I too entered the foyer.

The show on that night was simply called 'Camera Obscurer'. I asked the usherette if she had seen a lady in a blue dress pass by a few moments ago.

"Oh yes. She has just gone in," she replied in a commanding sort of way. I followed her outstretched finger. "There she is on the front table."

Against my better judgement, I purchased a ticket from the desk and found a table at a discrete distance away. My eyes were drawn towards a stage set. Two photoflood 'Blondes' lit a high-backed wicker chair, which was positioned centre stage. Off to the left was a Hasselblad on a tripod, with 'Redhead' lights positioned either side.

On the walls were black and white photographs of glamour models. I couldn't help but admire the simple but effective stage-set.

A tall black coated man with silver buckled shoes walked past me and headed in the direction of the blue lady but sat at an adjacent table. They appeared in deep conversation but I was too far away to hear. When the lights eventually dimmed, a third figure joined them. Abruptly a multi-coloured spotlight filtered across the tables followed by a spotlight that lit centre stage. When the band struck up, I guessed it was show time.

From behind the chair peeped a devastating short-cropped blonde. Even from where I was sitting I could see the high cheekbones and petite nose of an angel. It was Auster's girl! She climbed up until she was positioned on top of the chair. Wearing black fishnet stockings, the ghost of a white sequinned dress, and elbow length gloves she stared provocatively. Her hand toyed with a microphone and then she gently swayed gracefully onto the stage with sequins that flashed through the semi-darkness. From stage left and right two male dancers joined her. All black tuxedos and swinging Nikon cameras for neck chains, they grasped and then flung her recklessly into the air.

Their dance routine was slick, but my mind began to be focused more upon Silver Buckle and his companions, who were now in deep conversation. Their irritating drone was becoming obvious to everyone including the performers on stage. A spotlight followed Suzy as she left the stage and headed towards them. Silver Buckle shining like an angel appeared completely stunned. Suzy pounced, entwining her body around him and I witnessed her flapping hair and his choking panic. The companion to his left covered his face in embarrassment, but the lady in blue threw back her head and gave a deep throated laugh that must have been audible a mile away in Rougier Street. Velvet blackness brought with it tumultuous applause. As the house lights went up, I noticed that they had all gone.

Later, at the bar, Silver Buckles staggered towards me and we almost collided. His black glasses slid off his face, but I grabbed hold of them. The smell of alcohol draped around his body like a shroud.

"Enjoy the show?" I said handing back his glasses.

"No I did not." His hand and eye co-ordination seemed out of step as he attempted to refit his glasses.

"You should feel honoured: men usually hurl themselves at her feet. They'd kill to receive the treatment you've just had." The look in his face gave me quite a turn: like that of a vet examining a sick animal.

"Why the adoration which is so short lived? I see an old woman, in a residential home. She is scorned, neglected and easily confused."

"Perhaps you need a change of glasses," I remarked dryly.

He appeared to ignore me and glanced down at his watch. I followed his gaze and became fascinated by an outer bezel of his watch that seemed to pulsate with flashing red numbers. I caught him saying "16minutes. 29secs."

"Are you late for a bus?" I enquired, but he had already staggered away heading to join his companion. It was Major Gallagher! What was he doing here?

I went backstage in search of Suzy.

I knocked at her dressing room and a muffled voice beckoned me to enter. The thrill of delicate perfume immediate and intense was my first impression of Suzy's room. It was small with pink wallpaper. The carpet, if you could call it that, was threadbare revealing wooden flooring.

Across the room there was a woman who was slowly being seduced by Mahler. All flowery dressing gown and long legs that stretched to eternity she appeared to flow over her gnarled wooden chair like paint. A full brandy glass drooled from her hand. Abruptly the contents were pivoted down her throat; she gave me an accusing stare. "Who the 'ell are you?"

"I am a friend of Auster's."

She sighed in a disappointed way. "Oh! You're not a fan then?"

I gave her my best coy grin. "Is the Pope Jewish?"

She giggled and wiped her mouth with her hand. "You're as crazy as Auster. Pour yourself a drink." She stretched out her foot and there was a screech of a chair being pushed towards me. Her voice held amusement. "Have a seat."

On her dressing table was a slim bottle. It was half full, but then so was she. Beyond that was another brandy glass, I wiped cobwebs off the rim and filled it. My voice held admiration. "This is 'Five Star' Metaxa. I see you have taste."

Unfocused eyes sought mine. "It's a present from my sister."

I pointed the bottle at her wrist before re-filling her tumbler."I see we share the same taste in watches."

"Small world," she cooed.

"Quite,"I said trying not to notice her revealing cleavage. "That's quite a double," pointing to her glass.

She gazed down at her chest and slowly back at me; her lips pouted. "Cheeky."

"I was referring to your drink!"

Her laugh rippled like a drain. "Well you can admire all you like; I'm beautiful and I know it!" The contents were tippled down her throat. I refilled it before placing the bottle next to her and then perched myself upon the dressing table edge.

"So what's the problem with our mutual friend Auster?"

She inhaled sharply. "Auster is a rat! I should really throw you out." Her voice was slurred but coherent. "What's your name?"

"Ross," I said politely.

"Oh", She said in a knowing way adding, "I remember him talking about you now."

"Nothing bad I hope?"

She tried a cool, level stare but failed. Her attempt to bend her body towards me almost failed but I readily helped her; our noses touched. Her breath stank of garlic and alcohol, but even so, I wanted to dive into those inky fathomless pools of hers.

I sucked in a deep breath. "Tell me all about yourself – who are you really and what were you before?"

Her eyes lit up like bonfire night. "Do you think me sexy?"

I nodded encouragingly. "Lots of women try – but you succeed. You've quite a fan club out there."

She threw back her head and gave a laugh. "Bah! You would be surprised."

"Surprise me."

"I am also very sensitive. All my girlfriends come to me if they are in trouble; I have many friends."

I nodded again not realising her intention.

Her face twisted in contempt. "Austerfield: he's a rat!" She spat on the floor barely missing my foot.

I leant over and lightly touched her arm. "All I can say is more fool him. He must be deaf, blind as well as dumb".

My words hadn't registered. I could tell by the way she tried to focus on her glass; swaying slightly.

Eventually with another deep breath she said wistfully, "everyday he used to call. There would be pubs; clubs... or we would stay in. I can be very homely you know. Now all I get is that infernal answering machine of his."

My voice held urgency. "We need to find him because he might need our help."

Her long legs opened and shut like a pair of tongs. Her voice held caution. "What kind of help?"

"When was the last time you saw him?"

"I can tell you exactly. It was last Wednesday: the day of my birthday."

"Yes that was the first time we met too. This may seem like an odd request," I paused, "but do you know any of his friends or acquaintances?"

She feigned a yawn. "I'll have to think about that one, maybe check my diary when I get home."

I gave her my telephone number. "If you do remember anything I would be grateful."

She threw me a coy look. "How grateful?"

"The Police and Interpol are after him you know."

A startled look swept across her face. "You're telling me he's in trouble?"

"Maybe; I'm not sure yet, but the sooner we find him the better."

The awe in Suzy's face made me realise that I had clearly gone up in her estimation. "My sister will collect me soon. We have arranged a taxi for one o'clock. If you like, you can come home with me and I can check my diary there."

I glanced at my watch. If her sister was coming she was cutting it fine. My ears didn't detect the soft swish of a door opening but the hard sledgehammer perfume betrayed the figure that had entered.

"This is my sister Anya."

I turned and felt the world had stopped turning. It was the lady dressed in blue.

CHAPTER EIGHTEEN

Ghostly Laughter

Time Loop Red

In the taxi I was squashed next to Anya. Her body felt hard, warm and very sexy; the nearness was as cloying as her perfume.

I caught Anya taking a lipstick out to prune herself. An idle glance into the open handbag put the fear of God into me. Was it a replica; a cigarette lighter – or perhaps an ornament? Whatever it was, a gun is still a gun. What was she doing with it? We travelled into the suburbs of York and finally pulled up outside No 26A Huntington Road. The only attraction Huntington Road had (apart from Sainsbury's) was the Foss. On a good day it flowed with less rubbish than usual. I was pleased that it was dark, misty, and couldn't see it.

Suzy's flat was reached by climbing very weary steps. Peeling orange wallpaper, an ill fitting threadbare carpet and an oversized sofa, summed up her abode. Apart from the smell of damp, I liked it. A single bulb hung from the ceiling and cast harsh stark shadows against the far wall. A drinks cabinet – a relic of the Victorian past – snuggled there. Opposite the sofa were a couple of wooden chairs with green bound backs. I took one and promptly sat on a squeaky toy. Suzy removed her leopard skin jacket and wrapped it neatly around the other. She appeared irritated.

"I'll go and find my diary." she said.

"No hurry," I remarked and meant every word. I didn't fancy being alone with this gun toting Annie Oaklie.

In the next room I heard an indistinct cry and then a shuffling noise. A small boy aged about five or six suddenly flew into the room and leapt into the arms of Suzy. He was sobbing. "Mummy, mummy. Where you been?"

I must admit it caught me off guard. For some reason I was surprised that she was a mother. What sort of parent leaves her young son alone at night? My look must have portrayed what I was feeling; her reply was a guilty stare.

She bent down to hug him. "Hush now child," she cooed.

The boy's eyes suddenly focused upon the toy I held and tried to reach for it. I walked over and placed it in his outstretched hands. His eyes were pools of innocence. "Have you been playing with mummy?"

I crouched down and smiled at him. "Your mum's helping me find my friend."

"I've got a friend."

"Really?"

"Of course, he only comes when mummy goes out at night."

"Does he read bed time stories to you?" I said relieved that it might have been her baby sitter.

He coyly sucked his forefinger. "He's an Angel and we fly through the window together on adventures."

Suzy gave me a look of disgust. "Hush now Robbie." she scooped him in her arms and headed out of the room, presumably back to his bed. I was left alone with Anya.

She stood facing me, eyeing me up and down. I did likewise. I wasn't fooled by the smart double-breasted jacket, the type with deep padded shoulders; I wasn't fooled by her black leather trousers that showed off the rest of her curves. I wasn't fooled neither by her baby doll face or sensuous lips. Lurking behind big dark eyes was pure malevolence. If she possessed a soul it was out on vacation somewhere.

The light caught the gold bracelet of her watch. It appeared as lethal as the gun in her handbag. I could be wrong of course: perhaps that article was the real thing. She painted on a smile for my benefit. "I want to ask you about your friend David Austerfield: have you known him long?"

I sensed this was audition time. "We knocked around at school together. Never felt so lonely until he showed up. Kids can be cruel to those that don't fit." She remained silent so I continued. "He couldn't speak much English then, and I..."

She cut in sharply. "My sister said you are looking for him?"

I was taken aback by that. "I've only spoken to your sister this evening."

She smiled in a knowing way and moved towards me. She grasped my right arm. "Come and sit with me on the sofa and I will show you some photos. I think you may find them interesting."

I allowed Anya to keep squeezing my arm as we sat down. I made polite conversation. "Nice watch you are wearing. Can I see it?"

She held out her wrist for me to admire it. I was right. It was as phoney as the boyfriend who had given it to her. She saw that I too had the same make of watch. "I had to buy mine," I said. We both laughed at that.

She retrieved a pack of photos from her handbag and these were shoved into my lap. Her hands grappled around before pulling one out. It was the picture that Gallagher had shown me. It made me feel uneasy. She pulled me close and I could smell garlic on her breath. "Is this your friend?"

I gazed into the bloated face of Smythe and then at the phoney 'Rolkex' she was wearing. With my voice deadpan I replied. "I have never seen him before in my life."

My body was pushed aside like a rag doll and I saw her hand dive into her handbag. I heard a sharp metallic click.

"You are very stupid Mr Ross. Have you anything else to tell me; anything at all?"

An ill-advised drop of sweat trickled into my left eye. It was then I heard behind me the door opening and light footsteps.

"Anya! Please talk more quietly until Robin goes to sleep."

The angry face of Suzy made me inwardly laugh. I faked concern as I said: "Trying to calm a sobbing child is no joke at this time of the morning."

Anya appeared to nod as she closed her handbag. I noted resignation as she said: "I need a drink, anyone else?"

I gave her my best smile: the one reserved for Auster when it was his turn to buy a round. "I would love one," I said.

She climbed off the sofa heading towards the drink cabinet. My chance had come. I didn't look at my watch. "My goodness is that the time? I must be going."

The photos spilt onto the floor in my haste to reach the door. It wouldn't budge. I grappled with the lock and managed to prise it open. I wished I hadn't. The light that spilled out of the open doorway illuminated a figure almost as wide as he was tall. All white flowing robes thick black beard and mean ferret eyes that glared with menace. He wasn't moving. I hesitated and then stepped back: obviously out-weighed. He pushed me roughly towards the sofa. His jet-black hair was as false as his smile; I sat down meekly

"Is he troubling you lass?" His voice growled like a rabid dog.

Anya cooed her reply. "Salaam alaikum."

His reply was instant. "Wa Alaikum as-Salaam."

"Malik! Your timing is impeccable." I caught the insanity in her eyes as she turned towards me. "He seems to be having memory problems about his friend." She picked up the pictures and singled out the mug shot of Smythe again. "You know this man don't you?" Her voice screamed now. "Don't you?"

Suzy, who had now sat next to me, sniggered loudly. "That photo is definitely not his friend, *or* mine. The rat – I'm glad he's dead."

"Was he your boyfriend too?" I said incredulously.

"Ex," she exclaimed hotly.

Anya appeared amused. "My little sister – what have you been hiding from me?"

"I meant to write, but anyway, it's all over now. I have a much better boyfriend now; there's a photo somewhere."

I was intrigued. "You're both Greek then?"

Anya gave me a haughty look and Malik straddled the settee. His hand popped into his pocket and produced a fistful of peanuts, which he proceeded to shell.

I heard a cry from the bedroom. Suzy stared wildly at her sister and leapt to her feet and towards the room door.

"Can't this wait till morning?" she said.

Anya had her handbag open again; Malik was smiling in a sickening way. I looked at the gun that now pointed at my chest and then more appealingly back at her.

"A Browning 9mm; I see you have taste!"

She held an eyebrow smile. "Talk – and make it convincing."

"Can't we even discuss this?"

"I'm listening."

"If you set that off, you'll have more police buzzing around than you can deal with. I can assure you of that fact." I tried to sound convincing.

Anya laughed as with deliberation she carefully removed a silencer from her bag and screwed it onto her gun. "Crimped bullets, polished bore and this delicious silencer make no noise whatsoever. Now Malik and I will take you for a little walk towards the River Foss. You will blend in nicely with its floating rubbish. Who will come to your aid then Mr Ross?"

My stomach did a "U" turn. "I don't understand why you want to kill me. I have no business dealings with Austerfield at all. He owes me money and that's the simple fact." My bottom lip started to quiver like a double bass.

"Come, come," she purred and pawed my arm. "No harm will come to you, this I promise. Just tell me what we want to know. Why did this – Mr Smythe have your passport on him when he – so unfortunately," she spoke softly here, "met his Maker?"

I knew I was pleading for my life, so I told her the whole story of my encounter with Smythe; however I felt it wise to omit Gallagher from the picture.

A quick glance at Malik registered that he had stopped cracking his shells. He was clearly thirsting for more information and interrupted me.

"Ask him about Red Mercury? Go on. Ask him if he's got it." His eager voice was irritating.

She looked me straight in the eye. "Well?"

I looked in all innocence. "Red Mercury; what's that?"

She signed. "I thought so. Let's leave now and give my sister some peace shall we?"

My protested ignorance fell on deaf ears. I felt my left arm being held in a vice like grip by Malik. That however was lucky for me because my Judo training was my saviour. All his weight was behind that cruel twist he gave to my arm. I sagged, let him heave and then simply jumped upwards, pushed outwards and sideways which threw him completely of balance. I held the initiative now and spun him around and then pushed him hard into Anya. They fell in a crumpled heap. I heard a thud of a metal object. Across the room, lying next to the sofa was the gun. Unfortunately, there was no time to reach it.

I leapt towards the door leading to the bedroom and promptly collided with Suzy. In her hands she carried a diary and a picture which fell out of her hands; it slid across the floor towards me. If I had more time, I would have said how well composed it was, and that it was a young couple embracing. There was a gasp from her as she saw the gun and then a cry from Anya as she looked at the picture. "Dimitri?" she cried.

Who the hell was Dimitri I thought? Instinctively I bent down and picked up the photo as I ran upstairs and into the nearest bedroom. I saw the window was slightly open. From under the bed covers a little head peeked.

"Sweet dreams Robbie," I said as I opened the window fully and hurtled into the dark.

I knew these flats from my misspent youth. In my hospital days, I gate-crashed nurses' parties via this beautiful mode of access: the fire escape. With the sound of running feet behind, I ran towards the Foss knowing it to be dark and safe; my lead could only be a few minutes. I ran as silently as I could along the riverside path, skidding every now and then on the duck shit. There was a fleeting cry as someone slipped and fell. A smile graced my lips and I thanked the ducks for giving me extra time. My feet and lungs ached.

The path ended abruptly with a high bridge wall. From behind, I heard a 'swish, swish, swish', and I realised Anya was firing at me. Since I was still alive, perhaps crimped bullets were inaccurate at range! That academic thought held cold comfort as I stared at this barrier to my freedom. I veered sideways and crossed over the road and into Sainsbury's car park. This afforded little refuge because heavy breathing behind me indicated they were still on my trail. I headed into Peasholme Green and from there clambered up and onto the Roman walls grateful that the wall keeper had forgotten to lock the gates. I did his job for him that night.

From this high vantage point I could look to see if they were still following. Alone amongst the silence, I shivered but not from the cold. Somewhere behind me were a gun-crazed woman, and her bodyguard. That fleeting glimpse of Suzy's nicely composed picture and Anya's exclamation puzzled me. I examined the photo again and recognised a familiar face. Why was Auster posing as Dimitri?

The walls curved into the centre of York. I knew the exit gate should be locked – and this time it was – so I climbed over the low wall into Goodramgate. If only I could find enough human company to blend with, I would be safe. The nightclubs would be closing now, but that was at the other side of town. I ran towards Goodramgate, and then left through the medieval archway into Bedern. It was then I heard high-pitched laughter.

I hoped it was only the ghosts.

CHAPTER NINETEEN

Throat and Dagger

Time Loop Red

Bedern is a restless place to be in after midnight. It has a reputation for being haunted by laughter; dead children's laughter; so I had a choice.

Bullets or ghosts?

With raw fear I leapt towards these ghostly sounds that ebbed and flowed with the night.

In the mid – 19 Century, George Pimm, Master of the York Industrial Ragged School in Bedern, murdered his intake of homeless children so that he could collect more church income from the readily available waifs and strays abandoned in York. He worked and starved them to death. They were then buried under the floor boards or locked in a large cupboard ready for the next intake. Shortly afterwards ghostly laughter and screams haunted him until he eventually committed suicide. Their restless spirits have still lingered on down the centuries.

Between the walls of the red brick mews, I too drifted like a phantom, feeling drawn towards Andrews Gate and finally to Merchant Adventurer's Hall. All dull brick, thatch roof and sweeping driveway, this proud building beckoned me onward. I became aware that the noise issued from a particular upstairs window that glowed with ashen light. My hand tried the front door handle and found it unlocked.

With awe and relief I stood and gazed around me: all oak beams; wooden floors and time worn plaster, but no ghostly children. Inside, the hall was awash with ballroom gowns and expensive penguin suits. In my white overcoat I stood out like a polar bear amongst a flock of penguins. At its entrance, a huge matron like woman eyed me up and down before addressing me in a thick Scottish voice.

"Are yee a guest?"

"I guess I am."

"Awe yee come wi' someone, or are yee visiting fro' another Lodge?"

My God, I thought, I've walked into a Freemason gathering. From inside the hall, I heard guffaws and then a twee voice. "Mary Wesley, is that really you, and after all these years?"

It gave me an idea. "I'm with Mary," I exclaimed with a beaming smile.

The barriers lifted in her voice. "Awe a ken noo! Yee'll find her in there."

I eased past her and suddenly became entwined within a swirl of red and blue sequins of a five-piece jazz band. They were busily tuning up. "'Eyup lad, wot's tha' game?"

I retrieved my nose from within a trumpet cone and into the accusing eyes of a grey haired man of medium height. The "sorry," I gave him was not curt but sharp enough for him to back off. In the far-left corner, I located Mary's voice and steered towards it. Surrounded by so many admirers, I could just make out her wheelchair. With purpose in my stride, I moved towards her.

"Can I help you?"

A tuxedo clad man asking the question blocked my view of Mary. He was tall, elegantly dressed and seemed the easily shocked type so I casually remarked. "I do hope so. I am looking for an extremely sexy girl, who is an easy pick-up and likes to be pushed around."

His reply was trained in eloquence but you could cut a knife with it. I smiled at him but said nothing.

There was a gasp. "I know that voice. Move out the way Timmy. Is that you Ross?"

I brushed past him and knelt down in front of her wheelchair. Beneath curly chestnut hair, large brown eyes sparkled with excitement. There was only one thing on my mind as my gaze wandered recklessly over the black evening dress that complimented her demure figure: I held her in my arms and drank a perfume of delicate oriental mystique. She trembled when I caressed her lips with mine and they were generous in their response.

I tried not to gasp as I said. "I'm so thrilled at seeing you again. How many years must it...?"

"Too long!" she said nearly crushing the life out of me.

"Where've you been all my life?" I said fondling her lithe body.

"Not waiting for you! Dump that coat and let's dance."

I threw my coat over a chair and followed her onto the dance hall. In pure adoration I watched the way she spun her chair round in time to the music. It was poetry in motion. Looking back at Timmy I noticed pure contempt directed towards me. Another enemy I could well do without. I began to tremble.

"Are you alright?"

"Someone tried to kill me tonight."

"Nonsense! Is this one of your tall stories?"

I could feel my body shaking. "They go by the names of Anya and Malik – I was too polite to ask for their surnames."

Her pretty brown eyes looked worried. "I've heard of them somewhere – perhaps they belong to our York Lodge."

Cautionary bells started pounding in my head. "Forget what I just said – it's just my little joke."

"Some joke – accusing Lodge members of...."

"I must have trod on their feet on my way to the bar to get a drink."

"What are you like; always playing the fool?"

I feigned a smile. "How are Bess and Jake?"

Her face fell. "Bess died about a month ago but Jake is still around, must be fifteen now. I don't take him for such long walks now. Do you remember them?"

My thoughts returned back to the days of heady summers being dragged across the fields by red retrievers, kisses under the weeping willow. Then bad memories surfaced of the 'hit and run' accident that resulted in two deaths and her being confined to a wheelchair. She had slowly recovered helped by her favourite horse Sasha; 'getting back in the saddle' she had called it. Watching her shine and become well again seemed to add purpose in my life too. I held her close. "I certainly do: especially your dappled grey and those romps in the stables. Sasha how is she?"

She gave me a playful look. "She's gone lame, but dad looks after her now," Her voice trailed off and I noticed a wistful tear brushed aside. "You helped me to cope with this infernal wheelchair Ross; I will be forever grateful for that."

Her stare was direct like an arrow. "I do hope you haven't done anything stupid and got married again have you?"

I thought of the fun times with Mary; my agonised broken marriage and so I faltered before replying. She picked up on my blank expression. "I had heard that you had got married to Elizabeth...Thanks for not inviting me to the wedding!"

"I got divorced last year."

"No excuse – I received no invite to that party too – and what a silly girl to let you escape. " There was a wink in her eye. "I'm free for the next ten years." She tapped my arm. "Do you fancy it?"

"Mary you don't change. How many other men have you proposed to this evening?"

She glanced around the hall and I could see she was making a mental count of the male population. I could testify to her as being pure dynamite on wheels and any man who hadn't agreed to her proposal that night was a fool.

"You are only my fifth tonight."

"Well personally I know you're a tease: nothing would prise you away from your beloved horses.

"Dead right," she said as her face twinkled with excitement.

"Were you ever into horse racing?

"I loved to go to the York Races."

"Have you heard about a horse called Red Mercury?"

She pulled me down to eye level and kissed me. "Can't say that I have. Why?"

"I heard it was a good bet."

"What race did it run in?"

"I was hoping you might enlighten me there?"

Her hands caressed mine. "Who do you think I am: a bookie's tout?"

I could see by her look that she was highly amused by my ignorance and so I allowed our conversation to drift into other directions.

"Are you still a Freemason?" I said at last.

I caught her surprised look. "You mean the York Lodge here?" she declared cautiously.

My reply was cut short by Tim who grabbed her arm.

"Come on. It's my turn for a dance."

She gave me an apologetic backward look and was wheeled onto the ballroom floor.

To the tune of Glen Millar's String of Pearls, I made my way out of the ballroom; there were Anya and Malik questions that needed answers. Soon I was alone in a long corridor that had three oak doors to my left. The first two were locked; the third opened to the shove. I went inside and was immediately aware of a faint musty smell as I closed the door behind me. Moonlight spilled through a solitary window highlighting a jumble of boxes, crates and chairs. It felt dank and cold. My breath became frosty. Abruptly I heard a buzzing sound reminiscent of a bee swarm. A chink of light drew me to the far wall which appeared to be partitioned in the middle. Holding my face hard against the join I could just see into the other part which was occupied.

There appeared to be some sort of ceremony going on, because I could see a ring of men and a woman. It was Anya! A light blue sash hung from their necks and they wore aprons embroidered with unusual glyphs. Each wore white gloves. They began chanting in a monotonous tone which sounded like Latin. In the centre of the ring was an open coffin. A solitary figure stood in front of it. He looked comical with his left trouser-leg rolled up. But then I saw the noose around his neck, a bag over his head and a dagger pointed at his heart by one of the men. This man wore a pointed white hat. My heart pounded with anticipation.

My view was suddenly spoilt by two of the group walking towards me. The man on my right was someone I knew. I squirmed to see and realised it was Gallagher. I couldn't see the other man's face but I caught the flash of a shoe buckle. His wrist appeared to glow with a blue ashen light and I realised that it must be coming from his watch. In a voice above a whisper he said: "It's just been confirmed. Red Mercury delivery; 11.15 tonight at Arras Hill." Then they rejoined the circle. Abruptly the incantation ceased.

I wriggled my face in an attempt at seeing more of the room and just caught sight of a gold watch as the white hooded figure stepped into the coffin. Behind me I heard the creak of the door opening which flooded the room with light and warmth. In silhouette, I saw Mary.

"I thought you had got lost. Come on, they are playing the Last Waltz."

A feeling of guilt overcame me. "You go on. I'll catch you up later."

"Why are you in here?"

"I needed the toilet."

"This is a peculiar looking toilet!"

"Ah." I said. "Actually I'm a cat burglar."

She looked square at me and declared. "Oh no you're not: your face is far too honest."

"Haven't you ever seen an honest cat burglar before?"

She laughed and said. "You're not in the Brotherhood either – are you? I've sussed that much out. You are a common gate-crasher. I too remember those nurses' parties of old!"

"I give up," I said, holding my hands high, "arrest me."

She smiled. "I will. You're mine for the evening."

"What about Timmy?"

"You're jealous."

"He's very possessive over you."

"What do you take me for? Timmy is a dear friend, that's all."

"What are you doing here – I thought the Freemasons were a male only domain?"

"Not always," she declared. There was a look of annoyance now. "We have our Lodges too. However tonight is the Grand Lodge Ball."

I thought quickly. "Do you know a man called Major Gallagher?"

"He deals in global rail journeys I think with another man called Mr Michael Tombs. Why?"

"The man with black glasses. Do you know anything else about him?"

She shook her head "You seem very inquisitive?"

I gave a knowing wink. "Ah! Must not divulge secret names of The Secret Society, heh?"

"It is a Society with secrets, that's all. Gallagher is fine; but it's Tombs who is a bit creepy because he is always trying to give me books to read!"

I threw her a shrewd glance. "It's a Secret Society all right: one that enjoys black magic rituals."

"I have no idea what you are talking about."

I wagged my finger. "If you look through that partition, you might."

She looked worried. "If you are correct, it is most irregular. This is supposed to be an Open Evening."

"The only thing open was a coffin and a man with a bag on his head. People dressed like monks were pushing this unfortunate victim into it with a noose around his throat and a dagger pointed at his heart."

Her jaw dropped. "You've got to be kidding me."

"I'll show you if you like."

I took her to the crack in the partition and she peered through. "Where – I see nothing?"

She was right. The ashen moonlight lit a room bereft of life, apart from a stack of chairs in the far left-hand corner.

I shook my head. "I don't understand"

"Let's be sure shall we?"

Between us we forced open the partition and went through. She guided her wheelchair over towards the door and rattled the handle. "The room door is firmly locked." She declared. "And surely anyone entering or leaving would have been seen?"

"It's very baffling." I conceded.

Mary took hold of my arm. "Look there." She pointed towards a stack of chairs. I walked over and retrieved a white silk glove from between the chairs. She took the glove and examined it. "It's quite distinctive. This is nothing to do with the Freemasons – of that I'm sure."

"Detection is my business," I replied looking quite mystified.

She shivered. "Let's get out of here; this place gives me the creeps."

As we entered the passageway it was now awash with people, coats, scarves and an icy wind that howled from the open entrance way. Through this sea of humanity I noticed a pair of silver buckled shoes. The owner was in deep conversation with Gallagher. What was he up to? Mary pulled me down and whispered in my ear.

"Do you fancy coming up to Arras Hill tonight for a bit of a shin dig?"

Before I had time to reply, we were caught up with the crowd heading towards the door, brushing past the back of Gallagher in the process.

"Well – are you coming?" she enquired.

"I wouldn't miss it for the world," I replied giving her a squeeze.

CHAPTER TWENTY

A Deathly Film Set

Time Loop Red

The man behind the Polaroid glasses had only one thing on his mind: to be somewhere else than this cold hostile cockpit. Radar would have picked him up by now, but that didn't bother him. He pulled back on the controls and climbed up to 1500 feet. He tapped the heater switch hoping that might stir it back into life.

"Give me my Cessna anytime," he lamented hitting the control panel. "Useless crap."

At least his flight plans were in order. Officially his flight was only an internal English one; unofficially he had taken off from a rooftop in Marousi Greece; landed in Crete; climbed on board a Cessna fixed wing aircraft and had flown to a secret French coast location. Here he was supplied with yet another helicopter which he had personally piloted virtually at wave height over the Channel. In total, it had been a gruelling journey only occasionally stopping to refuel.

"A piece of cake really!" he muttered aloud to himself as finally he saw a few bright lights which indicated England was getting nearer. "And all paid for by the Anya Corporation!"

Perhaps he could use that empty coke can that rolled around at his feet? What a time to feel the need. He suddenly cringed at the thought of hitting an air pocket whilst at that critical moment. If he could only stretch everything possible towards the air vent and pee through that? The thought of protruding anything out into that sub-zero gale outside caused him to wince. Then of course, the effort of flying straight and level might become a problem?

He slowly banked the Bell Jet Ranger helicopter, clenched every muscle possible and followed the ashen full moon on his way due north. Below him the White Cliffs of Dover peeked through the pre dawn mist. Was he re-enacting a WW2 fighter pilot on his way home? He wondered how they coped with their bodily functions. This thought dissipated rapidly amongst the blazing city lights below him. He checked the fuel gauges, patted the Heckler and Koch 9mm held firmly in his shoulder holster and gazed poignantly at the briefcase at his feet. A short time later a full warm coke can lay delicately balanced on the cockpit floor. In a few more hours he would reach his destination just beyond York. He felt at peace within himself; a destiny fulfilled.

The City of York lay below like jewels on black velvet as he banked slightly towards his left. The lit up Minster, even at this angle looked splendid as he flew over her and onward towards his final destination.

The bright lights forced him to re-live painful memories of his childhood. He remembered peering through the stage footlights and watching the rapidly diminishing form of his father. It wasn't his fault that he had lost confidence. His father wanted a musician in the family and had paid good money in tuition fees for him. How he hated that violin. He had tried hard for his father's sake to master the instrument, but to no avail. Tears welled up forcing him to release one hand off the Yoke to wipe them. Once more he was re living the agony and shame of playing at the school concert and flunking it. Shaky hands now gripped the controls as he relived that awful moment of watching his angry father storm out of the hall.

Ten miles and closing. Nine, and then eight. At four, he climbed up to 5000 feet and allowed Market Weighton to glide beneath him. His landing checks had him preoccupied as the distance finally melted away.

Below his vantage point, an enigma now presented itself. Clearly by moonlight, and in the shape of the Star of David, he hovered above a pristine crop circle. He switched on his landing lights and slowly began his descent. At 500 feet, he saw that the circle held visitors. With an ego on overdrive, he chuckled to himself. If only his father could see him now. Soon at Arras Hill Upon -The Wolds, a visitor would arrive.

"Come on Ross!" I followed the rapidly diminishing form of Mary as she threw her crutches over to the fence and waited for me to lift her up. Close up and a trace of perfume seduced my senses.

"Almost like the old days?" she said as I scooped her agile body into my arms. I smiled and hoped that she didn't see the tears in my eyes. If only all this had been before Elizabeth?

It was a weary haul up the hill sifting through the ripening barley. Occasionally I slipped which caused much amusement to Mary. "Butter feet," she scoffed.

Suddenly we entered a clearing and I saw human shadows. "Mary. What's going on here?"

We stood along the edge of a huge wide crop circle. Judging from the wide expanding arches running either side of me I approximated the size at two hundred-foot. This formation was highly complex with pristine cross shaped avenues of barley running inside. The stalks had not been flattened but had been curled and platted as if within the hands of a skilful hairstylist. The only broken stalks I could see were the resultant trampling by humans. Abruptly a wind swirled amongst the stalks, giving a low moaning sound.

Grouped in the centre were the monks I had seen earlier. Their arms were linked and heads bowed in monotonous incantation. Mary motioned to release her and once more on her crutches she went over to get a better view.

"Is this what your Freemasons get up to then?"

She turned and shouted but I could hardly hear because her words swirled in the breeze. Awe overcame me. It was then I had the idea. Perhaps my pre-conception of a horse called Red Mercury was rubbish. Red Mercury was not a horse after all: but something Alchemists use to attain the Philosophers Stone. I was involved with another ritual, a dark and satanic one, which somehow involved this crop circle and Auster. There had to be money in it because he was definitely not religious by any stretch of the imagination. I didn't like my idea, but the facts pointed that way. My God he'll have some explaining to do. I became aware that a solitary figure had now left the group and was walking towards me.

"Ross!" I gazed through the ashen light into the eyes of Gallagher.

"Are you surprised to find me sir, amongst your Devil worshipping friends?"

"You daft fool. Have you no idea what danger there is in coming here?"

"It's about Red Mercury...?"

His face held disbelief. "You know all about this shipment coming tonight?"

"You sent me to find Auster. They seem to be linked"

He took a deep intake of breath. "You don't know anything do you? Look, there's no time now to explain. You must trust me to deal with this. Get out, now, whilst there's still time on your side."

Above our head a blaze of light illuminated the entire area. I felt I was on the film set of Encounters of The Third Kind. His voice raised into a screech. "GO! NOW!"

I ignored his advice. It was as if an unseen film director had called 'Action' and safety to me meant sticking closely behind him as he ran and rejoined the group. I gazed up in terror at this dark descending swirling shape. With relief I giggled when it turned out to be a helicopter!

A hooded figure suddenly broke away from them and ran towards the craft, waving his hands furiously. As the downdraft swept his hood away, a black wig quickly followed and was swept into the field.

Malik!

I had a bad feeling about all of this.

Black Glasses moved towards the helicopter also waving his hands and then Gallagher sprinted towards them shouting. "Stop! Not so fast."

The pilot leant out waving a small hand gun. I heard a sound like a car backfiring which appeared to cause Gallagher to convulse and drop to the ground. Black Glasses attempted to grapple with the pilot but I heard another 'bang' and he too fell to the ground. I watched helpless as Malik grabbed the suitcase and escaped into the swirling confusion of the Freemasons who had scattered like rabbits. Suddenly I realised that I too had become close enough to become his next target. I froze in my tracks staring into a long black muzzle. Abruptly a face emerged from within the cockpit shadows. I recognised it immediately. "Austerfield!" I growled.

Instant abrupt pain like that of a mule kick caused me to gasp. I buckled to my knees; blood gurgled out of my mouth. "Why shoot me, you daft wassock?"

"You!" he mouthed, as horror swept across his face. I fell backwards onto the stubble.

My last sounds were that of the helicopter receding into the distance. An intimate silence followed and then a woman's face swept into view. Abruptly blackness engulfed me like a tidal wave.

CHAPTER TWENTY ONE

Close Encounter

Time Loop Purple

"Are you rested?"

CHAPTER TWENTY TWO

A Hard Rain Falls

Time Loop Red

I awoke to the sound of the skylark that must have been hovering nearby. As my consciousness returned I felt the prickly sensation of sharp barley stalks upon my neck and arms. The morning sun felt warm and conflicted with the chilly breeze that rustled through the open field. My whole body felt different.

My last recollection was being shot at; I should be dead. I wobbled onto my feet and looked down at my stomach.

Not a mark!

Close by, I saw the body of Gallagher. He too, should possess a ruddy big hole through him; yet he was breathing, and also appeared unscathed. We were totally alone. I heard movement behind me and span around in sheer panic, but it turned out to be a rabbit scurrying into a hole.

There was a groan from Gallagher. I saw him attempt to stand but his left foot gave way. He collapsed in a heap "I'm in agony." he howled.

I brushed the straw off his coat. "You've been shot, but you're OK now!"

"That's not possible...!"

"I don't understand it either. Do you believe in miracles?"

He didn't answer but scanned the horizon searching for clues. "Have we been here all night?"

In the distance I saw a parked car glistening in the early mist. "I hope that's yours sir?" I said pointing towards it.

He gave that faint little smile of his and nodded. "Let's get out of here," he said.

At Betty's, we drank coffee and allowed the flow of York tourists to pass our window. It felt soothing: like sitting upon a riverbank. Then the 'Black Zombie' peered through the window and I nearly shit myself.

"Bloody street performers!" I mouthed beneath my breath.

It also drew Gallagher's attention and he laughed in a fashion that made me realise that his nerves too, were badly shaken. Inwardly though I smiled. Betty's Cafe was a nice touch of mine. Waitress service and served with elegant china. Gallagher couldn't fail to be impressed. So I felt relaxed as I briefly recounted what I knew (which was still very little) and my reasons for being at Arras Hill. He didn't like my next statement.

"I deserve to know what's going on: after all, whose side are *you* on?"

He pasted on that Buddha smile of his. "I suppose you do deserve some explanation."

I felt patronised and scowled. "Either that, or do you want me to spill this 'hill of beans' to the newspapers?"

He looked more like a bulldog now as he moved closer towards me until our noses almost touched. "I have the power to slap a 'D' Notice on *any* paper you may approach."

I leant back in my wicker chair and carefully scrutinised him. His hands were fidgeting, his face quivered like a cornered rat. All that was on my mind now was attack; take advantage. "What would they think if I told them about satanic rites which somehow involve illegal shipments and Freemasons? They'd have a field day. It's your call...Major?"

"I do not respond very well to blackmail, Mr Ross."

My hand quivered slightly around my cup as I downed its contents. "I don't respond to Red Tape and Officialdom," I snarled.

There was a heated exchange of glances; we ordered more coffee.

Outside I heard the sound of the squawking Zombie followed by raucous laughter. Gallagher turned to look. After a long pause he replaced that careful smile, leant back and said, "Please call me Ben."

I nodded carefully; my voice guarded. "Ok Ben."

"Mr Ross. In the short space of time I have been acquainted with you, I have begun to realise your true worth. Can I trust you? I think so. You have the intelligence to realise the panic that would be caused to the general public if this Operation was leaked."

I cocked my head. "Which is...?"

He gave a polite cough; paused whilst swirling his coffee, then smiled again, very coyly this time.

"The truth?" he said.

"Oh, I am all ears."

"I can only tell you so much. After all: it could get you killed."

I almost sniggered. "We both seem to be immune to bullets."

There was a sharp intake of breath; he didn't answer at once but swirled his coffee again before carefully replacing the spoon back in the saucer.

Faintly irritated I persisted: "Well Major... sorry, Ben; try and have more faith in me?"

He sighed gently as he appeared to fight some inner turmoil. Eventually he said. "All right, I'll tell you what you want to know but this is strictly confidential." I noticed resignation in his voice. "My Department received a little whisper concerning a British SIS Operation." He looked amused as my mouth slowly opened. "S.I.S – stands for Secret Intelligence Service or MI6."

I nodded encouragingly. "That serious then?"

"Apparently they had infiltrated an organisation that dealt with smuggling Russian military hardware."

"Military hardware?"

"Shut up and listen will you!"

I flinched and bowed my head.

He leant across and briefly gripped my hands. "Just hear me out." There was a slight pause again before he continued. "Where was I? Ah yes – military hardware. They tried to smash that organisation, but failed. However what they uncovered was chilling enough. A shipment of a special type of quantum trigger was in the process of being sent to England. Have you any idea what that means?"

I gave him the look I reserved for inquisitive DHSS inspectors. "A quantum trigger? What's that?"

"You've heard of the name, Red Mercury?"

My face must have looked very stupid. "So it's not a horse running at York Races, or an Alchemist potion?"

He laughed involuntarily. "I really wish it was that simple. No, this device: Red Mercury, refers to a type of trigger that is used in a unique form of bomb: a viral quantum bomb."

I felt out of my depth here. "Physics was never my strong

point, but don't you need a critical mass of Uranium 235 before fission to take place?"

"Top marks Ross, but this is beyond fission or fusion for that matter. The know-how to create a nuclear device is common place to your scientists. I am sure any six-form pupil in the school of terrorism could design one. This device however is different; much different. It is unique because this unleashes the quantum or zero point energy that is locked up inside the very structure of matter. That makes this device a very powerful bomb. If this device was detonated here it would make a sizeable hole in Britain and the resulting pressure wave would destroy the Earth!"

"Really," I mouthed.

"Of course it's the compact size that makes this bomb so attractive to the terrorist." Gallagher took out his fountain pen. "The bomb is in two parts. There is the quantum trigger which is approximately this size and shape." He waved his pen. "And a locking mechanism which it fits into." He pointed to the flower vase upon the table. "All of that fits inside a cooling chamber of liquid hydrogen. I have only seen the 'blue prints' but I guess it's the size of that service trolley over there." He pointed to an adjacent table where the maid was about to serve coffee.

I looked thoughtfully at it. "So that's the size of Armageddon is it?"

"The quantum trigger is dangerous enough. If you point it at anything it locally strips matter apart. A human being would be mummified in seconds." He paused and looked thoughtfully at me. "I think that's about as much as you can take for now?"

My mind felt numbed by information overload. An errant thought trickled through though. "How does Auster fit into all this?"

"He had a good smuggling business in operation behind the Iron Curtain, until it all fell apart." Ben looked hard at me. "As Russia fell, your friend Austerfield had unscrupulous friends who during this confusion, managed to steal the weapon from their military base."

I looked wide eyed. "How did Russia acquire the weapon?"

Ben took a deep intake in breath and hesitated before speaking. "In the years leading up to détente, Russia learnt about a crashed UFO that had landed in New Mexico. Only our organisation knew that it contained a deadly form of weapon. The Americans naturally kept it under tight wraps, but that type of secret doesn't stay secret for too long. The Russians then demanded this vehicle be given to them to be studied." He took another deep breath, "And when it went 'missing', this hastened our organisation to act quickly. Although we are not known to any of your world security services, by covert means we could steer them down fruitful avenues of investigation. In short we helped them liaise with each other! "

"So that was why the Cold War thawed so quickly. I never did quite understand all of that until now."

Ben appeared clearly embarrassed. "That's enough to be going on with. This Operation is ZETA Classified, and you my friend are now bound by those Regulations..."

I held up my hands. "OK! You've made your point: I'll promise not to tell a soul. Have you made any progress?"

"The shipment was routed via Albania into Greece. Unfortunately the trail went frozen at Athens."

"Frozen? You mean cold don't you?"

Clearly embarrassed he snapped. "Yes; I meant that as well."

We exchanged mutual glances of amusement. "I hate to state the obvious but in the wrong hands this weapon could destroy all life on Earth."

The enormity of what he had just said made my stomach flutter. From deep within I began to feel sick. "It seems an impossible task to undertake. Can I really help you?"

Gallagher leant forward and looked intently at me. "Listen very carefully." he said. "I must liaise with my intelligence officers to ascertain if I can find out where that 'copter was heading and the delivery. Your task is to find Auster. He's our valuable link."

I blinked. "I believe he is in Athens posing under the name of Dimitri..."

He cut me short. "Dimitri? Really!" He fingered his chin. "Of course: the English Athenian connection. If that is correct it complicates things. Anya is the Head of a terrorist cell in Athens. I think you've stumbled upon part of their English connection."

My face fell. "Yes he's a rogue, but a smuggler for terrorists? Anything to do with Auster is phoney. See this watch?" I held up my wrist. "Who do you think I bought it from?"

"That's what I'm afraid of," said Gallagher shuffling within his chair. "I think your friend has double crossed me; he is a fool to think he can get away with it." Gallagher gazed out of the window at the gyrating Zombie. "We live in dangerous times Mr Ross."

"Well I for one, admire him," I said. "Perhaps he's trying to save the world?"

His Buddha smile became prevalent again. "Wait there: I am going to make a phone call to London."

I watched him walk away to enquire where the phones were. He was gone about twenty minutes or so and so it gave me time to reflect about what he had said. What people tell you is not so important as what they don't tell you. That's the one to watch out for. To my mind that meant one thing: the connection between Black Glasses and Gallagher's organisation meant something far deeper. And that thought chilled my bones.

He strolled towards me but didn't resume his seat. "You're on the next flight to Athens. I've arranged a taxi to get you to the airport. Your tickets will be waiting for you at the reservation desk."

"You're not coming?"

"No. My assignment is to track down our Mr Malik Hamid." He tapped his watch. "Put your skates on: your plane leaves in four hours time." He poured serious money into my hands. "Take a taxi!"

We walked out of Betty's and without a backward glance, he drifted into Coney Street. With my nose to the wind I walked towards Museum Street and the Railway Station.

It began to rain.

CHAPTER TWENTY THREE

The Sleep of Death

Time Loop Red

There is something magical about stepping off a plane having left behind the fridge of Britain and to immediately feel the sultry breeze of a foreign destination.

Bathed in this cocoon of warmth, I paused at the foot of the plane's stairway and took a deep breath. The smell of aviation fuel was mixed with a subtle fragrance of pine. To my left I heard a thundering roar and turned to witness yet another miracle of aviation leap into the morning sky. Thoughtfully I walked across the tarmac towards passport control. Once through, I entered the airport lounge and carefully looked around, hoping to catch a glimpse of the contact Gallagher had arranged for me.

The way he described TRINITY Athens branch as a bunch of over-weight, wine burping diplomats, made me cringe at the thought of spending a few days in their company. They were the team who had held twenty-four hour surveillance on the 'players' (a term I had picked up from him).

"Liaise with them, find out what they know and see if you can locate the whereabouts of your friend," he had said. I pretended to look casual as I nervously glanced around the lounge. Could this be my contact?

A huge man, dressed in a white suit casually walked towards me. I braced myself, but all he gave was an indifferent stare and then a girl, all fair hair and complexion to match, ran towards him and grasped his arm. She looked young enough to be his daughter, but I reasoned it was probably his mistress. I began to feel abandoned, and walked towards the entrance wondering what to do next. Once outside I felt overwhelmed by the noise and hubbub of downtown Athens. Amongst the swirl of cars and blaring horns I became fascinated by a lady driver in a white open sports car. With as much skill as any matador, I gazed in admiration as she skilfully negotiated the traffic and then began to head in my direction. Glistening sunglasses and wind tossed auburn hair; I was surprised when she pulled up beside me, and leant across.

"Mr. Ross?"

"Yes," I said defensively.

"I have been sent to collect you. Get in."

I threw my travel bag onto the back seat, and squeezed in beside her. With both hands she decisively pushed up her sunglasses until they perched on the top of her hair.

"My name is Stella Hunnybun. Welcome to Athens."

My Mata Hari was dressed in khaki shorts; open necked tee shirt and designer trainers.

"Please call me Ross," I said.

She cocked her head at that. "Your name is Ross?

"Just Ross."

"You're kidding me?"

I watched her long legs wiggle as she changed gear. "If you must know, it's Farquhar, Reginald Ross. My mother was Scottish and named me after her grandfather. Now do you understand why I prefer, just Ross?"

She replaced her sunglasses on her face and I could see an attempt to mask laughter.

The ghost of a smile still remained when she said. "How very English," she turned to gaze into the traffic and back to scrutinise me. "Now tell me: what are your first impressions of Greece – Ross?"

I drank in the warmth of the late morning, gazed in wonder at the distant Grecian skyline and then became lost in the depths of her ice blue eyes."I just might retire here," I murmured.

She threw back her head and laughed out loud and then with the clutch screaming, we hurtled into the rustling traffic. We drove towards the centre of Athens.

"Do you normally leap into any strange girl's car?" she enquired as we paused at the first set of traffic lights.

The slip stream had carried her delicate perfume which intoxicated my senses. "When they're as pretty as you – yes, but then you did give the correct password."

"Well I should throw you out because you didn't."

"Really?"

The correct response was "I have come here to retire."

"That didn't make any sense to me."

"It's not supposed to!" she retorted.

I glanced outside at the heaving traffic as she accelerated away again. "Why didn't you: I'd end up pretty messy out there?"

She inclined her head towards me. "Your boss gave a good description of you and anyway, perhaps I like picking up strange good-looking men!"

Inwardly I laughed at the complement: at my time of life you grappled with scraps like that!

"I hope I've not disappointed you?"

"Do you like to disco?" she said as we paused at more traffic lights.

"Is that a question or an invitation?" I remarked.

Her reply was a pout of the lips as the lights changed.

Her next conversation seemed more directed towards the Gallagher and his Department. She assumed that I was part of his recently acquired 'Twelve' team and I let her carry on with that notion; I liked the admiration in her eyes!

However I was left extremely puzzled concerning this line of thought. I knew nothing about my boss or his background. Why were they so special? I decided to fish for clues.

"Our lot has the same problems you have," I suggested.

She threw a questioning look. "Then why has he such control over the other Sections?"

I shrugged. "Gallagher has been in the business a long time."

"Oh come on! We both know your lot was only set up last year. Within months, Six, Seven and Nine were practically eating out of your boss's hand – and now Twelve?"

"So what?"

"Usually they are at each other's throats!"

"He can be very charming."

"Hmm! Now, you're pulling my leg."

I looked down at her voluptuous thighs and half joked. "Given half a chance!" I whispered.

She took her hand off the wheel and gave me a playful tap on my knee. "Now you are making fun of me."

"If only there was more time," I murmured. Her answer was a raised eyebrow.

My travelling bag was dumped in the hotel room that had been reserved for me, and within the hour we were hurtling through the busy suburbs of Athens, towards our first stake out.

Beneath a huge red neon sign of the Moulin Rouge cafe in Imittou Street, we sat around a wicker table cuddling beers and looking like nicely behaved tourists.

She introduced me to her fellow 'Watcher' teams, Artemis and Pericles. I eyed them up and down as they sat opposite and agreed with Gallagher's assessment: overweight, over drunk and over Stella given half the opportunity.

Stella was a real pro however: one look was all it took to put those young flat cap and flannels to heel!

To my right, I gazed in admiration at two men trying to move a sofa along a busy side street. Amongst the confusion, cars honked their frustration and motorbikes played kamikaze around the hapless duo. A pigeon too tried to get in on the act by proudly riding upon the front arm of the sofa. I was quietly amused by it all and tried to convey as much to my companion, but she had twisted her back towards me concentrating intently on something across the road. Matisse would have loved those curves.

"Take a look at this," she said and thrust a pair of minute binoculars in my hand. "Across at the apartment block opposite. Third floor up; fourth balcony from the left. It's the one with all the plants."

I trained the glasses where I was directed and was amazed at the clarity of image. Through the sunlit window, two men were pacing the floor. Occasionally they would pause in the middle and it appeared as if their attentions were drawn to that central point. From this angle I couldn't see anything else, but much hand gesturing was being displayed.

"OK I see it," I said. "I can see the two players through the apartment window. Wait though: I can also see a woman. Have you any idea what is going on?"

She nodded her head. "Artemis said three men had entered the building about an hour ago. The third man must be seated. The woman is called Anya and a real cruel bitch by all accounts. It seems to me that the conversation is quite heated at times."

"Anya!" I shivered involuntarily. "I've met her before. Can you identify the men?"

"The thin one is called Yannis." I felt her shiver. "He is a nasty piece of goods. The other guy I am unfamiliar with. Is he your man?"

I scrutinised carefully through the binoculars and I caught a glint of gold upon his left ear. Auster thought earrings were sissy. "No. I don't think so."

Abruptly I saw Yannis raise his hand and thrust it downward upon the unseen person."Good God!"

"What's happening?"

"All hell seems to be letting loose," I exclaimed as I saw the other man's fist rise up, and then fall. For a brief moment, the third man's upper body came into view and I could see that he was tied to a wooden chair. In desperation he was trying to shield himself with it.

"We have got to get over there," I snapped. "They are trying to kill him."

"Don't be foolish," she exclaimed. "This isn't time for heroics; we could both end up dead. Anyway it's probably one of their men. Not our concern."

She was right of course but I felt strangely compelled to watch spellbound and helpless as the thugs rained blow upon blow on their unfortunate victim. A sound like a car backfiring caused me to jolt violently. I felt the glasses being gently removed from my hands and then Stella grasped my head and snuggled me into the depths of her bosom. I was so traumatised by the violence I had just witnessed that I just stayed there like a limp rag doll.

"It's OK," she said. "You're not used to this are you?"

My thoughts dwelt back to Anya and her amusement in trying to kill me and muttered. "No I'm not!"

"I hope you don't mind me holding you like this? It's good 'cover' anyway."

I looked up through her semi-exposed bosom and twinkling eyes and slowly whispered, "I'll give you all the time in the world to unhand me!"

She smiled and I laid bets that it was a halo and not the low sun around her face that made her look saintly. We allowed the twilight to fall into night.

Sometime later, she shook my arm. "Look! They're in the foyer."

I raised my head and strained to focus my eyes. Across the road Anya, Yannis and Gold Earring had entered the cloud of traffic. They were attempting to hail a taxi cab.

"Shall we follow them?"

"No. Our team will do all of that."

"They're still here?"

"Well of course! Moulin Rouge is the best club in town."

A momentary flash of light caught my attention towards the window. I detected movement.

"At least he is still alive poor beggar."

Stella replaced the binoculars to her eyes. "He appears to have staggered over towards the window. He's taken quite a beating, poor sod."

I grabbed the binoculars off her and gazed up through the window and into a bloodied face of despair. The flash of gold upon his wrist, when it came brought with it a premonition. "We are breaking in."

"No we're most definitely not."

I grabbed her arm. "Yes we are!"

Within minutes we had crossed the road, entered the foyer, climbed the stairs, and picked the lock at No 84 Imittou Street.

I was not prepared for the gruesome sight of that blood spattered room. In the middle, next to a leather settee, a mangled body lay sideways on the floor with his back to us. He was still strapped to the chair of his torturers. Just out of reach, a phone with its receiver lay sprawled across the carpet. Stella brushed past me and knelt down beside him. She was visibly shaking, but then, so was I.

My voice croaked. "Is he still alive?"

She felt for the pulse in his neck, and then turned towards me, wide eyed and tense. "Barely," she whispered.

I glanced at the phone. "The sodding line's been cut."

She ran towards me and gripped my arm in a vice-like grip. Visibly shaking only her voice was in command. "I'm going for help."

I nodded and limply watched her rush out of the apartment. Her footsteps caused my heart to race in step to their urgent path down the hall. "Please be quick," I whimpered.

From within the room, I heard a shuffle and a moment later, a gasp. I turned towards the body on the floor. His blood soaked head had now turned towards me. My premonition was correct.

"She's going for help," I pleaded.

"Bit late cock, but I knowed someone would come."

That voice gave him away. The opened black eye and that attempted smile against all the odds could only be..?

"Auster?"

There came another gasp; urgent and desperate: "Why you here kid?"

"I'm the only one who could find you."

"Tha's sound, bah no mistake."

"Don't speak. Save your energy." I walked towards him and knelt down so that I could put his head on my knee.

He coughed up some blood and then tried to speak, the words gurgled and indistinct. "Tha say Ross: cat's pissed on't matches bah no mistake."

"I should have guessed you would pull a stunt like that."

"Gallagher put me up ta'it."

"The Major?"

"Anya's got the real goods. She..." He would have said more and attempted to struggle with the words but blood gurgled from his mouth.

"Don't exhaust yourself." I pleaded: "You'll soon be in hospital."

I wished I could speak to him: so many questions; so little time. Within a short space of time and cuddled within my arms, he gave a final deep hollow rattle that seemed to last forever.

Then there was stillness.

Like an automaton, I kept rocking him in my arms, willing him to say something; anything would do. I heard footsteps behind me. It wasn't Stella with the cavalry. I stared up into the stony face of Tombs.

"Hello Ross," he whispered. "Don't be afraid. I can help your friend if you'll let me?"

"He's beyond your help, you bastard."

"He's merely asleep," Tombs declared.

Idly I observed his black rims glisten from the nearby lamp as he leant over and placed a hand on my forehead. His wrist watch bezel appeared to pulsate with red and a then a deep purple. I held Auster in a close embrace and wondered where the hell Stella was.

"You bastard," I simpered. "You bastard."

A silent scream filled my head, and then my world swirled from purple haze into blackness.

CHAPTER TWENTY FOUR

Dream Time

At Time Loop Purple-Blue

A still life acrylic.

Of Van Gogh style.

Such hues of deep orange and verdant greens.

Then blue.

Then red.

Lots of red; deep red; splattered like Polka dots.

Red splashed on walls, carpets and mostly smeared over victims all too soon to become corpses.

Human blood and guts are messy stuff.

Michael Tombs stopped his free fall of thoughts, as he became further intrigued. Thoughts – human emotions, invaded his mind; they were immensely stimulating and he could bathe within their intensity and depth. However there was no pleasure whatsoever to be derived from such base instincts. He recoiled in disgust. How did this culture ever evolve at all? Even amidst stumbling within their cave of shadows, only relatively few could face and scramble up into enlightened truth.

The basic axiom of civilised order; hidden from them.

He cast a glance at his watch. The purple flashing bezel troubled him. TL P-Blue was the prevalent Time Loop. Using too much purple could fragment this loop, perhaps permanently hastening the end sequence which would result in total destruction of planet Earth. And that would be far too early. With a decisive twist his watch bezel now displayed a room occupied by three occupants. What manner of truth was this?

The distance between Anya and the slumped form of Austerfield was carefully measured with his hands. Then the ropes that held her victim to the bedroom chair were also scrutinised. These were slacker than last time. Yannis however still boiled with passionate hatred: it was obvious even within this TL. Purple veins, threatened to erupt from his face and blood had trickled down from the nose. Next for his attention was the bullet that appeared frozen within mid air. This too was also minutely examined; all angles noted. Would it miss its mark? Behind that bullet lay a multitude of histories. Summed up what would be all of their outcomes; could one become precedent, changing the dimension again?

He walked back towards the bullet and once more examined it. Last time he was here, he had influenced the outcome by adjusting the bullet's trajectory. It disgusted him to wallow in human affairs, but if this meant being closer to mission completion, it was justifiable. For all his attempts however, he had failed.

Why cannot all human emotions be quantifiable?

Time Loop Purple-Red

With careful adjustment of his bezel, suddenly below the purple ring a red hue appeared. He noted a slight scene change but nothing more. The red now deepened in intensity and then within a few seconds, a blue ring of light formed below it.

Time Loop Purple – Red-Blue

Tombs appeared satisfied at this self-made rainbow that slowly pulsed with energy. Another watch button was touched and abruptly the room displayed two figures of Anya; identical twisted faces of Yannis and twin roped forms of Austerfield. Although displaced in their dimensional shifts, they were surprisingly close to each other. The figures from each dimension appeared to be sharply focused with an occasional ripple between their layers as if connected in time space and causality. Further away however, the surroundings blended into a Gaussian blur that stretched as if like a melted cheese canvas.

To Tombs this was irrelevant. His entire concentration now centred on the bullets. He meticulously studied each and as if making up a decision he stood facing along the trajectory of one. He pressed his watch, and this macabre scene danced a sickly routine as each figure appeared and disappeared to be replaced with its counterpart in quick succession. Tombs gaze however, remained fixed upon this one single instrument of death: the bullet. With a determined twist of the bezel the original scene returned.

Time Loop Purple-Blue

His attention now was upon the girl. The lack of a smile on Anya's face fascinated him. Slowly almost pirouetting around her, each skin blemish, even the mole on the left-hand side of her face was minutely examined.

Almost by accident Tombs stumbled upon an enigma. Why was it present? A teardrop was about to be released. In her left hand a gun was pointing straight at Dimitri's chest. Or was it? The bullet was examined again and then he realised that his intervention was not required this time.

What was paramount was this more enlightened experience. Something or someone had tipped the balance of this mission from failure to success? The necessary inclusion of David Austerfield had not done this. In fact it had turned into disaster. Why are these aliens so self-centred and uncontrollable? The puzzle however was that there had been change and it wasn't by his design. Who had altered this dimensional loop so dramatically? The prevalent TL P-Blue was slowly changing into Green? What startled him as he scrutinised this scene were the occupants. They slowly began to fade into non-existence.

Time Loop Purple – Green

At TL P-Green he gazed around at an empty bland room with bare walls, exposed floor boards; bereft of all life. In short, this would be a blank canvas; a new beginning.

Time Loop Purple – Blue

As way of experiment he replayed TL P-Blue again to its final conclusion in slow motion. He observed once again the door opening and seeing the two faces of Stella and Ross as they looked like puppets being jerked by invisible strings. They entered and bullets flew like confetti as the room filled with smoke, then blood and guts spattered everywhere. Abruptly that macabre scene became still life again.

"This just will not do!" he exclaimed. "This just will not do at all; I *cannot* allow this." With a forceful twist of the bezel he replayed the TL but then abruptly cut the Loop before the final death scene. "I must put this 'cat' back into its box." He muttered under his breath, "this just will not do."

Time Loop Purple – Green

Back in TL P-Green he walked over to the window and gazed out through the open door onto the balcony. Walking outside, and peering through the verdant plants he noticed below a group of people at a table of the Moulin Rouge nightclub. He smiled at seeing Ross in deep agitated conversation with Stella. They were like still life gargoyles. An errant thought caused him to pace the room for several seconds before returning once more to the scene below.

He gambled that this time; his intervention would be the correct one.

Time Loop Purple – Blue

With commitment written across his brow, he re-programmed the bezel for TL P-Blue. Abruptly he now entered yet another room; another beginning; another possible future.

A voice questioned: "Do you play chess?" There was no requirement to answer: he merely moved a few pieces into their relevant positions and hoped that his interference *this* time would be successful. The figure next to him looked surprised at his arrival but said nothing. He whispered quietly in his ear. "Well done Ben: I think Ross is our man for the job." He then took "Highfield' from within his hands. "There is a young lady who needs this book." With a sigh of relief, he then reprogrammed his watch for Purple.

"I do so want to go home," Ben Gallagher declared with sobriety before they swirled into blackness.

"You will – eventually. Now where have I left Ross?"

CHAPTER TWENTY FIVE

Double Cross

Time Loop Red

All white suit and straw hat Dimitri walked with purpose. To his right, in the marina the yachts seemed to sway and dance with the dappled sunlight across the water. To his left the narrow street was awash with cars sounding their horns at every opportunity.

He approached the straw roofed wooden Appaloosa Taverna and went inside. Pulling up a wicker chair he sat perched like a pregnant hen. Nervously his gaze flitted around the Taverna whilst errant fingers drummed monotonously upon the glass topped table. A tall dark haired waiter came over to his table; he ordered beer and waited.

The urgent sound of car horns caused him to turn swiftly. A battered white sports car seemed to break away from the line of traffic and roared towards the Taverna, and screeched to a halt. The sole occupant a voluptuous, curly auburn haired girl climbed out of the car exposing delicious looking thighs. She paused. From the corner of his eye Dimitri watched her enter the Taverna. He was held captive by the way she carefully edged her green fluid dress between the light wicker tables and chairs. He smirked as every male turned to admire her. She was heading straight towards him now and he smelt a seductive light perfume that preceded her. As she approached he got up and held out his hand. She shook his hand gracefully and sat opposite him.

"Kalimera Dimitri?"

He reclined back into his chair. With a trace of an English accent he replied. "Kalimera Stella. Tekanis?"

The girl nodded and briefly smiled. "I am well thank you. Sorry I am late, but I was held up with this accursed traffic."

"Tha's a pert lass bah no mistake!"

She flinched. "Signomi?"

His Greek returned. "Parakalo. What a nice dress you are wearing. I'll order beer?"

Her face held suspicion. "I think I will do that."

At her raised hand, numerous waiters cascaded towards the table. One was a clear winner however and the others enviously held back.

"Theloume duo bires Amstel, Parakalo."

The waiter wrote down her order, whilst occasionally gazing wistfully at her. As he hastened away she looked sternly at her companion.

"Ben has been most concerned about you. Where have you been hiding these past few days?"

He dismissed her with a wave of his hand. "Something is amiss with one of our couriers."

"What do you mean?" she demanded adjusting her hemline as she caught him drooling at her.

"The usual man didn't show at the docks, and then I was set upon by thugs and then the police arrived. This wasn't a chance thing, they knew what they wanted and just grabbed it."

"How could this have happened?"

"One of these thugs was a man called Smythe who was supposed to be working for me; the double crossing scoundrel!"

"You seem to attract them. What was your merchandise?"

He looked indignant, "I don't know. I was under strict orders not to open it."

"What shape was it?"

"Beneath the brown wrapper I would say it felt more like a book than anything else.

He watched in amazement as she inwardly laughed.

"What have I just said?"

Stella shook her head. "Sorry. Yes, you are quite correct. That parcel you were carrying was far too important to be misplaced, or stolen." She observed him wince. "It was however- a worthless item."

Dimitri sat bolt upright. "Worthless?"

"Yes worthless. Concealed inside the book – as you correctly describe it – was the plastic decoy of a 'Trigger' device!"

He looked indignant. "Look here, if Ben is making a fool out of me..."

"Don't be so childish!"

Abruptly there was a rattle of a waiter's tray. The drinks had arrived. Stella nodded towards the waiter. "Efharisto," she said.

The waiter nodded lustfully into her eyes "Parakalo, " he murmured before hurrying away.

In the bay a motor cruiser engine chugged into life. Wistfully Dimitri gazed after it. Cautiously he turned to face her. "What precisely is this 'Trigger' device anyway?" He watched her flinch uncomfortably in her chair. "I deserve to know something."

"You know I can't tell you anything." She saw annoyance in Dimitri's face. "The less you know the safer it is for both of us."

He shrugged. "Give me a day or two, and I can reschedule the shipment if you can obtain another duplicate."

"Ben wants this deal completed sooner than that."

Dimitri gave her a coy look. "This whole thing is making me nervous. Anya is now expecting me personally to help make the connection. I can only fool her for so long."

Stella eyed him up carefully. "What was it you kept telling me about how infatuated Anya was with you?"

Dimitri shuffled in his chair. "What is so important about this package that nearly got me killed?"

Stella leant back in her chair and thoughtfully sipped her beer. Almost as if on impulse she leant forward to place her hand on his. "As I have just said: the less you know, the safer it will be for you." She hoped he would pick up on her seductive whisper; this was no time for back tracking. "You are quite safe in my hands. That plastic replica of a device: the Trigger is not worthless but very vital to your mission. Anya has acquired the genuine article. Your job is still to locate and swop the replica for the real thing and then pass it on to me. That is not too difficult for a man of your obvious calibre is it?"

The distinctive smell of freshly made coffee caused both of them to be aware of a man in a light blue suit who sat at a table next to them. Stella realised Dimitri had become extremely nervous and noted that beads of sweat began to form on his forehead. They watched closely as the man drunk from a petite Turkish cup and then with precision the cup was replaced back on the saucer. With delicacy he removed his glasses. A white handkerchief was retrieved from inside his trouser pocket. Slowly his fingers worked around his black rimmed glasses. The glasses were examined and re-fitted. Abruptly he stood up and turned to face them. It appeared as if he was going to acknowledge Dimitri, for smiling he walked towards them. However, he merely swept passed their table and out of the Taverna.

Stella looked anxiously at him. "He might have overheard us speaking. Do you know him?"

He wiped his forehead. "I don't think so – but I swear he knew me."

She swung her legs from under the table and stood up. There was gravity in her voice. "I'm putting a lot of trust in you."

He gave her a sly grin. "You supply me with the replica, I'll make the switch. My price of course has increased to one hundred thousand Stirling!

Stella opened her mouth in shock. "Do you expect me to agree to your blackmail?"

"What else can you do?"

With a scowl she turned and without a backward glance walked away. Dimitri watched her retreating figure before also leaving.

At the bar a waiter took an order from the man in the light blue suit who had now returned. A little later Stella joined them; they had a lot to say to each other.

CHAPTER TWENTY SIX

Gold Earring

Time Loop Blue

The man in the shabby brown suit couldn't believe his luck. Much to the consternation of the people who had walked into Rowntree Park that day, hoping to feed the ducks by the pond, he began to sing in a high tuneless pitch.

Huddled on the bench with a cider bottle at his side, he didn't care. In his wearied tattooed hands was a brown package, a passport and a flight ticket to Athens. He struggled to contain his excitement; his face twisted into a grin.

He took his precious picture from his breast pocket which showed his 'mug shot'. It showed tattooed arms and his Armley identity number; he had enjoyed that prison stretch. Now that was a holiday; he had felt safe there like being a child again cosseted by his mother. Of course that was before her new boyfriend came along and toppled him off his perch. They both then had to be taught a lesson. Why do people bleed so much after road accidents? His prison sentence was a necessary evil; unfortunate but predictable due to a witness getting in his way.

Smythe's face twisted back into an idiotic grimace that caused yet another of the Park's visitors – a young couple who were entwined in romance – to completely change their direction. Dreams of dollar and sterling signs started flashing before his eyes and that spelt sleek American cars and fat breath-taking women, almost now within his grasp. The only thing that disturbed him was the idea of posing as someone else. That was awesome. However his business mate Robby, had made it quite plain how that was to be accomplished. "I've cleared it with the Job Centre Alan. So do exactly as you're told. It's so important that you do. OK?"

Of course it had all been so easy, he wished now that he'd gone into the acting. That Ross: what a gullible punter he was. He poked a grubby little finger between his brown decayed teeth and dug out a piece of chicken that had troubled him. Opening up his flight documents, and for the umpteen time that day he checked the flight tickets and then the phoney ones that would make him appear as if he had flown from Bulgaria. That puzzled him a little.

He started once more on that tune which had bugged him all morning, and reached once more for the bottle at his side then cursed when he realised it was empty.

Later that day, sobered up and fresh faced he caught a taxi that would take him to Manchester airport and the night flight to Athens.

When Alan Smythe emerged from passport control, he walked purposely through the airport lounge but had only one thing on his mind: food; he was ravenous.

Through the swirl of human traffic his thoughts mimicked this turmoil: where was the female contact, he was supposed to meet? Robby described her as a short-haired auburn carrying a copy of the Times. They would make the exchange and then the job was done. His plan then would be to grab an excellent Greek meal and take the night flight home. The only thing that sounded promising after the money had been paid: was his meal.

Was that her?

A woman, whose slender form was draped over a chair, seemed very interested in him. Under a chic white hat, her dark eyes beckoned. When her legs crossed then uncrossed pulling up an already tight blue skirt, Smythe almost had forgotten what he had come for.

He strutted over to her like a bantam cock on heat, chat lines at the ready. Abruptly he felt his left arm being grabbed.

"Mr Ross?"

The voice sounded monotone and impersonal with a coarse foreign accent. He turned and looked into bulging neck muscles and a bulldog face. The man wore a white flannel suit that strained at every joint.

"Do I know you?"

"Come with me."

Smythe looked into eyes of liquid steel and noticed in a fascinating way, that the man wore a golden earring.

CHAPTER TWENTY SEVEN

A Secret Smile

Time Loop Blue

"You said what!" Stella responded furiously as she threw her hat violently upon the sofa. It bounced and landed upon the red carpet. "Are you trying to get us both killed?"

"Don't talk pisspottical lass! How wer I to know that great clartead Smythe would turn up bold as brass with that phoney parcel under his coat. Anya's not stupid tha knows. Ah knows that if tha dern't."

Her eyes were narrow slits now. "What sort of gibberish language is that?"

Dimitri gazed up at her from his armchair and slowly mellowed. Within her apartment he felt safe and warm; soft yellow wall lights reinforced that feeling. Her screams sounded like an orgasmic release. He watched captivated as she now removed her high heels, which allowed the matching blue skirt to ride high over petal-soft thighs. In his mind's eye he was caressing her; holding her; kissing her. Desperately they were making love."

"Dimitri?"

"What?" he murmured softly.

"Have you listened to anything I have said?"

Slowly his brain rejoined the real world. He sighed. "When that Gawpead Smythe turned up at Anya's apartment I nearly wet myself."

"All I could do was watch helpless as he was being dragged out of the airport lounge by Anya's thugs."

Dimitri rubbed his sweating forehead. "The greedy fool was hoping to make off with the money. What was I to do? He nearly blew my cover."

She waved a finger. "I was supposed to meet Smythe for the transfer with Manolis!"

"I'm scared."

"You are a Greek businessman and as long as you stay in that role, you will be safe. There is no room for panic."

"If you say so."

"I do say so and I want you to think *and* believe it; convince me of your sincerity."

"Do you think Anya suspects me?"

Stella laughed involuntarily. "I am sure her adoration of you blinds her to everything. Now repeat once more, what had happened?"

"You are probably right." He rubbed his sweaty palms anxiously and tried to gain solace by looking at the picture of the Dauphine hanging upon the peach coloured wall behind her. "Someone must have tipped off Anya regarding Smythe as a plant; it was sheer survival on my part. I only told Anya, that in my opinion the package looked a fake; she knew it had been tampered with."

She gazed unbelieving at him. "What on Earth were you playing at?"

"Maybe it was the wrong thing to say, but they were on to him reet quick." He looked sheepishly at Stella before continuing. "All right!" he paused and took out a white handkerchief and mopped his brow. "I mean – how stupid he was to have both passports on him. I had warned you before that he wasn't the brightest tool in the box."

"So he was cutting his own deal?"

He shook his head in irritation. "Alan has no brain to save his life at all. You have to give him simple tasks and then watch over him."

"So what do you think happened?"

"Well I had heard talk which I must admit worried me a little."

Stella observed him carefully before replying. "What talk?" she said leaning forward.

"I'd overheard Yannis say that Manolis was coming by boat, not flying in as we had expected. Since I had set up the deal, I had to cover my back. I tried but failed to contact my English connection to say the deal was off."

She noted cockiness in his reply which troubled her. "Was there no time to warn me?"

Dimitri snapped. "No!"

Stella's reply was a measured response. "I find that switch very suspicious don't you?"

He rubbed his hands nervously. "Smythe was one of my best men. You must take my word for that." He shivered. "I watched in horror as he turned into a mummified corpse by that pen-like device. Anya screamed with pleasure as he..." He looked pleadingly at her. "What sort of woman is that?" He quit talking then, and just gazed at her as she perched on the edge of the sofa, waiting for him to go on. There was silence. The seconds became so significant that he felt drained at their passing. He shifted position looked down at the rug and then back into those accusing eyes. "He never stood a chance." He murmured.

Stella leisurely sat down on the sofa, crossed her legs, but never took her eyes off him. "That wasn't the plan, was it?" she said slowly. "We agreed that Smythe would hand over the package to me and take the next flight home. I would then make the transaction with Manolis – as you agreed – and then he would meet Anya to clinch the deal."

His eyes wandered playfully over Stella's body once more and temporarily missed the drift of the conversation. She sighed and hastily pulled her skirt to a modest length. "An unfortunate mistake: I *had* expected Ross!" he remarked casually.

Stella's face turned crimson. "Oh! You wanted your friend to walk into that obvious trap did you?"

Dimitri raised his voice. "I keep trying to tell you how unexpected it all was! Anyway I have arranged to meet Manolis and make the exchange again."

Her eyes opened wide. "What with?"

He looked downward. "I managed to convince Anya to give me the fake Trigger and dispose of it. So that means I can still do the switch for you." He gazed up and watched with satisfaction that her expression was one of admiration.

"I won't ask how you regained that much confidence, but can you trust Manolis?"

Dimitri gave her a cheeky grin. "He and I go back a long way. We used to negotiate all sort of dea...."

Stella waved her finger. "Considering just what has happened; can you really work safely with your friend Manolis?"

He shook his head vigorously. "No, no, it's not like that at all. He wouldn't con his best business partner. Manolis and I are good..."

"You must be very wary of him and especially Anya. She could turn on you at any minute."

"I'm her lover aren't I?"

Stella nodded slowly. "She killed Smythe in cold blood. Now do you realise the danger of not following orders? Tow the party line in future."

Dimitri was only half listening: his thoughts were with the next phase of his enterprise. Carefully he said. "I can see why that Trigger is so important to you."

Stella was about to reply but decided against it. She got up as if to go, but hesitated as she reached the door handle. Swiftly she turned. "Oh!" she put her finger to her lips in mock surprise. "Ben has uncovered a piece of intelligence about your friend Manolis; surprised you didn't know it?"

He looked guiltily at her. "Oh?"

"Manolis appears to have been Anya's ex lover. Ben couldn't be definite about whether it's still 'ex' or not. Can you be?"

Dimitri looked deadpan "Nothing I can't handle."

"Await my phone call." She commanded.

He nodded with mechanical precision.

It was a deceptive breeze that almost took his breath away, or perhaps it was the company he kept? Yannis, still in the Rolls, was casually exhaling cigar smoke (he had smelt the fragrance of Havana) and Manolis, only inches away, was wheezing heavily.

Dimitri with his back turned, stared out from the Lycavitos like a king surveying his vast empire of silver stars.

Athens lay sleeping far below, hiding beneath twinkling diamonds. They had the place to themselves. From beyond the distant mountains came a peal of thunder. He felt the hate that bore into his soul; there was no need to turn to witness it.

"You've messed with my woman. I don't like that."

Outwardly calm, inwardly the catgut vibrating his heart, Dimitri turned and looked straight into the raisin eyes of Manolis Paterakis. He could smell his rotting breath now, hot and rasping upon his face. "You've got it all mixed up: Anya and I are only business partners. That's all. Where's your problem in that?"

"You think you are a clever little man don't you?" His nose now brushed against Dimitri's. "Let's finish it here and now: I'll give you first blood and then my pleasure will be smashing your head in and then throwing your body over this parapet."

Dimitri gently backed off until he felt safe from the reach of those gorilla like hands, he almost had a problem in speaking his native tongue. My God he was convincing.

"I've no quarrel with you. Why don't you inform Anya about your concern, I'm sure she'll smooth away all your fears."

"Yannis too is a close friend of mine. Did you know that?"

Dimitri felt his pulse race. "We are all close friends; calm yourself!" They had been so careful. Anya never mixed business with pleasure. Yannis must only suspect. Perhaps it was jealously? "I can assure you that there is nothing to these allegations. I think Yannis is the one you need to watch." Dimitri feigned a laugh. "He's always has an eye on her, you know."

An indignant voice perked up. "Hey! That's a lie and you know that."

Dimitri could see that Manolis wore the face of confusion and so he followed through with, "Believe me. Your fears are groundless."

Manolis wrapped his paw around Dimitri's throat, pulled and lifted until he was gasping upon tiptoe. "Let us make the deal and then we'll talk again."

At this Yannis climbed out of the car and ran over towards them. "Stop all this can't you? I can hear a car approaching and we can't afford any trouble here, can we?"

Manolis dragged Dimitri back towards the car. Yannis, a pace behind, was skulking like a whippet. Dimitri was thrown into the back seat.

Yannis started up the engine and selected auto, but before he released the handbrake he leant across to Manolis and whispered.

"Personally I've never seen anything improper going on between those two. I can assure you of this. So let's leave all this ill feeling behind, shall we?"

"I'll think about it," declared Manolis as they roared down the hill towards Athens. "When I have rested."

Yannis scowled with frustration, but Dimitri merely turned and peered out across at the black velvet Mountains.

He smiled a secret smile and said nothing.

CHAPTER TWENTY EIGHT

Triple Dilemma

Time Loop Blue

Stella's phone call, when it came around eleven-fifteen, caused not a trickle of emotion for Dimitri: he knew straight away who it was. The code: a single ring preceding the call caused him merely to observe Anya.

How would she respond?

There was no indicative expression. Perched upon the throw-covered sofa she appeared cocooned amongst her embroidery, oblivious even to the dappled sunlight that played upon her hair. He looked mesmerised as her hand continued to weave monotonously to and fro, but then suddenly she stopped and looked across at him. Slumped within his armchair he noted the glance of irritation, the raised eyebrow. His response was well calculated: the slow move upwards; his walk casual; the expression equally so; the handset lightly lifted, like that of plucking a rose.

"Yes?" he said rather disdainfully.

"Mr Perrakis?"

"Can I help you?"

There was a slight pause before she said: "Your suit is ready for collection."

"My suit? So it wasn't ruined after all?"

"It dry cleaned perfectly."

"Can I come for it now?"

"We are open until three-thirty, sir."

"Thank you."

He replaced the handset carefully, but inwardly Dimitri's heart was pounding. Stella must have done that for him and he vaguely remembered that 'dry clean' was code. The little incident with Smythe had given him the jitters but she had 'dry cleaned' him which meant his cover therefore was still good.

So he was safe after all and Anya was not playing cat and mouse. It had felt like that, the last couple of days. Was Ben on to him? Had he been recognised; had he assisted with Smythe's murder; had he sold his soul to the Devil? His mind was a whirlpool of thoughts and he wanted badly to escape them. If only he could blot out that unearthly scream as Smythe died by the destruction of that strange weapon. If nightmares could be exchanged for poverty, he would gladly do so now.

His immediate thought before picking up the phone was to disappear to a safe house for a while, one that only he knew. He allowed himself a deep intake of breath, and then another glance at that woman. How could they have made such passionate love whilst each owning a heart of glass?

With meticulous precision he surveyed the Laura Ashley decor that blended so tastefully with the Georgian-styled furniture. Neatly placed upon a dresser there were crafted crystal goblets which sat proudly upon silver mats and then of course there was her: he realised that he had become infatuated. For the second time in his life he had re-experienced the stability of a loving relationship. His father (if only he could see this) would fervently approve.

Their rampant lovemaking had been exhilarating and never ending. She was insatiable. Abruptly however during these last few days, her mood had changed into being aloof and cold. Perhaps her coolness would thaw in time? Decisively he stood up and made his way towards the door.

Anya ceased her embroidery and looked disdainfully at him. Crisply she asked, "Dimitri?"

He turned cautiously. "Yes?"

"On your way back, pick up some Feta cheese will you?"

He wore the smile for her benefit as he slipped through the door. Once outside and the moment he entered the lift he became grim faced and worried. There was a strong smell of diesel that grabbed his nostrils as he entered the downstairs foyer. His heart jumped as he saw Yannis walk into the building. They brushed past one another without any sign of acknowledgement. Once more that nervous chill racked his body as he walked out of the apartment of 45A Constantinople Street and headed towards Marousi railway station.

Had Anya set him up?

Could even Gallagher be trusted?

There was a weakness in using the train. It was either that, or a taxi. With relief he noted the platform was empty: that was a good sign. Dimitri contemplated his next move from the bridge over KAT station. A sultry breeze caressed his hair as he gazed across at the blue wash of the mountains. In his jacket pocket he fondled a rail ticket as out of the corner of his eye he glimpsed the yellow taxi that had just arrived. The scar-faced driver, all greasy haired, middle aged and plump as a melon, was scrutinising for his next fare. As the small orange train pulled into the station, Dimitri glanced at it, then at the taxi and only then, made up his mind.

There was a tension in her expression; an anxiety that would not go away.

What had gone wrong?

Blending with the tourists of the Acropolis, Stella tried once more to see if Dimitri was amongst them. Fifteen-minutes late was a serious affair. She smoothed down her denim skirt, perched herself upon the parapet overlooking the Parthenon and thought with regret about that morning phone call.

Her white blouse caught the afternoon breeze. The Athens Team had assured her that Dimitri's cover had not been blown over the Smythe affair. Without that assurance, she would have phoned and used the code, 'not dry cleaned' to abort, and he would have gone to one of their safe-houses to be collected and shipped home.

Behind her, a greasy haired, barrel-shaped man appeared to scrutinise her closely. Casually then, he lifted a camera to his scar lacerated face. At the 'click', Stella turned, but all she saw was the back of a shabby suit scurrying towards the five sculptured figures perched in the Erechtheion. At her feet was something that she had previously missed: a glowing triple red-ringed cigarette. Upon closer scrutiny she noticed it had burnt to half of its length. That meant approximately thirty minutes had passed. What caused a flutter of panic was the meaning of that triple ring.

The 'fall back' meeting was in a poky orange-fronted souvlaki bar situated near the Plaka. As she sat near the window and ordered from the menu, she noted a middle-aged man in a black leather jacket sitting near the window. They were the only occupants. He seemed occupied with his newspaper. She waited for what seemed like an eternity, allowing the sun to slide into the distant horizon; it briefly caught on the earring of the man who she noted was now giving her far too much attention.

She left abruptly.

Even with the usual swirl of tourists, the long street of Pandrossou made her feel naked and vulnerable. Tonight felt all wrong. Finally her instincts caused her to hasten but she resisted the wild panic from within.

Leaving the tourist packed streets behind she carefully back tracked then made her way up towards Tripodon Street and turning left at Scholarhio Restaurant towards the Parthenon. High above, the lonely ruins glowed white and virginal. It was the murmur of solitary footsteps that first alerted her that someone was discreetly following. In a doorway she paused and glanced quickly behind. Abruptly then, a chunk of house wall exploded into the gutter a few inches away and less than a heartbeat later, the ricochet sound of a bullet.

She was being shot at!

Suddenly a loud bang made her jump. Into view came a battered white Yugo that turned into the street. Effectively it had shielded her. She ran in front of the bonnet and as it roared past, she tried to flag it down. The occupants were a young couple; the boy held a pleasant grin and had black hair; the girl was all flowing blonde and rounded face. She heard unintelligible words and laughter as with billowing smoke, the car swept around a narrow corner. Ahead were stone steps that would lead her up to the walls of the Acropolis.

She leapt up two at a time only briefly pausing for breath at the top. The ringing footsteps followed closely behind. To the right were railings and further along this path, there would be a gate. It led down a steep grassy incline but there would be olive trees to hide her.

Would that gate be locked?

She arrived there just as a figure emerged from climbing the steps. There was a lock and chain around the gate. Her assailant grew closer.

Hugging the contours of the railings she hurried as silently as she could further up the path until Saint Paul's Rock towered above her. Here she knew there was another gate. Her assailant seemed to be closer now; the footsteps louder and more urgent. She crouched down to examine the chain and lock mechanism. With shaking hands she examined it closely. It hadn't been snapped shut. Sloppy caretaker she breathed, but blessed and thanked him as her fingers worked the lock apart.

The gate creaked! How close now?

With survival instincts kicking in, she grabbed her hair spray and sprayed it into the hinges. Blending with the shadows of the Rock, she watched a shadow sliver by her, but then it paused, and backtracked towards the gate. She imagined those eyes penetrating the darkness, hunting her down like a fox with a rabbit. Then she heard the noise of that chain rattling through the night. Thank God, she had locked the gate behind her.

A distant car light flooded the path momentarily and highlighted a face that hung there for eternity. It was the man from the souvlaki bar.

Her nerves were in tatters by the time she arrived at her apartment. Pausing at the oak drinks cabinet, Stella hurled a brandy down her throat and refilled her glass again. Slumped onto the settee extremely tired, she eventually became aware of the alcoholic numbness that was now taking hold. At her feet were Larry and Barnabus. Stella grabbed her cuddly toys and hugged desperately nursing her mental wounds through them.

Someone had tried to kill her tonight. Why?

Around her apartment she idly gazed, devoid of feeling. The red-suited Dauphin portrait to her left; the phone upon the coffee table at her feet; the wooden bookcase adjacent to her, and then back to the phone. "Why?" she murmured. "Why shoot at me?"

After what seemed like an age she reached down to pick up the phone and punched numbers.

"London Desk? I want to speak with Major Gallagher. Yes, yes, I know it's late but please ring his extension will you: he'll still be there. He always is," she muttered thankfully under her breath. A few minutes passed before she heard a click and then his comforting voice. "Hi Stella. How can I help you?"

She wanted to appear calm but her words tumbled over one another. For the first time in her life she desperately wanted his comforting arms around her. "I'm worried about our dry cleaning service."

His response was reassuring as a father should be. "I'm sure there's no need for your concern, but your voice sounds rather shaky. So what's happened?"

"I believe the Team has become rather slip-shoddy."

"That's a serious accusation to make?"

"All our appointments seem to have been undercut by other operators."

"Really!" What makes you think that?"

"Let's put it this way: one of your own suits may have been ruined. There's a cigarette burn, a triple ring cigarette burn in it." She could tell by the gasp from the other end that the message had got through.

His voice was crisp when he said. "That does not surprise me in the least; it's happened here too!"

"You could have warned me!" she said angrily. "However that can mean only one thing?"

"No-one but you and I know of this side of operations... and York Desk."

"We have a problem," she said carefully.

"Can my suit be salvaged?"

There was no restraint in her voice now. "Oh yes," she replied. "Oh yes."

CHAPTER TWENTY NINE

A Lonely Gunshot

Time Loop Blue

The step casual; the poise elegant; the glance easy, almost flippant, beguiled the truth: his bowels were playing up.

His Metro ride was more uncomfortable than he envisaged. His irritating forty minute journey had been accounted for; the need for the loo had not been. A toilet in this city was a rare event and Auster mused that Athenians must be an alien race with concrete bladders and bowels. He remembered there was a toilet at the station but when he arrived at Thissio, a cursory glance at the poky little hole that professed to be one, didn't inspire him at all. He headed out of the railway station towards the Plaka and eventually the Acropolis. Stella had better be early. On the way he had stumbled across a burger bar with toilets. "Thank you God!" he exclaimed whilst leaping inside.

The Plaka Flea Market is a swirling market place of leather goods, Greek statues and postcards. Every shop window appeared crowded with these tourist trinkets but they complimented the narrow haphazard streets with their drab tarnished buildings and derelict houses.

Auster doubled back and forth 'dry cleaning' himself of would be assassins. However he felt at home here, blending within the dense heaving populace until finally he felt comfortable that he hadn't been followed. As he sat upon the parapet overlooking the Parthenon, his thoughts dwelt upon the five sculptured maidens perched in the Erechtheion. Within their faces, Auster felt enchanted by their world-wise beauty.

A click of a camera caused him to turn. Hurrying away was a greasy haired, barrel-shaped man in a shabby suit. A Polaroid camera was not a usual tourist accessory and he looked suspiciously like the taxi driver. To his left, walking into the museum was Yannis. Abruptly he turned and stared directly at him. The smile, cruel and very meaningful, caused a sweat to break out on Auster's brow; this was no time to feel complacent. Before he fled the Acropolis, a friendly tourist helped him light a triple ringed cigarette.

Stepping out onto the platform of Faliron railway station, he reasoned it all away with a touch of rationality: hadn't he been 'dry cleaned' by the elite professionals? Auster performed his own ritual now, sweeping up and down the arid roads until he felt satisfied and confident enough to make his way towards the Port of Piraeus and then onwards towards Microlimano. Dry cleaned or not, Stella was not his nursemaid.

Darkness had fallen before Auster had reached the Appaloosa Taverna, and beyond that, the yacht Rigel. He paused momentarily and admired once more his cabin cruiser that was sleek and long, with the muscle for tremendous speed. Casually Auster walked up the gangplank and stepped on board, unlocked the hatch and reached for the Ouzo bottle that he knew was waiting for him.

The night was wonderfully silent as he gazed up at the fierce starry brilliance of Orion; there was not a breath of wind, just an embracing balminess in the air. Across the Port the bobbing yachts silhouetted against the sky and seemed to be listening perhaps to the occasional mournful cry of a sea bird that pirouetted above his head. Abruptly, a gun barrel poked into his back. He turned to witness a gold earring that flashed in the shadows.

"Not saved me a drink?"

Peeping from within the cabin doorway was Manolis. Hands held high, he followed him into the cabin. Once below and out of sight, the gun was thrown casually upon the brown blankets of the bunk bed. Auster nervously giggled at him; there was nothing else to do.

"Phew! Tha's sound, bah no mistake."

Manolis slapped him on the back and howled with delight. "Katalaves! Your Greek is dreadful!"

Auster brushed aside a bright red plastic Father Christmas and flopped down. "Red Mercury shipment; is it safe?"

Manolis walked down the cabin until he faced the far wall that contained a row of books and pointed to the central yellow volume. "What do you think?"

"Thank the gods for that!"

He knowingly shook his head. "And I thought they were worthless metal junk."

Auster heard a creak above his head but ignored it.

Time Loop Red

Auster heard a creak above his head but ignored it. "Do not concern yourself with what I am about to tell you but one of my English colleagues has betrayed me by interfering with one of my business deals."

Manolis scowled. "What do you mean?"

Auster rubbed a hand across his perspiring forehead. He walked over and extracted the yellow leather bound book and waved it at Manolis. "I think it very wise to move quickly on this business deal with our English buyer. Have you fuelled up the helicopter as I requested earlier today?"

Time Loop Blue

Auster heard a creak above his head but ignored it. "We have enough dummy Triggers to sell to our English as well our Greek connections. And then of course I'll sell the real one to my naive boss Ben Gallagher."

Manolis scowled. "Explain yourself?"

Auster rubbed a hand across his perspiring forehead. "OK – you must trust me to deal with our English contacts." He looked suspiciously across at him. "Why did you sell directly to Anya – didn't you trust me?"

Manolis shook his head. "Anya was tipped off about the courier Smythe – therefore I felt it prudent to act carefully for both of us; you played your part well. I don't think she suspects anything."

"We have a mole somewhere; we must be doubly careful"

"What now?"

"The most important thing we must do is to keep up with this deception."

Manolis laughed. "Yannis trusts me like a brother now, it will be easy." He grabbed the Ouzo bottle. "Let's drink to our success."

"Good idea; with fake Triggers and the real one we can triple our profit. I'll drink to that!"

"I went to check if the helicopter was secure, but it had gone?"

"Under the circumstances I thought it wise to re locate it to a far safer place after my little trip to England. My hanger might have been too obvious a place."

The voice of Manolis had the cutting edge of barbed wire as he said: "so where have you put it?"

Auster was about to answer when he was disturbed by another noise: that of a cabin door opening.

"Can I join your party?" said a familiar voice.

Yannis grinned like the Devil on vacation as he stepped inside and closed the door carefully behind him. For an hour there were heated exchanges of words before there was silence within. Abruptly the cabin door opened spilling light out across the deck of the Rigel.

A lonely gunshot echoed far into that starry night. Then silence. Eventually as if to cover this deadly deed, the wind howled and a sea bird cried out her forlorn sigh, as if in protest.

CHAPTER THIRTY
If We Shadows

Time Loop Purple

"Are you rested?"

CHAPTER THIRTY ONE

A Diamond Cage

Time Loop Purple

I awake gently to the tang of ozone, which reminds me of the sea. The only sound that I can hear is that of a low-pitched humming. Both however appear faint and non-threatening. Carefully I open my eyes and find myself in a small darkened windowless cavern; I appear to be on a white slab which is soft to the touch like leatherette. The only light I can see comes from above; a white parallel beam of light spills from a huge porthole in the domed ceiling onto the floor. My next disturbing experience is trying to sit upright. This causes me to glide upwards and I grab onto the side of the slab to stabilize myself. I realise now that I had been here before, but that recollection is hazy and distant. My last memory I could recall with any certainty is Tombs standing over me whilst I nursed the dead body of Auster.

Peering through the gloom I notice that along the near side wall to my left, I count six stainless steel cabinets. Protruding from each are thin swan-like necks. I begin to shudder uncontrollably. Around my head I slowly become aware of a strange swishing sound like a badly tuned radio. Abruptly then a subtle fragrance of cinnamon wafts into my nostrils.

A whispered voice fills my head. "Are you rested?"

I frantically try to locate its source. "Where are you?"

"I sit near the window."

I sift the near blackness. "I see no window."

"Then find it, human."

I peer through the gloom, but find nothing. What was that? Something moves between the light and dark! Taking a deep breath I resolve to escape this awful place. As my legs swing off the slab, my action causes me to float gently downwards. I lose my balance and spiral forward. Gently however my face makes contact with the floor. I stay there awhile feeling somehow safe. From this viewpoint however I notice that the floor comprises of a jagged rubber-like material. Regaining my feet I realise its purpose because, although my body is swaying from side to side my feet stick like glue. By prising each foot off the floor I rock and sway my way forward with a gentle swishing sound as each foot releases from that clutching material.

Ahead of me is an alcove set in the wall. My approach although slow gives me too much momentum to prevent me from stopping. I brace myself for impact, but suddenly the alcove becomes an open doorway and sucks me through. I emerge into a long sweeping corridor stretching in both directions. Looking back, I am surprised to find merely an alcove wall again. In stark contrast to the gloomy cavern I had vacated, the entire surface of this corridor appears translucent and vibrant with colour and light. It reminds me of pure diamond. Set into both walls, are more of these enigmatic alcoves which are placed at regular intervals along its path. Some appear as windows and through them I see outside onto an awesome spectacle. I am swimming amongst a myriad of brightly coloured stars.

"What's keeping you?"

That curt voice feels like a lightning strike. "Where are you?" I plead.

"Hurry."

"I'm doing my best but at least tell me the way!"

My protestation went unanswered and so reluctantly I undertook to obey this command. I sway along a gently sweeping inward arc. The corridor ends abruptly with yet another of these puzzling alcoves blocking my path. Again I tried to stop, but the micro-gravity has me fooled and so my mass propels me forward. As before however, I am sucked through this materialised portal. When eventually I steady myself it becomes apparent that I have entered another cavern, but one that is so huge there is no ceiling. As my eyes adjust I am amazed to discover more gothic shaped archways, seven in all, set along each wall. Coupled with the crisp cool air, there is a faint trace of mustiness; an age like quality. I had the overwhelming feeling that I was within a church, or a sanctuary of some kind. Within the seventh archway I see an antechamber, and holding dominion is a peculiarly shaped table. Triangular in design with an uneven leg at each corner, the top is not flat but has a steep inclined 'V' shape, which holds what looks like a shoebox. The whole contraption should have fallen over, but enigmatically it didn't.

I detect movement and along with it, a strange calm anaesthetises my senses.

Reclining within a small alcove beyond the table is a man dressed in a simple white monk's habit. His face appears transfigured with light and I could have taken him for a saint. He is asleep. As I draw closer to him I realise that the glow comes from a huge Catherine like wheel outside the window.

What an awesome sight! Nothing that I had seen previously through astronomical telescopes could prepare me for this grand spectacle. Piercingly bright points stud this spiral cloud-like structure. What rich colour greets my eyes! Pirouetting from the yellow bar-like centre, are deep red, pin-sharp stars that melt into subtle graduated shades of salmon pink. Further out and blended as if by a master artist, there is a flourish of azure that succumbs at the extreme edge into a finale of ice-blue stars. Intermingled throughout like a swirling smoke trail, are deep-coal dust lanes. From the corner of my eye this figure abruptly moves. Words invade my mind.

"*Aoccdrnig to waht yuo can haer I am tlaknig total gibbreish, yet yuor huamn mnid can undrestnad me prefcetly. My prfered way of coumnciation is mny tmies fster tahn yours and that is why yuo haer me in this way.*"

I turn to find that this stranger is gazing intently at me yet there is no mouth movement at all as he continues.

"*Wihtn yuor mnid yuo ansa with amzmt?*"

I feebly nod.

"The region that slows your mind down is called the Brocas Region. I have now bio engineered your brain to accept my speech. You are free of this constraint."

"I can understand you; I can understand you perfectly at last!"

He ignores my exuberant outburst and turns to look outside. "The system you describe as the Milky Way is simply breathtaking do you not think?"

For the first time since I had awoken from my slab, it began to dawn on me the sheer magnitude of my surroundings. My body begins to shake with emotion as I turn and gaze outside.

"Where am I?"

He shrugs as if he is reading a dinner menu. "From this Transit Station you are approximately thirty-five thousand light-years from your Earth."

I suddenly feel light-headed and repeat myself blubbering softly. "I am where? I am where?"

He gives me a disdained impersonal look and then points his finger airily along one of the nearest highway-like arms that appear to sweep before us. "Behold your home galaxy. Your sun is a mere speck upon that galactic spiral arm down there."

Raw uncontrollable fear causes me to drop to my knees and curl up in a foetal ball at his feet. I shake with fear. "Please let me go home?"

He gently raises me up and I look into hazel eyes that twinkle with amusement. "Do not be distressed. You are in a place of safety. Consider me your friend."

As if a cloud had lifted from my mind I examine his face and realise it was familiar.

"You're Michael Tombs?"

He lifts an eyebrow. "Yes, I am. Please call me Michael."

I look in disbelief. "An alien called Michael?"

"I am closer to your species than you'd believe."

I feel an iceberg sliver down my spine. "You murdered my friend." I gasp out the words feeling completely out of control.

He sighs heavily. "Come come! Can't you perceive anything? Nothing what you have seen or heard is real in your terms of reference! Your friend is not dead. You must understand that."

"How do you expect me to?"

"I observe you are perspiring. Therefore you clearly are shocked by this. Take deep breaths and you will calm down." A pregnant pause follows. His reply when it came held an intensity of foreboding. "You and I are the only occupants on this Station. Am I a murderer? Am I your friend? Which scenario can you comfortably live with?"

I give a cool level stare before replying. "I'll have to trust you then won't I?"

There was a mysterious twinkle in his eye. "We both must trust each other. Believe me when I say that I have no real interest in your affairs. In truth I am as caught up in this mess as you are."

My mouth opens but I totally fail to speak. Did it matter anyway because he must sense my inner turmoil.

"Clear your mind by observing outside; your entire existence now is the exact present time: no past, no future, just the raw passing moment. You have experienced Earth beaches, but now see a celestial beach of multicoloured grains. Each is a sun. There are suns that are as huge as your entire Solar System and also there are those, smaller than your Earth, possessing tremendous energies. This transit station can harness these inexhaustible energies. One thimbleful of their mass would weigh many, many tons. Then of course there are many suns very similar to your own."

Curiosity, raw and strangely exciting compels me now. "Do they have planets revolving around them like Earth?"

"Yes, but that was not your question?"

I give him a puzzled look and pause to think over what he had inferred. I instantly regret my next response. "Which planet do you come from?" my words tumbled out and I noted his immediate distain.

"Our species requires no planet to exist on."

I sense he is laughing at me but it is more than that: he was the master and I merely the pet dog attempting to communicate. I take a deep breath and feel his words invade my brain.

"By answering that more fully I would alter the course of your future and I cannot do that."

"I don't understand. Can you explain?"

He gives a curt reply. "No! That is none of your business."

"There is no need to be rude to me?"

I experience hurt as he revaluates my answer. "Is that being rude? I thought I was stating an obvious fact."

"What can you tell me then?"

He ignores my question and looks outside. "On a clear day, relatively speaking of course," he briefly turns giving an impish smile. "You can see for light-years. The black hole at your galactic centre for instance is barely perceivable as a mottled dot with a spike attached. It's lost of course amongst the brilliance of millions upon millions of closely packed stars that surround it."

"Really?" I must have looked stupid with my mouth sagging, a vacant stare on my face as he once more faced me. His finger points accusingly.

"And now to more important things: I want you to help me accomplish my mission on Earth."

"Will that bring Auster back to life?"

I notice a deep sigh followed by a shrug. "I am a doctor that specialises in human anatomy," he turns towards the window. "Back there in the barley field I brought you back to life and thus have given you a new beginning. And your unsaid question 'why' will be answered by yourself – when you do my bidding."

My familiar iceberg returns. "What do you want me to do then?"

"I present you with a paradox. Your Earth is now held in the balance between death and life. Will you help me stop this stalemate? We do not have much time."

I see again that look of his: like that of a vet attending his sick patient, and so I thought carefully before replying.

"Of course." I answer simply.

"Then we must go back; back to Athens."

"Why there?"

"I want you to be enlightened Mr Ross. It will amuse me!"

CHAPTER THIRTY TWO

Schrödinger's Cat

Time Loop Purple-Blue

Looking down from the right-hand corner of a ceiling was an experience I could not easily explain. I had no body, but felt blasé to this fact.

"Observe and learn my inquisitive friend."

Michael was somewhere in the nearby vicinity, but I couldn't see him. Strapped to a chair wriggling in pain was Auster. Both Anya and Yannis were standing over him; Anya screamed.

"Who are you working for?"

"No one you stupid cow."

Her entire body convulsed now in emotion. "I don't believe you. Yannis, hit him harder this time."

With meticulous care he aimed a blow at Auster's face. I heard a sickening thud.

"Talk you bastard. Talk."

"I don't know what you mean. Go to hell."

Abruptly I heard Michael say. "Observe the brutality. What are your thoughts?"

"What?"

"Observe and learn."

Anya had now pulled a gun from her handbag and directed it towards Austerfield. With its gleaming metal silencer it almost touched his chest. She grinned maliciously. "Have you anything to tell me? Anything at all?"

"There's nothing further to tell."

She backed off and there was a swishing noise and I realised that she must have shot him because his face twisted in a soundless scream. 'Swish.'

Everything then seemed to slow down and finally like a jammed film reel in a projector, the entire scene stopped in mid frame. Suddenly I felt an invisible force take hold of me and I floated downwards to eye level. In front of me, hanging in mid flight was a solitary bullet.

"Notice the trajectory. This time it will obviously miss its target."

The room smelt like an abattoir and I retched violently. "What kind of unfeeling creature are you?"

"It's you who do not comprehend."

"What is there to comprehend?"

"Observe at the door."

As if frame by frame, the door jerked open and then I heard another "swish" and several frames later, a yelp from Auster. Then the frames appeared to jump because now there was only Austerfield sprawled across the floor. In amazement I watched myself appear at the open doorway and peering over my right shoulder, was the wild face of Stella. We looked like puppets being jerked by invisible strings. Abruptly that macabre scene became still life again.

"Am I a spirit?"

The reply was condescending. "That question is too simplistic for me to answer. See yourself as a virtual identity: neither here nor there. You are in reality observing Schrödinger's cat."

I looked around the room. "What cat?"

His voice now held amusement. "One of your scientists, Schrödinger, deduced an analogy to explain the 'Uncertainty Principle' in quantum physics. Imagine a cat in an enclosed box, which also contains a vial of poison gas and a radioactive atom. This atom has a 50-50 chance of decaying, emitting a deadly Gamma ray which triggers the breaking of the vial, thus killing the cat."

"Run that past me one more time?"

"Observe the box now. Is the cat alive or dead?"

"How would you know that, without first opening the box?"

"Have *you* opened the box?"

I began to feel very frustrated. "What box"?

"Really! What cat? What box? *Think* human. Think".

Was this my first day at quantum mechanics kindergarten I thought? I tried to solve the problem he had poised and finally gave him my best answer.

"You mean the 'box' in reality then, is this room?"

He sighed. "I have become bored with you. Look around. Be quick now. Why is your friend in this predicament?"

"That question at least is obvious. He's been set up by someone."

I heard another deep sigh from him and so without any more ado, began to search around the room. There was a frustrating nothing.

"Look there!" exclaimed Michael.

"Look where?" I growled. "You're invisible!"

I heard a brief laugh. "Mmn, human comedy again; how intriguing."

As if by a poltergeist's hand, Anya's bag levitated upwards spilling its contents on the floor. Amongst the pile of lady terrorist knick-knacks: makeup, paper hankies, comb, spare bullet clip, there was something else: a single white glove. Upon closer examination I noticed an unusual motif on the back: a black dot surrounded by a setsquare and compass.

"I remember seeing that somewhere else," I said.

"There's your deadly atom," he announced.

I still felt mystified but was too proud to admit the fact. "What now?" I declared soberly.

"Watch again and observe carefully this time!"

Suddenly the entire room changed and I watched mesmerised as the front door opened and Stella and I entered. Auster's startled face stared at us. It felt strange observing a scene like actors upon the stage of life.

"You experienced your friend die in your arms, yet also he is alive. You see Stella and yourself yet in a moment..." He abruptly paused and I heard him sigh heavily. "Tell me what the observed facts are?"

"I don't know; both cannot be correct."

"You must hold me on trust, as much as I with you. My next step is to now return you back into your body so that your tasks can be accomplished."

"You'll do what? I am not one of your experiments," I snapped.

"Can't you understand yet? Austerfield must remain alive if the world is to be saved! Now is it clear?"

"What tasks are you giving me?"

"Are you familiar with the Rubik's cube?"

I began to protest, but my words became blurred within an envelope of low frequency sound like bees. Abruptly I became engulfed with an intense wave of light that sent a painful lightning bolt through my whole body. After that, an intense calm befell me and gently I felt myself float over and sink into my body. That experience was not unlike climbing into a warm bath. Michael appeared at my side, his body translucent and flowing like a blue waterfall. "Look down at your watch."

I saw that Auster's watch had now an illuminated holographic outer bezel. Hovering above were numbers: '00:00:00:49' flashed the purple blue readout. My jaw dropped. "Wow!"

"I have redesigned your watch to give you an indication as to the time element you must stay in each Time Loop. If you are to succeed, your tasks must be completed within that limitation."

I looked in wonderment at him. "What happens if I don't?"

He sighed. "I must test your worthiness. You now, are our only hope – if I can but trust you."

Abruptly the room became alive with movement. Stella's breath, short and crisp pummelled the back of my neck; a staccato of bullets and cordite filled the room.

"What the hell do you want me to do here?"

His voice replied softly. "Remember. Your task must be completed within the time limitation."

"Why?"

"Do you remember Arras Hill?"

I caught sight of a bezel that flashed 00:00:00:00 and couldn't answer.

CHAPTER THIRTY THREE

Deadly Candy

Time Loop Purple-Red

00:00:12:00

Sometimes memories can play funny tricks on you: this evening, mine was working double overtime. I stood amongst the ears of hissing winter barley staring intently below. An aroma of mowed hay, fresh on the night air intoxicated my senses. An arctic wind moaned. At my vantage point high up on Arras hill, I saw below a small perfectly formed crop circle of about 30 feet in dimension. From this angle it looked like the Star of David.

Within the circle a young couple, all bobby hats and anoraks, were looking around them. She suddenly gripped his arms and they embraced passionately. Even from this distance this man and women looked familiar. That revelation however came as no surprise: I had expected them to be there. My convictions had been right all along because even without binoculars I knew her to be my wife Elizabeth. However this wasn't how I had remembered it at all. The last time I was here I had been too late and had to return home nursing my suspicions. Like an upturned saltcellar I had endured a loving relationship that had from that moment eventually trickled away into nothing. Now here before my very eyes was the proof of it all.

So who was her lover?

With intense resolution I leapt down the hill two steps at a time and hurled myself into the crop circle.

If it wasn't for their ecstatic embrace, I would have been surely discovered. I approached closer and closer until I could aim a blow to the side of his face. My fist swept straight through his face like a phantom.

00:00:00:00

Time Loop Purple -Blue

00:00:07:00

A chill wind groaned like a dying animal whilst a lazy moon straddled the horizon. I was much closer now. Their passionate embrace gave me the chance to plant a blow at the left side of his pulled down bobby hat. All it achieved was that I fell in a crumpled heap at their feet. My reaction now was intense anger as I regained my feet and aimed a kick into his side. Again, this was a futile attempt; my leg swept right through him.

A familiar voice enquired. "Have you forgotten this?"

I turned and saw Michael; his hooded face covered in shadow. In his outstretched hand was a stone of deadly proportions. "Hit him with that. You'll kill the 'tomcat' for sure!"

A trickle of guilt caused me to stammer. "What do you mean?"

"Search your soul Ross; then give me your answer."

My heart pounded. "If you were me, wouldn't you too try for revenge? Can't you understand: I still love her you unfeeling sod."

Within my mind I felt swamped with emotions of curiosity and puzzlement. "You cannot alter this future, whatever you do. Their destiny is set, but then so is yours. Embrace it."

"I cannot," I cried and snatched away my gaze.

"Love is neither selfish nor restricting. True love is oneness. Divine love is forgiving and then letting go. If you really love her – then let go. Open your mind and comprehend infinite love."

When I eventually turned to look at him, he had gone.

Dumbfounded I stood amongst the swirling windswept barley and watched the setting moon as it slowly draped the landscape in silver shadow. I heard the growl of a car starter motor. In the distance, the flash of headlights swept across the hill and the black shape of a car headed off back in the direction of York.

00.00.00.00

Time Loop Purple – Red

00:00:10:00

My next recollection was standing outside my house – but this was the house from my past.

Today was yesterday.

I reached out to open the garden gate but there was no need: my hand and then body glided through like a spectre. As I looked around, bitter-sweet memories were conjured up like on a movie set. However my viewpoint appeared slightly above normal height which unnerved me a little. There was a draping sunset with Elizabeth sitting on the garden bench; the aroma of fresh coffee and laughing voices on the lawn; barbeque smells that also intertwined with intense fragrance of rose and wood bark and as quickly these apparitions gently -evaporated. Now the flowers were in autumnal bloom with the birds in final rehearsal before their winter ordeal.

My heart ached as I entered this house of the past. It was home but not home; familiar but not familiar; a displacement in time, but not emotions. In the kitchen the same leaking tap trickled water into a bowl full of crockery. Fresh scented clothes hung over radiators.

Why was I here?

I climbed the stairs and entered a marital bedroom that spat cold and hostile. Racked with painful memories, I felt that Michael had sent me here for a purpose. This was not my house anymore and felt more like a cage. Why was I being ruthlessly tested in this way? I paused and thought how I was about to solve this particular problem that had evolved from within an alien mind. The different colour shifts of my watch gave me cause for concern. Each dimension probably was given a different colour, but to solve Schrödinger, I too, must learn to think alien.

After several minutes of thought, an idea congealed and took form. It was time to test it. I searched through every room knowing that Michael was behind all this. Was it innocence or goading that had me searching every nook and cranny for that important clue of the deadly atom kind? It was coy in revealing itself; but I knew that I would find it eventually. Under the bed a new novelty presented itself: a ladies handbag. An unusually motif white glove reclined over it. Abruptly, a door slammed downstairs.

"Hello?" The voice held nervousness. "Is anybody there?"

"Only me," I shouted, but immediately realised how futile that response was.

From the top of the stairs, I gazed down into short red hair; blue denim shirt and brown corduroy trousers. She climbed the steps up into the bedroom and I became aware of a delicate fragrance. Her hands danced across her shirt buttons to reveal a black sheer bra. Quickly her trousers were unbuttoned and fell to the floor. Her gaze was now full on me and my heart skipped a beat at seeing once again those sensuous eyes and that cute upturned nose. My body broke out into a trembling sweat.

Abruptly the room faded into flickering shadow and materialised back again revealing an empty room. Her dressing table held a box of a few cue tips and a full rubbish bin. My observation abilities were never brilliant but this felt like the passage of time had taken place. Heavy footsteps coming up the stairs alerted me to a presence. Someone paused on the landing; they were breathing heavily and then silence. I heard crunching sounds. Abruptly peanut cases rolled into view.

A door opened and then slammed downstairs. Lighter footsteps entered. Now the heavy footsteps moved quickly into our bathroom; that familiar slight creak of its door shutting.

Light footsteps now climbed the stairs; they paused at my bedroom doorway. I looked into the anxious face of Elizabeth. Something beneath her left foot crunched. A clawing apprehension kicked my senses into overdrive. I retched. We both heard a noise coming from the bathroom. My stomach suddenly contracted in ice cold fear.

"Who's there?" she demanded.

She left the room and turned towards the bathroom. I heard a stifled scream and then scuffling. I ran towards the doorway and saw a white hooded male figure standing over her. Huge paw like hands were around her neck. Briefly she managed to turn so as to claw at her attackers face. They both fell upon the landing floor; her writhing body tried desperately to escape this death grip. The hood and a black wig fell off onto the floor revealing a red birthmark upon his head; he intensified his grip around her neck until she abruptly stopped wriggling.

All this time raw fear had held me in a stupefied trance but now I hurtled my body in a futile attempt of rescue. The wild godless face of Malik stared vacantly at me. My anger was up and I thrashed my fists into this evil shape.

Cinnamon instant and sharp upon the air abruptly held dominion. As if in response, Malik's entire body convulsed like an electric shock. He sank down upon the floor moaning softly and began to rock her body.

"Not candy mummy; not candy mummy; not candy..."

This ceaseless incantation was suddenly cut short as the world became freeze framed and then a swirling vortex smeared out this entire room.

I was somewhere else now and a dank smell invaded my nostrils. My next perspective was seeing a flight of stairs and two figures huddled beneath them. It appeared to be a cellar of some kind. Grey peeling wallpaper and soft silvery moonlight were held captive by bewitched shadows that moved by passing car headlights coming through a skylight immediately above us. Then the pungent odour of piss and excrement became dominant. Suddenly a particular bright pair of headlights focused briefly upon one corner and highlighted a slumped shape of a young girl with long black hair and dishevelled clothes. She looked about sixteen with arms that were bare and revealed dark undulating lines which I took for blood. There was a brief glimpse of a vacant waxen face. Grasping urgently on to her body was a young boy stabbing an addict's syringe into his left arm. He was rocking to and fro as black ribbons of blood trickled down onto the floor. This nightmarish scene abruptly became encompassed within shadows. I heard his pleading sobbing voice.

"Not candy mummy; not candy mummy; not..."

Mercifully this hellish room swirled anticlockwise like water down a plughole and I became sucked into it.

00:00:00:00

CHAPTER THIRTY FOUR

Which Girlfriend?

Time Loop Purple

I gaze out across 35,000 light-years and wonder. Only a moment ago I was at Arras Hill and then within my house witnessing a murder. Perhaps it is shock that allows me to stay calm and cosy within the confines of this alcove? At least this cavern-like room is familiar now, having first met Michael here. Ashen light drapes across my face and spills over the black mottled floor. The awe at seeing my home galaxy outside still causes me to draw breath.

Is it the faint smell of the sea, or that of the gentle hum of air conditioning that gives subtle reminders of home? Below on one of those insignificant dots that comprise our galaxy is the Sun and swirling around that, my Earth. It is the Earth of my father and my father's father. And now some stupid sod is trying to destroy it.

The enigmatic three-legged table still continues to intrigue me and so I return to it. How can it remain upright? With its uneven sized legs it should have toppled over by now. Further scrutiny of the shoe-like box leaves me baffled as to its purpose and design. My close approach however causes the box to hum and glow with a light blue phosphorescent colour. At the top, I notice a crystal lens ball. When I peer into it I become amazed at seeing a smaller view of what I had just seen outside. What surprises me now is seeing a smaller 'Z' shaped galaxy close by to our own. Could this be an unknown galaxy hidden from our Earth's viewpoint by the galactic centre and am I the first human to see it? Mathematically I use proportion to try and discover the apparent distance apart these galaxies could be. My approximation is about 75 thousand light years which would make this our nearest galaxy to Earth rather than the text book answer of the Andromeda galaxy at 200 million light years. Abruptly the scene changes and I now see our Sun. However this view reveals yet another unknown phenomenon: it possesses a dull yellow ring that swirls around the disc like a skipping rope.

This alien experience begins to unnerve me and I shake violently. My whole body arches into stomach cramps and nausea. A subtle trace of cinnamon reminds me that I am not alone. I look up to see Tombs standing close by; he beckons me to withdraw.

"It is draining your vital life energy; step away quickly before it kills you!"

The lens fades as I move away from the machine; I faint. His arms catch me and then guide me over to sit within the alcove. I sob uncontrollably. "Oh, my head thumps with pain."

"It was lucky I came when I did. That machine works on brain wave energy and is not configured for your alien biology; you could have been killed."

I attempt a smile. "Perhaps it was worth the risk. I saw puzzling views through it though. The Sun appears to possess a ring and there is a galaxy close by to our own, both are totally unknown to Earth science. Can you explain these strange phenomena?"

"Yes, but your knowledge must evolve from yourself; I cannot interfere with that process."

"How does your species learn then?"

He reveals a mischievous smile. "We learn by self development." I detect an air of superiority. "The end result is a more established group unity."

This was a revealing avenue to explore. "What you are telling me then is that each one of your kind learns by their *own* experience?"

"Yes – but that would only be an approximate surmise. Let me give you an example." He moves over towards the strange box and revolves the dial. Abruptly a new view materialises: that of an outside perspective of the Transit Station. It looks very much like that of a huge toilet seat of solid translucent crystal. "On Earth this shape would merit laughter and yet if I tell you it is constructed of the most purest solid diamond, then other more earthly emotions might surface; avarice, corruption – to name but a few. Your species are disharmonious to each other. For example your friend Austerfield, if given the chance would try and sell this for maximum profit!"

I feel mesmerised and overwhelmed. "I am just stunned by its beauty."

"I would expect nothing less from you; I am proud of your evolutionary progress!"

For a moment I inwardly smile at this complement. "You claim non-interference," I said finally. My next sentence holds caution. "Are not these 'Tests' a kind of interference?" I pause to see how he would respond. "Is that why you have brought me here?"

He gives a direct stare that I find very disquieting. "The confused mind stumbles: scan the horizon, not the immediate rocky path." He turns to gaze outside. "You must perceive the solution, not stagger over the problem my friend"

I cock my head. "What problem?"

"Schrödinger's cat: is he alive – or dead?"

"Oh! You mean that again!"

"Yes that. Time is too short and we must focus our minds more succinctly."

I think back to Gallagher and Tombs; Stella and that room; the barley field and then my mind focuses upon a single white glove. All appear disparate information. And yet there was another explanation, a very simple one.

"Why are you torturing me?"

I witness a fleeting emotion of shock. "Me? Torture you? Explain yourself?"

His obvious embarrassment permeates my mind too. Unexpectedly I am overwhelmed with his discomfort. To hold advantage I press on. "I don't believe the world is in danger of a Viral Quantum bomb at all. There is however another explanation to all this façade: a very simple one!"

Michael looks at me intently. "Oh! Go on. Surprise me." His voice holds a trace of amazement.

"All these experiences of mine have been either painful or pleasurable. Yet like a vampire you've sucked them from my mind, delighting with their intensity. In short you're an alien voyeur!"

I watch aghast as he holds back his head and laughs. Within my mind I feel strange conflictions. Abruptly then he turns away from me to gaze intently out of the window. After an embarrassing silence he said. "The threat of destruction is real I assure you, but I will confess that your reasoning up to now has been sound. You had to be tested to prove worthy of your assignment here. He holds up a hand to dispel my protest. "Our other attempts have proved how very little we understand your species; I tested you to your breaking point. I too have learnt and evolved from that experience."

"Please explain?"

"Some time ago you posed the question regarding why I had picked on you to help me. I gave only a part-answer. In truth, although you and I have many differences and the gulf between us is vast, there is a common link which intrigues and fascinates me."

"So the human race merely amuses you then?"

He sighs and a long silence follows. When he speaks again his voice contains sadness. "It is too hard for you to understand. Both of our species have an inherent curiosity; an innocence of gaining knowledge. You are indeed as guilty as I. There is a bridge that may unite us yet: a resonant chord."

"I'll give you that," I concede.

"My ignorance to human emotion has caused you pain; I have learnt from it." He points a finger at me. "Now it's your turn. Your viewpoint can be changed." He walked over towards the machine upon the table. At his approach the lens becomes alive with an intense blue phosphorescent light. "Let me show you Earth, as it is at present." From outside, the spiral galaxy fades into blackness to be replaced with a mottled blackened planet. It appears completely lifeless.

"Oh my God!" I scream. "Is that Earth?"

"Like your friend Austerfield, the planet Earth too, is held transfixed within dimensional Time Loops. This is the view in both those red and blue loops. We call them TLs. The VQ bomb caused Earth's time line to fragment and all I could do to save your planet was by time freezing that process. Your total history of everything you once knew is now jumbled up like jigsaw pieces. You are trapped inside a zoo-like cage; an Earth zoo. In fact I have designated this mission as Operation EarthZoo. Perhaps now you can understand and comprehend?"

"I'll help you anyway I can."

"Which girlfriend would you like to visit first?"

I stare open mouthed "Will that help?"

"Put simply – yes!"

"I never knew I had a choice – or was that popular!"

CHAPTER THIRTY FIVE

Ghosts need to be Exorcised

At Time Loop Blue

00:00:20:00

The sky was pink powder puff; a limp wind blew. I changed down a gear of my bike and braced myself for the cobblestones of Micklegate. Gallagher had contacted me to say that he had gone down to London hoping to find solutions amongst his Registry files. I could have told him he was wasting his time. However he was the boss and I merely his assistant.

It was a tortured soul that morning that scoured the empty streets seeking solace, finding none. Only the smell of freshly baked bread from a nearby bakery appeared homely. My bezel flashed twenty minutes and only a few minutes before that, I had been sitting within the Transit gazing into the infinite.

Something that Michael had said began to gradually make sense now: each dimension he had thrust me into seemed to affect others and I appeared to be the instigator of that change. I did not like being treated as a laboratory rat running around a maze. No I didn't like that at all. His Rubik's cube analogy with all its crazily arranged colours was an apt analogy– however this was only partly right. It felt more like being the ball that bounced crazily around a pinball machine. The more I thought about that, the more that idea appealed to me. A terrible thought surfaced: was he really being honest with me?

At the waterfront I parked and began my walk up to Mary's flat, No 72A Postern Close. She was an early riser and one for disappearing off for the day. This early bird was hoping to be in time. I gazed up at her balcony (hers overlooked the river) and noticed movement amongst the profusion of plants.

"Mary?"

"Who's that?"

"It's Ross. Can I come up?"

"Oh! This is an unexpected pleasure. I'll put the kettle on."

Mary's flat was a picture of rustic contentment that comprised of a flowery wicker settee, one matching chair and on the facing wall a painting depicting the sea. The opposite wall displayed an antique Grandfather clock. On top of the television was a photograph that I didn't particularly notice. That was a mistake because it could have saved me much valuable time later.

Her voice was faint. "Refresh my memory again. Was that one sugar and milk with your coffee?"

"No, just milk please Mary," I shouted.

I heard a scurry of cups and minutes later she bustled through carrying a full tea tray. What completely bowled me over was that she walked through the door. I politely waited until she navigated onto the settee before picking up my sunflower cup in its genteel saucer. She grinned like a jackpot winner.

"You were lucky to catch me in. I had just about finished cleaning the fridge and watering my plants and my next plan was to be off to visit my mother."

"How can you manage without your wheelchair now?" I enquired trying not to sound too inquisitive.

Her cup quivered within her hands and she threw me a puzzled stare. "What wheelchair? If this is another one of your pranks, it is in very poor taste I can tell you."

I must have looked sheepish as I stammered, "I am glad you have finally proved all the doctors wrong."

"What doctors?"

"After your hit and run accident all those years ago; they said you'd never walk again."

With a strange touch of dignity she answered: "I have never been in a wheelchair in all of my life." She paused and reflected upon what I had said. "You've spooked me though..." She shivered. "What made you say that?" She shivered again. "Whilst riding my horse recently, I nearly got killed."

With my curiosity aroused I moved closer. "Why is that?"

"Well if you insist." She paused deep in thought. "I was riding Sasha along the back roads towards Acaster when I became startled by a speeding white sports car that hurtled around a sharp corner. He appeared to be deliberately steering towards two walkers." She visibly shook. "The strange thing is, my mind flashed back to something I had read recently which prompted me to rein Sasha out of his way – as if invisible hands guided us away from danger." Tears rolled down her face.

I sat next to her and held her close. "I am very insensitive. Sorry to rake up such obviously bad memories."

Her voice trembled. "I'm glad you did. Ghosts need to be exorcised." She paused and drew a deep breath. "Only that day I had been reading a book about a murder. The heroine uncovered a plot to kill someone by causing a startled horse to throw and kill its owner. The perfect crime except for a witness." She gave me a level stare. "That day I became a witness – at a murder trial of those two walkers! Fiction and fact becoming all mixed up." Her hands covered her face. "The driver was called Smythe. Why do you want to know all of this?"

I picked up her exquisite bone china tea cup and thought deeply. I had no sensible explanation to give, but this was another Tombs mystery to solve. I took a sip and smiled sheepishly as I looked back at her. "You wouldn't believe me if I told you – but it might make sense in the end."

Her intense scrutiny bore into me like a hellfire preacher. "You always were a mystery Ross. Now please tell me as I am very curious to know what happened the other night?"

The loud tick of her wall clock intruded upon the petulant silence that followed. "What other night?" I enquired whilst stirring my coffee.

"I looked all over for you but you'd scarpered. You could have at least said goodbye."

I hesitated for a moment. "I'm sorry Mary but I haven't quite been feeling myself lately, could you please explain?"

"Surely you remember being up at Arras Hill in the crop circle?"

I returned her puzzled expression. "I appear to be a little confused Mary. All I remember is the blazing lights of a helicopter..."

She threw me a startled look. "What helicopter. I wish there was, it might have livened a dull evening. All we had to contend with was all those prancing gatecrashers taking over our meeting."

"Did Austerfield turn up at the crop circle Mary?"

She cocked her head and looked puzzled. "Strange of you to mention that but I noticed there were two people who weren't part of our group. There was some sort of exchange. A package I think – but I wasn't that close. There was a bald headed man and another man which could have been Austerfield I think."

I glanced down at a flashing bezel indicating nine minutes and panicked. This line of enquiry has got me nowhere with Mary.

"Fancy another cuppa?"

My face flooded with frustration. "Another time Mary." A thought occurred to me and wouldn't go away. Perhaps it was important. "Who gave you the book that appeared to save your life?"

She laughed. "That strange man Michael Tombs from our society; in fact he insisted that I should read it. When I think of it now – it gives me the shivers.

I was compelled to ask: "Was it 'Highfield' by Maria Bronte?"

She looked wide eyed at me. "You simply amaze me: have you a crystal ball or something?" Abruptly she walked across the room to pick up a photograph from the top of the telly. This was placed in my hands. It depicted Mary, Elizabeth and then Auster – all anoraks and bobby hats pulled well over their ears. Discretely in the background were the faces of Anya and Malik.

"It's funny how they never included you in our pagan group," she remarked brightly."

Slowly I nodded. "Yes it is – but playing with dark forces that you cannot understand can be extremely dangerous."

She patted my hand. "Oh it's only a bit of fun. There nothing sinister about it."

I gave her back the picture. "This might have solved a mystery for me. Thank you."

Her eyes followed me as I stood up to go. "I do love a good mystery!"

Outside Mary's flat, with about five minutes to go I located a phone box and rang the number Gallagher had given me.

An enquiring curt voice said: "Good afternoon. How can I help you?"

"London Desk please; I'd like to speak to Major Gallagher."

"Can I receive some identification caller?"

"My name is Ross; he'll know who it is."

"And your Service Number is...?"

I felt as if she'd hit me with a rubber bullet. "Ah. Is that really necessary?"

"You mean you've forgotten it haven't you – you naughty boy?"

I tried to sound very humble and grateful. "Sorry."

Her voice reflected the female role of women on top: "I'll put you through.... this time."

I heard the phone connect. "Hello"

"Major?"

"Ross?"

"I've found out some very important news regarding..."

He cut me short. "I'll have to hold you right there. Please remember this is an open line."

"It's about the package."

There was a pregnant pause. "Really?"

"I've identified the couriers and recipients."

"What's this got to do with finding your friend?"

"Spanish boots. You'll have to work out the connection yourself: this is an open line!"

I could almost feel him thinking hard. "Oh you mean the song by Bob Dylan?" he said whilst humming the tune. "A fickle woman?" he commented at last.

"Yes. Let's just call it the marital love triangle. I think you've met them all." I began to enjoy this intrigue. "Let's say they were your friends who were taking a Lodge Degree in 'funeral services'."

"My God! You *are* observant."

My chest puffed up. "Just doing my duty sir."

"OK. I'll put feelers out this end. Be at the York Minster about 5pm tomorrow."

The line disconnected.

CHAPTER THIRTY SIX

Chinese Whispers

Time Loop Red

00:00:10:00

The official name of York Minster is: 'The Cathedral and Metropolitical Church of St. Peter'. It is the largest Gothic church in England. What the guidebooks can't tell you is the wow of it all. I paused in the doorway of the West Door, and allowed the history filter through me, like fine coffee.

My sharp intake of breath captured the hallowed mustiness that blended with whispered echoes, past and present. Somewhere in the mysterious depths I heard a choir singing: The Lord Is My Shepherd. I glanced down at my watch. It displayed five minutes past six and: 00:00:10:00 TL Red. I inwardly cursed my bad memory. Keeping track of TLs was vitally important.

Where was Gallagher? He stated emphatically that we would meet at 6pm prompt. "Don't be late," he had emphasised. My ringing footsteps seemed to mingle with the choir as I made my way beyond the glowing candles of the various altar rails until finally as if by instinct, to Zouche Chapel.

Through the black and gold metal filigree, huddled in desolate, silent prayer, I saw him. As the great bells boomed out, I entered this private chapel and drew closer. Surrounding his still form were peanut cases.

He appeared as if asleep, but the pink laceration upon his neck needed no autopsy report. That blow had done the deed, and more obvious, someone close to him had been a mole who had betrayed his appointment here. I sensed someone was behind me.

"I see you're admiring my handiwork?"

I turned and looked up into the dead fish eyes of Anya's henchman, Malik. Blocking my only exit, this hulk swanked towards me. As his gloved hands pummelled each other I noticed a gun holster protruded from his open jacket; a sickly smile followed.

"If you run you'll only die exhausted."

With more anger than fear I said. "This is God's house man. Have you no respect?"

His face twisted in mockery. "I'll say a little prayer over you both."

I frantically looked through the enclosure at the passing tourists that were seemingly too occupied to care about one dead body and the imminent creation of another. It seemed hopeless, but then almost by instinct; I placed my right hand into my trouser-pocket and felt a measure of small change. I grabbed a fistful and waited for a miracle. A scurry of voices caused him to spin around and then more slowly, back towards me. We both paused like statues.

The sounds came from a multitude of Chinese schoolgirls. All blue jackets and raven hair that flapped with excitement, they were gazing through the doorway. His foul breath felt sharp upon my face; that cruel calculating mind re-evaluating the situation. I gazed past him and tried to will those guardian angels to step through, but they merely hovered, laughing and joking. In despair I watched as their backs slowly turned. I inwardly whispered. "Please don't," but they began to walk away. Malik briefly turned to watch their retreating forms. Once more he focussed on me: his face showed no display of hatred, only the cold calculations of a professional hit man. My soul chilled.

"Zouche Chapel? Yue duo yue hao." (The more the better).

He swivelled around at that.

Proudly marching through the doorway of Zouche Chapel was a Chinese schoolteacher, the brood in her wake. My miracle had arrived. With all my might, I pushed against the middle of his side; my left foot behind his, catching him off balance in a Judo leg throw (Ouchigari) and then hurled my coins into his face as he collapsed in a heap.

"Yue duo yue hao – include me as well!" I cried loudly and squeezed my body amongst the screaming swirling children as I made my escape towards the South Transept.

I gazed down at flashing red numbers. They were all zeros.

Time Loop Blue

00:01:08:00

This seemed like a repeat of what had just happened. Once more I entered by the West Side and paused in the doorway, but this time I remained focused and more alert. A glance at my watch confirmed that things were different now: by time and colour. My bezel flashed blue and displayed the figures: 00:01:08:00. The blue display puzzled me but I had more important things to worry over. For some reason I had now been given a fifteen minute start. This was no time for conjecture or theorising.

My footsteps ricochet like machine gun fire as I hurried my way down towards The Nave. Startled faces accosted me in all directions but I didn't care: I had a life to save.

"Ross!"

I halted in my tracks and perceived to my left a huddled figure of Gallagher, sitting in one of the stone alcoves. My indignant voice rebounded off the walls: "Why aren't you at Zouche's Chapel?"

He looked astounded. "How on Earth did you know where I was going?"

"Call it intuition," I replied, expressing relief in my voice, "but you have a 'mole' in your camp."

"Oh come here man and don't draw attention towards yourself."

I hunched up next to him. "You're in grave danger," I said trying to squash the panic in my voice. "Someone has found out that you would be at Zouche Chapel today."

He shrugged nonchalantly. "You may be right. Someone has been following me ever since I stepped off the train at York; can't appear to shake him off."

"That would be Malik, Anya's henchman."

"Really! You two have met before then?"

"He has a strange habit of wanting to kill me."

He gave a furtive look around: "I doubt that he is working alone."

I followed his gaze and saw that down the central isle strategically placed were six very tall looking men in dark coats. Anya and Malik joined them and intense conversation followed. They seemed more intent on viewing us than Minster spotting.

"I suppose you could identify all of those thugs in your Registry files?"

Gallagher laughed inwardly. "We'll be safe here: they'll not try anything in such a public place."

"Don't bet on it. A few moments ago, Malik tried to kill me, and you were..." my mouth went dry and I looked away. "The sooner we get out of here the better," I said at last.

We gazed up and down the Nave; it felt more like being on a duck shoot. Something caught my eye. Amongst the thinly spread visitors I saw a multitude of blue heading in our direction.

"How good is your Chinese?"

"What riddle is this?"

I pointed towards my guardian angels as they swept past.

"Trust me," I said to his gaping mouth as I flagged the school teacher down. "I'm a professional!"

We blended in with their youthful giggles and fought our way through their bustle. Gallagher whispered something in the teacher's ear, which made her round face explode in a grin. She gave my back an almighty pummel; whispered to her girls, which sent them into hysterics. Our heading suddenly changed and we speedily made our way towards the South Entrance, gliding unnoticed past one of the thugs at the doorway.

"What did you say?" I said in awe as we stood at the base of the steps and breathed in the fresh air of freedom. All I received in reply was that quiet little smile of his.

We waited an hour skulking behind the shop frontage opposite the South Entrance waiting for the chance to tail them.

"Are you armed?" I said trying to sound calm.

His reply was an innocent grin.

"You mean you haven't a sawn off shotgun under your coat, a dagger in your sock and a gorilla for company?"

All he confessed to was having a crappy yellow belt in judo and faith in the British criminal that played the game. "My God," I cried. "What planet are you from?" Then I realised that in all probability this was an academic question!

He looked at me square. "This could be dangerous, but..."

I burst out in a fit of hysterics. "You're telling me," I eventually gasped.

He scowled. "Pull yourself together man: this isn't the time to be cracking up." He turned to look towards Deansgate. "They probably have a car parked nearby here. It will be difficult to tail them on foot so we will need some form of transport. Have you any suggestions?"

I never got the chance to reply because abruptly two figures, Anya and Malik appeared at the South Entrance, paused briefly in the shadows to discuss something and then ran down the steps. The other henchmen were streaming behind like a gaggle of geese. At the bottom of the steps further heated conversation followed before the six men hurried off towards Monkgate. Anya and Malik scurried in the opposite way towards Deansgate.

"We'll follow those two," commanded Gallagher.

To avoid detection we hastily made our way towards High Petergate and followed the street until it intercepted Deansgate. We were just in time to see them climb into a black BMW and drive off in the direction of Lendal Bridge. Gallagher frantically looked around for a taxi. The only available transport was laughable, but Gallagher didn't seem to mind.

In the distance I saw a haze of blue smoke which may have been the BMW, but I was past caring. George, our one horsepower transport, whinnied into gear and clopped through the traffic lights. Briefly looking behind, I could smell our hot pursuit as we steamed ahead. They say God is kind and maybe his Face shone that evening because York was entertaining us with an almighty traffic jam. Fast cars; slow cars; even expensive wrecks of cars: all have been a leveller in York's busy streets.

Our horse snorted which seemed to mean something to the driver because he climbed down and gave him a piece of carrot. "That's cheaper that unleaded," I remarked which caused a snigger from the driver.

"Keep your mind on the job," retorted Gallagher.

He obviously was clearly embarrassed by our predicament; a fact I wanted to relentlessly pursue. "Perhaps if I climb out and walk really slowly, I just might just catch them up?"

His face appeared unmoved. "Stay where you are," he curtly answered. "Perhaps you've failed to notice the obvious, but the beauty of this open carriage is its height. I can see perfectly from here."

He was right of course. A few cars ahead I glimpsed our getaway vehicle, growling like an angry bear at the red traffic lights at the bottom of Lendal Bridge. Miraculously then, the lights changed and I saw a haze of blue swirl left into Rougier Street heading for Micklegate. Our tail pipe also heated up briefly as we resolutely followed.

Eventually after what seemed an eternity, we merrily clopped our way over Ouse Bridge and then noticed the BMW had parked outside the Hotel Principia. On this side of the bridge was Yates pub and it was here, Gallagher told the driver to halt.

As we alighted, he seemed pleased with himself and even joked with the man as he paid him a handsome tip that made me gasp. He pointed firmly towards the hotel. "I think we've tracked them down to their lair. It will be a simple matter to ascertain their next intentions."

"What next?"

His nose quivered like a bloodhound. "I think I am going to treat you to an excellent bar meal; if that's alright with you?"

"Is the Pope Jewish?" I said.

He seemed puzzled by this revelation.

CHAPTER THIRTY SEVEN

Earned Privilege

Time Loop Red

01:12:00:00

It was the gently rocking of the parked van that had initially caught Olivia's eye. How could it have arrived there without her noticing it? Perhaps when she was inputting Mrs Liddell's room reservation it had slid by her and parked up? Surely that was a mere five minutes ago and prior to that she had hastened to the loo hoping the phone wouldn't ring. It definitely wasn't parked then. She closed the reservation book, placed her pen precisely by its side and stared once more through the double swing doors.

Outside the hotel, she could see that more late night revellers had congregated. A glance at her watch showed 2am which confirmed her suspicions: they must be chucking out at Dazzle's night club. With curiosity now firmly taking hold, she held the warmth of the Reception inside the wrap of her coat and descended the steps of the Principia hotel until she had joined the rapidly increasing throng. As the rocking intensified, was that a moan and then a gasp she heard? She joined in with the crowd's silent stifled laughs, yet these emotions conflicted with her morality: this was supposed to be a respectable street! A young man of about twenty, all flapping sleeves and straggled hair broke loose from the crowd and headed across the road; she followed him. In his right hand dangled a bottle of lager. "Wey – hey," he cried banging it down upon the van's roof.

The swaying abruptly ceased and a moment later the van doors flung open. Olivia leapt forward brushing flapping sleeves aside. From the dark recess of the van emerged something totally unexpected.

She screamed hysterically.

In the confined space I wriggled out of my shirt and trousers and prepared to don my wet suit. This was a one piece outfit of 8mm thick neoprene and an absolute beggar (even liberally talcum powdered) to get in and out of. First the right leg, then the left. I pushed and pulled; gyrated and heaved, and then repeated the process over and over again. Then I gasped because I was completely stuck and couldn't breathe. Maybe if I wriggled and then turned: that might just do the trick? That was it. Just a little bit more. Fresh air!

What was that? I could swear I heard a noise. Not at 2am surely? I rocked and rolled my body until I eventually slid into this extra layer of skin. "Damn! Where was I going to put my keys?" I growled. Eventually they fitted down my left bootee. I removed the Snark demand valve from my holdall, made sure that the hose horns pointed upwards before engaging the first stage onto the breathing cylinder at my feet. A dubious glance at the various bits and pieces of equipment that encircled made me think: what a load of antiquated crap. I must be totally crackers to be doing this. I breathed through my DV (Demand Valve) to check it, as I glanced at my pressure gauge. It read 120 ATS (Atmospheres). That should give me ample time below.

A bang on the van roof nearly frightened me out of my wet suit. I opened the doors and gazed unbelieving into the eyes of a short cropped blonde and a swaying youth. Both appeared in a state of shock. The girl screamed; I screamed and then behind them, a crowd of drunks suddenly clapped and cheered. All I could think of what to do was to bow gracefully!

It's called Zero Vis. That's frogmanese for underwater scary stuff. If you can imagine placing your head inside a big bowl of oxtail soup and somehow stirring it as well, then that might give you some idea of what it is like to dive in the River Ouse.

I waited until everyone had become bored and had left. In truth this gave me time to think and realise how stupid this whole episode was. Twice I had decided to chicken out and had stood poised upon the river's edge, checking my breathing gear again. Briefly 'Flappy Sleeves' returned to hurl insults but then I heard a splash.

"I don't approve of throwing bottles into the Ouse." I growled. However he must have gone. Eventually some inner courage took hold of me and I slipped unnoticed into the icy depths. Of course, the years of neglect took their toll: I spiralled down like an idiot amidst swirling heaving bubbles and landed with a bump at the river's bottom. Freezing water gripped my stomach causing me to gasp and then it became apparent that I'd lost my torch. I expelled a stream of frenzied bubbles.

Cramp in my right calf muscle, was the next misfortune. I nursed and pummelled my leg whilst staring into the flowing blackness. Nudging against my right leg was something hard: it was my torch.

Twenty pounds of weight belt obviously was the wrong number to choose: that was for sea water, not fresh which had made me sink like a stone.

Learn better next time I thought – if I survived?

Panic was the next thing to overwhelm me and I started to hyperventilate. Calm down I told myself. Calm down.

The low rattle of bubbles leaving my DV followed by the higher pitched hiss as I breathed in, eventually focussed my thoughts. Gradually my pulse and I relaxed.

My mission was simple in Gallagher's eyes, to find the proof that Smythe was murdered at the hotel and dumped into the river. I could still hear his words.

"I've got a hunch that Smythe's body was thrown into the river from over there at the Principia. If I'm right, Anya or her henchman Malik would have killed him there." He then rested his elbows on the parapet of the Ouse Bridge and surveyed the river bank below through his binoculars. A chill wind then mingled with his words. "As for the reasons why," he shrugged. "Perhaps he had outgrown his usefulness?" He turned briefly and gave me a questioning look. "His body held no personal belongings, apart from his passport. Don't you think that strange?"

I swallowed the bait. "What are you suggesting?" I had said lamely.

"I gather you have done a fair bit of scuba diving in your time?"

From our vantage point leaning over the parapet, my eyes had travelled from watching the sleepy river flow and onto the rippled skin of Gallagher's bald head. "Is that from your Registry files?" I commented naively, whilst alarm bells inside my head threatened to demolish my brain.

"It was merely a question," he said putting down his binoculars.

Then of course I started to wriggle upon the bait line. "That was a long time ago I'm afraid. It was primarily Auster's idea of a fun day out, only he never showed up at the training lesson. I was the one who ended up on the pool bottom learning fish talk."

"I suppose you maybe past it now – old man. Is it now just the frayed carpet slippers and all that?" I heard a sly laugh. "Perhaps I should buy you a pipe for Christmas?" He looked square at me then. "At the time though, you did alright: First Class certification or so I gather."

That got my gander up. "I enjoy a challenge," I retorted fervently.

Gallagher suddenly become preoccupied again and had turned his back. He pointed towards the middle balcony of the Principia. "I was counting upon you saying that!"

What a fool I was!

The whistling of my exhaust valve was beginning to annoy me now. Walter Bowman, my British Sub Aqua Club diving instructor, would have given me a rollicking for this. His words echoed down the years. "Remember the first 'Golden Rule': do not *ever* dive alone."

I bubbled. "It's for Queen and Country, Walter. Honest?"

During our many training excursions however he did have one peculiarity which he eventually passed on to me: an introduction to his silent dive buddies. Even at this thought I peered around nervously checking just in case I too felt that ominous, tap, tap, tap, upon my shoulder which was their call sign.

With my torch switched on, blackness became a flowing sludgy brown again. I held my wrist compass until it touched my mask and fiddled with the 'arrow' until it aligned with my chosen direction and began to lift off the undulating sand towards (I hoped) the Principia. Allowing for river current, five minutes by my watch should be the time I had calculated to be at my rendezvous checkpoint.

As the time approached, with great effort I left the bottom and attempted to surface. Once there, it was hard work to keep my head above water, but my navigation was spot on.

High above me was the hotel and nearby, upon the bridge, I heard cries and laughter from late revellers. The air felt chilled and somehow hostile.

A splash of light issued from the balcony above me. Even from this angle I could just make out the red hair of Anya as she appeared to stomp out onto the balcony, Malik in her wake. Heated voices ensued. I smiled. It didn't take much imagination to realise why. Their failed attempts of trying to kill Gallagher and myself had obviously irritated them. I allowed my leaded body to sink once more beneath the surface and into blackness.

As I reached bottom I became well and truly stuck between something sharp and clinging. Rusty bedsteads and flippers are not convenient fellows. I reached down towards my left bootee for my trusty diving knife and realised it wasn't there.

Damn!

Walter would not have been pleased with my progress. "Are you kitted up correctly?" These would be his last words regarding equipment checks.

"Wise words Walter." I bubbled.

Suddenly I felt a tap, tap, tap, on back which sent shivers up my spine. I turned to see if one of Walter's silent buddies had paid me a visit. With relief it turned out to be only a submerged tree branch. Once more I tackled the bedstead. With a heave I freed myself and after the initial palpitations had subsided, my quest was resumed.

The plan was to begin a search from the location of the Roman road which lay nearby. As I scrutinised the sandy ridges and clefts, suddenly within the narrow confines of my torch beam, I glided upon it.

If a large piece of Kirkgates's cobbled roadway was dug up and placed here, it would give a good description of that ancient road.

Almost by sixth sense I inched my way along the brow of the Roman cobbles knowing where to search. It seemed so surreal thinking that Roman legions in full march had crossed this once tidal river. Although the swirling mud kicked up by my gloves and flippers threatened to smother me, my inner compass didn't fail me once.

Patience brings rewards.

Gleaming within the restricted glow of my beam were two objects that had been wedged between the cobbles: one notebook and a tattered bulging wallet.

The riverbed gave up nothing else.

Back at the surface I heard the plaintive cry of a woman and realised it was the blonde girl I had seen earlier. As I drew closer she spotted me. She screamed hysterically. "I heard a splash and then a scream for help; I think someone has fallen into the water."

"I'll try and find him. Call an ambulance – just in case," I shouted back and sank once more beneath the waves. My thoughts bubbled heavenwards. "Come on Walter: we have one more job to do before the night is finished". My dive instructor was always grateful that he could render this last service to the suicides or unfortunates who had recently drowned. The Ouse appeared to be extremely gracious in giving up her dead to him; his silent diving buddies.

Once more I hit the river bottom hard and it felt like a re-run movie had been played because I also had got caught in that infernal bedstead. Cursing my luck I tried to untangle myself. Then, at the nape of my neck, I felt that familiar tap, tap, tap, of a submerged object and suddenly blanched hands wrapped around my neck. I span around and stared into the face of 'Flappy' Sleeves who too had been caught amongst the wire. His lifeless body abruptly had entangled around my own and to the bubbled music of the river, we swayed to a macabre dance routine. Salvation arrived in the form of a gleaming object trapped under the bedstead: my trusty knife! So I had packed it after all. Quickly I grabbed it and managed to free us both then with strong flipper strokes headed for the surface.

Once there I applied mouth to mouth resuscitation whilst swimming ashore. Abruptly I heard a groan from him.

"Walter – this one has been returned alive!" I proudly gasped above the waves.

Once within earshot I shouted across to the girl patiently still waiting. She helped me haul him onto the riverside landing stage and then hugged me whilst sobbing uncontrollably. To the blaze of blue flashing lights we both watched the crew place 'Flappy Sleeves' onboard. I turned and observed her tear swept face.

"Thank you for saving him," she said quietly.

She trembled like a captured bird as I held her close and whispered. "That privilege is all yours: he would be dead if it wasn't for you."

CHAPTER THIRTY EIGHT

When Thieves Fall Out

Time Loop unknown

I had got up at twelve, showered with the company of aqua gear at my feet, grabbed yet another cup of coffee, and then glanced down at the watch. The bezel display had disappeared. The second hand still ticked happily around which proved that Auster's low-tech watch had survived the night dive; the alien holographic one hadn't.

The combined effect of rain and struggling light was to bathe my lounge in drab monotones. The low pummelling sound of raindrops filled me with apprehension. I retightened the cord on my dressing gown and slumped onto my settee. It held another body! Gallagher, still in his mohair overcoat, appeared dead to the world. He received my full mug of coffee in his face.

"Ah!"

"Good God!" I exclaimed and rapidly stood up.

He licked his lips and looked accusingly at me. "Coffee? How considerate!"

I offered my apologies and tried my best to smother a laugh. "Let me get you a cloth to dry yourself."

He scowled as he sat up. "Your carpet drank nearly all of it; however a fresh cup would be most appreciated."

"Of course. And after that, how about breakfast?"

He chuckled. "Please – not in my face this time." He paused to brush himself down. "Give me a fighting chance to enjoy it!"

"I promise."

"I must say that your sofa is most comfortable. I've had a wonderful night's sleep." He paused and I caught him looking around my lounge. He then gazed through the open doorway as I was about to hurl a wedge of rashers into a pan. "How can you work in such a small kitchen?"

"Please don't criticise until you've tasted the goods."

The instant bacon smell caused him to take a deep breath. "Point taken." he said in a good natured fashion, whilst fighting my soft cushions to regain his upright composure. "I must say Ross you have quite a small library here with a broad selection of writers. I was spoilt for choice."

At his feet was a yellow leather bound book; another white volume was in his hands. "I see you've been reading?" I ventured.

"Stephen Hawking's 'A Brief History of Time' was amusing. I could have straightened him out on one or two things, but I enjoyed his reasoning: especially on 'String Theory'." He laughed good naturedly as my head poked around the doorframe. "I found it wedged between 'York Between The Wars' and that 'Curtain of Fear' by Dennis Wheatley."

"That Austerfield is always giving me books to read. 'Classics' he calls them?" I turned the bacon over. "Did you also get the chance to scrutinise Smythe's notebook and wallet that you were so adamant at snatching off me in the early hours?"

His answer however became mixed and congealed within the sizzle of eggs that I had added to a side pan.

During breakfast he said very little and could have won an Olympic medal by the way his food was consumed. The plate finished, he leant back and carefully drank from his coffee mug. "For a young un, you're a good cook – and I am allergic to food!"

I laughed. "I'm glad you approve."

He waved the diary in my face. "I shall reiterate then. Our Samuel Pepys here, kept a meticulous account. This notebook held various entries. The names are smudged, but readable." He scanned a rapid eye over the pages flicking them over with impatience:

"10th, 11pm Robinson to meet T.I.C. and arrange date for main transaction and receive payment for shipment.

11th, 8pm. Meeting Robertson -24 Bowers Glade- collect package.

The 12th, 6pm. Meeting Austerfield -Dino's.

15th. 8pm. Deliver package to Principia."

He scrutinised me closely. "Were you acquainted with any of Austerfield's colleagues?"

I smiled and shook my head. "Only his girlfriend and our mutual friend Mary."

Gallagher raised his eyebrows and appeared embarrassed. "Did either of them tell you anything?"

"On my recent visit to Mary she showed me a picture of herself with him and my ex-wife. Malik and Anya were there discreetly in the background"

I looked at him carefully hoping to see a flicker of sympathy. There was none. He stood up and moved towards the far end of the lounge. His voice was deadpan. "Nice garden you've got: I particularly like your garden well and bird table. Back to nature; I like that." We exchanged glances and I saw a pained look. "I'm so sorry that you found out this way."

I looked hard at him. "Perhaps all the signs were there regarding my wife and Austerfield. In a way I'm glad that I know the truth now."

He turned back to the garden. "That's not all. I am not very good at conveying bad news – perhaps you had better sit down."

I meekly did as I was told. "What is it?"

"I don't want you to read or hear about it in the news before I tell you – but your ex-wife has been murdered and we suspect Malik."

My mind cleared like fog on a summers day and I realised I had witnessed it; the actual event had been hazy and indistinct until now. "Strangely I do know that – but why kill her?"

He gave me a curious look. "We had employed her in our York office but it soon became clear that she was our 'mole' in camp. And once they too realised we had blown her cover they silenced her – permanently."

We both became distracted by a Robin that had landed upon my bird table. As it flew off carrying a huge piece of bread, he continued with: "What I'm about to tell you now is sensitive information."

"Secrets seem to be overloading me recently."

He briefly turned and looked bemused before continuing. "These terrorists seem to be working for a paymaster whose reach is worldwide. From your diary entries it may suggest that T.I.C. might be a valuable lead. Have you any ideas as to what it means?"

My reply was halted by an almighty electric shock that gripped my wrist and I spiralled into blackness.

Time Loop Blue

00:00:59:59

The extension to my bungalow only allowed a single photon to spread itself evenly around the room. It held that 'just died' look. Whilst still under the depression of my recent divorce, I bought it with that recommendation.

I glanced outside at the drizzle, muttered under my breath about the vulgarity of the British weather and moved over to the fireplace where I tripped over a book and crashed onto the sofa. There was a body on my settee! I got up sharply.

"Ben! Where did you spring from?"

He looked indignant as he sat bolt upright. "I took the liberty of entering your house whilst you were out last night."

I retightened my dressing gown cord and glared at him. "That's a bit of a cheek."

He brushed down his blue anorak, and then scrambled to his feet. "My apologies, but I've come here to warn you of the extreme danger you are in. Anya has arrived in York and is threatening to kill someone called Ross. Do you know anyone of that name?"

"I happen to be very attached to its owner."

He chuckled. "I think I'd better stick around for a few days and watch your back, don't you?"

"You were also on her list."

"How do you know this?"

I looked puzzled. "Don't you remember our close shave at the Minster last night?"

"Last night I was in London! I have made the journey here because I have recently found out that Smythe had an accomplice in York. It might be a vital lead."

"Yes I know it is a vital lead – and so do you." I felt faint and abruptly sat down. "It was on your suggestion that I was under the Ouse searching for Smythe's belongings."

His jaw dropped. "I gave no such command!"

"You did. You said that Smythe was killed at the Principia and then dumped in the river."

He looked at me with incredulity. "I most certainly did not because Smythe was killed in Athens!"

I gasped. "How on earth did you come by that conclusion?"

"They found him this morning in a burnt out car in Marousi. That's..."

"That's North of Athens." I said.

He paused and looked surprised. "You know your geography." Gallagher walked over towards my table and picked up a newspaper and gave a display of reading it. "You should pick your friends more wisely. Did you know that it should have been you in that burnt out car?"

My face felt cold and must have whitened like a tub of lard. I laughed nervously. "My stolen passport – it all makes sense now."

I could tell that Gallagher was enjoying himself now that he had regained his pedestal and was going to milk the story for all it was worth. "Well, it was through Stella's diligence in tracking down the couriers to a backstreet in Athens. Smythe's blood group was found within the fibres of a rug in an apartment there."

"That wasn't 84 Imittou Street by any chance?" I said and then immediately could have kicked myself.

Gallagher however merely raised an eyebrow. "Now that's very strange that you know that. You surprise me yet again."

"It seems to keep saving my life?"

He took a deep intake of breath "On my insistence the backroom boys re-examined him. They hadn't spotted that his body held an above normal radiation count, but he didn't die of that. Death had been caused by intense heat, almost like he had been fried like a chip. Of course that would have caused very little blood loss. Oh! I'm forgetting something." Gallagher gave that quiet little smile of his again. "Time of death was approximately two hours before he was found. And that was in Athens. This last point was heavily emphasised.

I was going to argue the point but decided against it. My mind went back to the trivial incident over my bookshelf. I looked up and saw a gap between 'York Between The Wars' and 'Curtain of Fear' by Dennis Wheatley. Perhaps that wasn't so insignificant after all. "Are you saying that Smythe was killed in Athens and *not* found in the Ouse then?" I suggested at last. "I would like to query that."

He glared at me briefly but then looked crestfallen. "They are the facts; live with them. With Smythe dead we have lost any hope of finding Red Mercury now."

I walked over to my window; it was always a comfort to see my feathered friends pecking food off my bird table. "Perhaps I'm too modest to suggest this, but it was my idea to dive into the Ouse last night and retrieve these." I walked over to the table, hoping to find Smythe's belongings but they weren't there. "I left them there last night; they must be still here," I lamented searching diligently around.

He looked mystified. "How on earth can that be important?"

My watch bezel now held a blue haze and abruptly there was an erratic green flash and I failed to answer.

00.00.00

Time Loop Green

00:00:05:58

Violin music slowly flooded my senses, and I found myself supine on my settee with Austerfield sitting opposite in the armchair. A violin cradled under his chin and he appeared in complete rapture playing the instrument. He stopped and looked expectantly at me. "What are you like?" he laughed. "I discovered you fast asleep here on the settee so I thought it a wheeze to play Brahms's Lullaby! What do you think to my rendition?" he asked.

"Since when have you learnt to play that?" I said in amazement, allowing my left slipper to fall off my foot and onto the floor.

"What sort of question is that? After all it was your encouragement at school that gave me the confidence to learn." He looked pensive. "Do you remember that school pantomime – I gained tremendous self reliance from that event; and all thanks to you?" He turned towards me putting down his bow and it was then I noticed he wore white gloves.

"You're quite – 'sound as a Pound' when you put your mind to it."

I looked at him with suspicion. "What do you really want?"

His face beamed. "I am eternally in your debt for saving my life back there in Greece. How on earth did you know where to find me?"

I looked incredulously back at him as conflicting

memories fought with one another. "I really don't know," I said at last.

He grabbed his bow and pointed it towards my library shelf. "I've entrusted you with that little yellow book over there. It's a rare first edition – at least my business colleague Michael Tombs says so. Perfect spot next to Maria Bronte don't you think?"

I replaced my slipper and walked over to the shelf indicated. "Well it does appear to fit nicely with a bit of reshuffling." My nose caught the delicious whiff of leather as I briefly held it. "Where's the catch, Auster?"

"When do you expect him to collect it?"

I eyed him suspiciously. "That all depends on what you know?"

He ignored my comment and walked across to my chess table where there was an empty whisky bottle. His face held amusement. "Queen whisky forces the Checkmate; how clever!" The bottle was now placed firmly within my hands. He laughed as he saw the full one beneath and stooped to retrieve it. "For the book," he said and nodded. "It's a stonking bargain if I say it mesen; you're robbing me blind – but yer' ma' mate." He slapped me on the back which caused me to gasp. Suddenly there was fear within his eyes and I realised that he was shaking. I pointed to the yellow volume.

"Thank you for entrusting me with this."

"What happens next?"

Suddenly the doorbell rang followed by a 'thump, thump, thump', on the front door. He patted me on the back. "Better be going: that's either your neighbours or the police! I suspect they will be objecting to a helicopter parked in front of your house! Oh and by the way, there's an invitation for my party that I'm holding. Your air tickets are enclosed!" A large white envelope was thrust into my hand and with that he left me open mouthed and walked towards the front door.

For some time I gazed in silence trying to evaluate the meeting. My eyes gravitated upon the chess set: those two vital moves slowly began to mean something.

00:00:00

Time Loop Red

00:00:05:59

I awoke to find myself slumped on the floor with Ben Gallagher's face peering over me. His forehead had more worry lines than Clapham junction.

"I can't turn my back for an instant. I was just making a coffee in your kitchen and you'd disappeared – and now you are back." He helped me to my feet. "Are you OK?"

I nodded. "What happened?"

"I can't stay now to explain." He made his way into the hallway and paused at the door. "I have arranged a meeting with a chap called Robertson at the Minster tomorrow. Since he was Smythe's colleague, he may have valuable information that will lead us to who is behind all of this and thus Red Mercury."

I began to feel very tired. "Don't go – you will be killed if you do."

"That's rather a worrying statement. Please explain yourself?"

I glanced at a bezel that registered red zero, and was unable to answer.

00:00:00:00

CHAPTER THIRTY NINE

A Pricked Conscience

Time Loop Red

Two glasses, one empty, the other half full of lager, graced the table of Charles Robertson. He was not a man to be trifled with. As a retired pig farmer, he found there was a living to be made in the shady deals that York provided – if you looked in the right places of course. A man called David Austerfield had introduced him to such places. Every so often he would prune his grey receding hairline, hoping like King Canute to hold back the tide of nature. He sat chewing his pen, then strummed his fingers on the table, eventually as if defeated scowled at the River Ouse as it flowed past his window.

Dressed in pin stripe and crocodile shoes, the weasel-eyed man opposite him displayed a face twisted with rage. His jowls quivered as he spoke. "My paymasters had great and let me say misplaced faith in your organisation. I am not going to tolerate this incompetence. You say that my delivery has been misplaced?"

Charles squirmed in his chair. "This isn't shopping at Sainsbury you know."

"What!"

Charles suspected the man wore a black wig and that unnerved him. He inwardly shivered but spoke now in smooth level tones. "I can assure you that your merchandise is safe and will be delivered on time."

The man carefully reached into his trouser pocket and retrieved some peanuts. He popped a few into his mouth. "Explain yourself?"

"There was a problem with one of our couriers who mixed up the venues; easily done and just as easily fixed." He felt confident now. "If you prefer, I can sell it on you know. There are always other outlets"

"I think you will find that avenue has dried up by now," he said coldly, whilst popping more peanuts, crunching them in a deliberate menacing way towards his colleague. "Your last courier attempted to sell me phoney stuff. Last seen he was taking a little swim in the River Ouse.

Visibly shaken Charles said. "Why can't we talk this over sensibly like businessmen?"

The weasel-eyed man grabbed his client's pen, snapping it in two before Charles Robertson's startled eyes. "My Organisation does not make deals. I buy businessmen like you and then sell them on at a fat profit. Make sure someone doesn't try and sell you out."

"What more can I do?" he replied trying hopelessly to fix his pen.

"Try me."

Charles trembled nervously but said in a firm clear voice: "I have been assured that your merchandise will be delivered very soon and to your requirements. A man called Smythe will be our liaison. What more can I say?"

The man removed a brown paper parcel from his pocket and placed it carefully on the table. "I want you to deliver this to your partner. You can call it insurance." He leant across.

"It is very valuable, so don't lose it or I might get extremely angry."

Greed dawned in the eyes of Charles Robertson. "Is it money?"

"Don't question. Just do it. Or is the deal off and I'll take my business elsewhere?"

"I can assure you that your wishes will be carried out to the letter, it's just that..." He fingered the parcel nervously. "I am so glad we understand one another. This unfortunate incident will soon yield good fortune for both of us."

"I pay for results, not excuses so you'd better be right because my worries will become yours and next time you may be looking up at this window, not out of it. Do you follow?"

Charles meekly nodded and thought about David's frantic phone call with him earlier that day. He had informed him that Smythe had tried to intercept the shipment at Dover thus hoping to cut out the 'middleman'. He shuddered at that thought because he was the 'middleman'.

The man then climbed out of his chair and without a backward glance sauntered through the swing doors and into the distant skyline of Ouse Bridge.

After a nervous interval Charles tapped glowing numbers on his mobile and was in deep conversation for a while. "Yes David!" he snapped finally.

Afterwards he moodily gazed out of the window. Nothing was going to plan. Abruptly a man in a brown tweed suit sat opposite him. His face broke out into a serene smile. "You appear to be in a spot of bother old boy."

"Who are you?" snapped Charles.

"Major Gallagher. Perhaps David has mentioned me?"

Charles thought awhile. "He might have done, but only briefly."

Major Gallagher edged forward and whispered urgently. "From your heated conversation with David I think you could do with my help?"

"You're very perceptive."

"When dealing with David, I need to be." He patted Charles's arm. "Perhaps you have realised just now that your business partner has cut you out?"

"David?"

Major Gallagher shook his head and looked surprised. "I was referring to Malik Hamid – the man who just left."

Charles trembled. "*That* was Malik Hamid? He is the worst crook in York!"

"Who arranged the meeting?"

"Smythe. He claimed David wanted this meeting in York. Malik must have been Smythe's accomplice." He looked pleadingly at him. "I really wasn't to know; you *must* believe that."

Major Gallagher looked grim. "This simple transaction was supposed to have taken place in Athens. David had gone there to use his contacts to swop a parcel I had given him for an identical one containing the real merchandise." He tapped his fingers on the table to emphasise his last point. "And then give it to my contact in Athens."

"The double crossing scoundrel."

The Major thought carefully before replying. "Not necessarily," he said at last. "Smythe might have been tempted to grab his own piece of the action at Calais docks. He wouldn't realise it was a dummy parcel."

"I was referring to Austerfield!" Tears welled up in his eyes. "I'll inform David..."

Gallagher gently grabbed his arm."No! Don't do that. It is of no matter – we shall let this run its course."

"What about Malik's delivery?"

"Let's open it shall we?"

Once the package was opened it revealed a book and a thin pen like instrument. Charles covered his face with his hands. "That's Smythe's delivery: I packed it myself."

"This is my fake package," Gallagher said. "I'll take that now."

Charles sunk his head in his hands and sobbed hysterically. "Smythe must be dead."

Gallagher patted his arm and then got up to go. "I would lie low for a while and let David deal with it."

Charles gazed after the retreating form and suddenly realised that perhaps after all, he should have listened to his conscience rather than his bank balance.

CHAPTER FORTY

Not a Lonely Drink

Time Loop Red

03:10:10:00

It was early evening and my watch flashed three days, ten hours, ten minutes, as I stood outside Robertson's house. I thought about many things.

In one TL, there was a book called Highfield by Maria Bronte who had died in early childhood and therefore couldn't possibly have written it but in another, there was a genuine article penned by her; both couldn't or shouldn't coexist.

My experience led me to believe that TL's were almost identical from a historical viewpoint, apart from subtle changes like random books upon bookshelves. The gap in my bookcase has or had held both volumes. Perhaps it merely 'holds' the book just like another mysterious 'cat' within a box? It might become a very useful indicator to TL shifts. I also reflected upon the fact that I had never been given three days plus to work with before. Perhaps it meant that I was close to solving this enigmatic puzzle.

Things were looking up.

Robertson's red brick detached house had a driveway in the same colour and a white gravelled garden that held a matching coloured rose bush at its centre.

The man who came to the door, all sweater, leather sleeves and fine snowy hair, held the expression of a rabbit being confronted by a stoat. He wore white gloves. I gave him my best smile, the one reserved for Auster when it was his turn to buy a round of drinks.

"Mr Robertson? Can I borrow a few moments of your precious time?"

He threw me a suspicious look. His voice had a culture all of its own. "What are you selling?"

I shook my head. "I'm not a salesman. My name's Ross..."

"You look like a salesman to me."

"I believe you know my colleague David Austerfield?"

At the mention of Auster, he glowered at me. "I have never heard of him. Go away!"

My foot received a battering from his attempt at closing the door, but I remained firm: he was my only lead and Gallagher would skin me alive if I blew this one. I tried a different track. "For your own good, you'll let me come in?"

At my words the fear returned to haunt his face. He cowered back inside the entrance hall. At this I practically jumped inside and closed the door.

"Please leave me alone." he whimpered as he edged into the dining room, "I want no further dealings with that scoundrel."

I followed after him and sat down upon a dark oak chair, rested my elbows upon its matching elegantly styled arms and gave the impression of absolute calm and control. "Please sit yourself down and let me try and straighten things out."

He stood firm. "It's no use; I'm through with the whole damn lot of you. I will not be a courier anymore; now get out of my house." He tried but failed to raise his voice above a stern whisper.

I nodded gently. "First things first. I'm not the police, but maybe I'm the next best thing."

He screamed. "Police! I don't want them to be involved."

I raised my voice above his. "I said I am *not* the police." The only effect this had was for him to shake like a jelly. My hands firmly encompassed his. "Please sit down."

He snatched his hands away but meekly obeyed my command. "What do you want from me?" he said curling up in a foetal ball, his eyes seemingly searching for an escape route. Eventually he looked up at me with interest.

"If you'll just trust me for one moment and tell me what happened, I might just be able to help."

His face slowly became crestfallen and he began to wring his hands rocking back and forth. "I've read in the paper about Alan. He has been murdered – I know he has. It's a bad business; a bad business. They'll come looking for me next."

I smiled sweetly at him. Confidence would be a hard earned thing. "Alan Smythe mixed with the wrong type of people – but you're different. It's important that you tell me all you know." I noticed a sharp increase in breath as he eyed me up and down for the millionth time. Somewhat composed he began to recount his tale of woe. It began and ended with Auster and sounded very familiar. There but for fortune I thought. There but for fortune.

I smiled again – perhaps it had turned to a grimace but it now held his attention. "I remember you telling me about 'they'. You said 'they' will come looking for you."

He began to rock again, cradling his face within his white gloved hands. Who could command that much fear? I waited patiently for him to answer. Eventually he did so, his words piecemeal. He claimed that Auster was dealing with an organisation called the Triethe.

"Who or what were the Triethe?" I asked innocently.

It was then that he surprised me by leaping up, grabbing my arm and pushing me towards and through the door. Before he slammed it into my face I managed to stammer, "Why are you wearing white gloves?"

The door and my nose, painfully met.

02:04:10:00

That night I was haunted by nightmares: I swam through swirling bodies completely immersed in thick brown soup. I awoke covered in cold sweat. The day was filled with regrets: I should have informed the police or even Gallagher about my meeting with Robertson. However there was really nothing I could tell him.

It was with grim foreboding when I opened the newspaper the following evening and read the headlines:

'York Famous Violinist Killed In Hit And Run'.

'Robby Robertson, York's most outstanding musician, was knocked down in the early hours of this morning.

He had been returning home after an outstanding concert performance at the Barbican, when he was knocked down as he waited outside for a taxi. Shocked onlookers chased after the car but it failed to stop.

Police are appealing for witnesses to this tragic accident', read the closing paragraph.

I was disturbed by a knock at the door. A middle aged woman, all fluffy black coat, white hair and makeup stood there, angrily eying me up and down. "Robert would still be alive if you had only left him alone."

"Who?"

Her face looked as if it would explode. "My husband, Robert Robertson. That was no hit and run driver..." her face cracked up. "It was pre-meditated murder."

She ceaselessly moistened her lips whilst agitated hands were clutching and twisting her handbag; I realised this was fear not anger she was expressing.

"Can't we talk about this over a cup of tea?" I suggested.

"Leave me alone!" she said turning sharply and walking away.

00:00:00:00

Time Loop Blue

02:04:10:00

My meeting with Robertson although pleasant had led me virtually nowhere. My sleep that night was interspersed by nightmares: I swam through swirling bodies completely immersed in thick brown soup. I awoke covered in cold sweat.

I heard the Press clatter through the letterbox and was surprised with the headlines. Somehow I was expecting bad news.

'York Famous Violinist Wins Prestigious Award'.

My jaw dropped. Abruptly I was disturbed by a knock at the door. A middle aged woman, all fluffy red coat, white hair and makeup stood there, eying me up and down; her face glowed with admiration.

"Hello." I said rather too meekly for my own liking.

"Robert wanted you to have this."

"Who?"

She looked expectantly at me and then thrust a white envelope into my hands. "After you left the other night, my husband, Robert Robertson wanted you to have this."

"Thank you," I stammered.

Her face looked briefly expectantly at me. "Robert holds great faith in you." She then swivelled around on her heels and walked hastily towards her Volvo.

I watched as it roared down my street and vanished around the curve in the road.

Back in my armchair, I finally opened the letter and was confronted by a blank piece of expensive embossed paper inside. For some time I stared at this piece of vellum trying to make sense of it all. These were two different TLs with two different outcomes and I didn't know why, but it was very important that I did find out.

I needed a drink but not a lonely one.

CHAPTER FORTY ONE

Cat got your Tongue?

Time Loop Red

00:01:45:00

Rik's bar was small, cosy with walls and most probably chairs, but I tended not to notice such trivia. My barstool next to Oscar Wilde was all I cared for, with a full glass of alcohol. Any type would do, I wasn't fussy. The bar top seemed more gleaming than usual, once you adjusted to the sombre orange tinged lighting.

"Are you there Rik?" I shouted and miraculously he appeared from beneath the bar. His weather beaten face and lean features could be interpreted as menacing – but I knew better. When he released a smile it would be as warm and casual as the clothes he wore. Within his hands was a polishing rag.

"Didn't mean to startle you Boss; the usual is it?"

I nodded. "Wish you'd get brighter lights around here."

"You sound rattled lad. What's up?"

When the glass was filled, I grabbed it and quaffed it in one. "Cheers". I said waving the empty glass at Rik and then to the wall poster of the reclining Oscar Wilde. Both of them appeared quietly amused by my little charade. "I'll have the same again." I gasped throwing down a fiver. We both watched mesmerised as it swivelled and danced along the bar top.

"I am very impressed with that shine." I remarked. "It's like an ice rink!"

"Come into money?" He enquired.

"You could say that. Auster's behind it of course."

After he had refilled my glass, he gave me a stern look. "So that's why you seem uptight. Be extremely wary of him: he's a barrel of worms." He flicked imaginary dust off the bar, before fixing his eyes back on me again. "Be afraid, be very afraid; but you already know that don't you?"

"Don't I just!"

As I took hold of my drink, he put a hand on my forearm. "Steady on will you. It's bad for business if my customers collapse at the bar!" Rik gave me a knowing look and started polishing the bar again. He allowed a few moments to discretely pass. "Something you need to get off your chest?"

I looked very apologetic. "I'll make it last." The drink swivelled down my throat. "It's about one of Auster's couriers Robert Robertson."

"Ah yes: I remember reading about that in the York Press this morning." He looked up sharply. "Dreadful business; how are you involved?"

"I may have got him killed; it was cold blooded murder and Auster's implicated up to his neck somehow." I cocked my head. "You haven't seen him recently?"

He looked thoughtful. "Strangely no; I haven't even seen him at the club for the last few weeks."

"What club?"

"The Rufforth Flying Club; you must have heard of it?"

I looked incredulously at him. "Flying club? You mean you're both pilots?"

Rik sighed. "Who do you think introduced that rogue to the sport?" He pointed to himself and began polishing again, this time more violently.

"Hold on – or you'll dig a hole?"

He had quite a sweat on before he finally stopped. "If he's coming at all, Austerfield is normally here before closing time." He glanced at his watch. "Its ten-thirty now – at least I think it is." There was concern in his voice. "It doesn't seem to keep proper time"

My amused look was instant and obvious. "Auster's bargains never do." I showed him my own.

He scrutinised both. "I do love this latest Rolkex technology, but it's my flaking chrome and the fact that its 'Made in Yunphuk' tends to suggest counterfeit!"

I laughed. "All that glitters."

"It's accurate to within a day!"

I began to feel faint and desperately I grabbed hold of the bar. "My stomach appears strangely empty. I must confess that with all this concern with chasing Auster, eating food was the last thing on my mind."

Rik scavenged around beneath the bar and brought up a plate of sandwiches. "You'll be doing me a favour. I'll only throw them out." He looked amused as I grabbed a handful. "Business deal with Auster is it?"

I rammed a sandwich down my throat. Food felt good and my mind seemed to come alive again. "No. I'm being paid by the cops to find him. I have a strange notion he's back in Athens."

Rik put both of his elbows on the bar, cradled his chin and remarked. "It's funny you should say that because the last time he was in here, he asked to use my phone. I knew by the money he poured into my hands that it must have been long distance."

"I suppose you didn't overhear anything?"

"Every ruddy word, but it won't make much sense: he spoke fluent Greek. I had the shock of my life. He generally talks more Tyke than we do."

"His mother is Greek. Didn't you know that he was born there?"

"His father came from Barnsley. How on earth did they...?"

I held a twinkle in my eye. "Oh that's easy: the RAF was responsible for their wartime romance." After a short pause I remarked. "I wonder what his conversation was all about."

Rik shook his head. "Rigel! It kept cropping up in his conversation. I found that quite amusing. Sprinkled amongst the Greek were references to Rigel. More Greek and then Rigel again. That's some sort of star name isn't it?"

I nodded. "It's the far right-hand star in Orion."

Rik looked at his watch, smirked and then in a very condescending manner said. "By my fancy new watch it's eleven o'clock. Last orders?"

I would have answered but suddenly there was a cold draft and we both expected someone to enter. All we saw was a rapidly retreating figure slipping through the door. We looked dumbstruck at each other.

"How did he get in?"

"I'm going to find out," I snapped.

Rik's comment: "Well I'm blowed!" was my only escort as I hurled myself after our eavesdropper.

Outside, a gusty wind threatened to take away my breath as I hastened up Grape Lane and into Low Petergate.

Ahead of me I heard footsteps, faint and distant. Who could it be and how had they remained inside for so long without detection? I hurried onwards towards Kings Court feeling very disorientated. Perhaps I had fraternised with too much alcohol but things seemed different. My poky restaurant for instance, had developed a face-lift and shops on both sides had unfamiliar names to them.

Something was definitely wrong.

I had reached Goodramgate (to my left) and in front, I was surprised to find Butchers' Church. A glance down indicated that I was in TL Red. Suddenly my bezel flashed Blue/ Purple.

The church abruptly evaporated like a flock of starlings at sunset and the now familiar King's Square swirled into existence. The area appeared empty, apart from in the corner was a tree rustling in the breeze. Everything else was a Matisse blur of rainbow colours. This had to be another TL shift. As I paused for breath my nerves tingled with expectation. Abruptly a figure moved inside Pump Court. Although shrouded in darkness, I knew that I was being minutely scrutinised.

"You stick out like a barber's pole, who are you?" My voice was sharp and clear but when there was no answer with more bravado than sense I bellowed. "Cat got your tongue then?"

Suddenly the darkness parted and a white face poked through. It was instant recognition: Michael Tombs! Then he was gone, leaving behind only an impish smile.

With a cry I chased after him and ran headlong into the enclosed Court. I became aware of a metal gate but then I tripped over something and fell heavily. But I didn't hit the floor. My next sensation was one of cold swirling weightlessness.

00:00:00:00

CHAPTER FORTY TWO

A Dead Man's Clutch

There was a moment of breathless anticipation that was mixed with electric static and burnt charcoal, and then abruptly through the swirling darkness, a human shape hurtled towards me. Close up its startled face was disturbingly familiar and then as it swept past I realised that it was – me!

Time Loop Blue

01.00.00.00

A woman's voice registered surprise. "Eesa Kala?"

My head throbbed; my body ached; I opened an eye and became aware of a plump wrinkled face inches away from me. She looked concerned and her short urgent breath stank of Ouzo.

"Eesa Kala?" There was more emphasis now.

I looked around me to find that I was slumped upon a cold metal bench. "It's alright, I'm English," I replied cautiously.

She didn't say anything else then but helped me to my feet and then abruptly left. I watched her black overcoat slowly mingling within the crowd.

I had found myself in a huge hall that seemed alarmingly full of Greek speaking figures and Greek advertising signs. It had all the hallmarks of Athens airport. A glance at my watch threw another mystery at me. Twelve minutes past eleven kind of mystery. My last memory was chasing after Tombs. If I had left Rik's at eleven, it must have been only another ten minutes after that, when I had run into Pump Court. Now a few moments later I'm here in Athens. Sweet gods, that's faster than Concorde!

Almost by instinct my next reaction was to walk outside and gulp in the warm breezy night air. It was at that precise moment I heard a horn blast and the squeal of brakes as a white sports car pulled up alongside me. The driver looked familiar. Her sunglasses caught the flash of neon as she climbed out of the car and hurried towards me; her long auburn hair flowing in the night air. There was no hint of recognition as she swept past.

"Stella," I cried, but she was already into the airport and running desperately through the swaying flow of people. I too then became immersed in the swirling throng apologising profusely as I bumped and weaved my way through.

Eventually I caught up with her denim-clad form as she appeared in deep conversation with a seated official at passport control.

"Stella? Stella Hunnybun?" I gasped as I stood alongside her.

Her face scowled as if I had owed her money. "Who the hell are you?"

"It's Ross."

"Am I supposed to know you?"

My eyes opened wide. "Yes, through Gallagher."

She threw me a look as if I was a dog begging for scraps. "We must stop that scumbag Dimitri from leaving the country."

"I thought Dimitri was working for us?"

"Don't you read your INTELS? He's taken us for fools and double-crossed us. Your boss is furious," she paused. "Of course, you should know that?"

I showed mock surprise. "Oh! I do."

She turned abruptly then and vented her anger upon the poor official. By the way he waved his hands, I realised Austerfield had already slipped through her fingers once more.

We were in her apartment and sat like bookends upon a white leather sofa. I tried not to become mesmerised by the thigh-length slit in her denim skirt. Our conversation ran like a trickling stream: a little bit about this, a little about that, and definitely about the other: the other being Gallagher.

By her antique grandfather clock it was 2am. A glance at my watch assured me against time travel. Giving a slow blue pulse, it read only midnight which was English time; Greek time was two hours ahead.

"Nice watch; looks expensive?" she reached over and held it up close. "Rolkex made in Yunphuk. Now that is an original make of watch!" Her laughing eyes sought mine. "Why it even has a pretty blue glow."

I looked sheepishly at her. "My boss gave me it to improve my time keeping."

Stella looked intently at me, hesitated, and apparently was trying to formulate a way of saying what was on her mind, without appearing foolish. Eventually she said. "I feel as if I know you from somewhere; have we met before?"

Instead of answering her (I didn't know how to) I feasted my eyes around the room.

Pride of place upon her warm pastel walls was a picture of 'The Boy In Red' by Goya and to the left, four smaller pictures, showing English scenes. In the corner was a mahogany bookcase and adjacent to that, another leather sofa. For a moment it felt homely but then uncontrolled panic kicked in. All of this seemed far too scary. Two thousand miles away, Rik would only just have finished closing his bar. I turned to look at her. Stella flashed a smile that finally precipitated my reaction: I blubbered like a child.

She moved across and buried me in her arms. "Hey. That's not the response I was expecting."

"I'm so sorry," I sobbed.

She caressed my face. "How very unfeeling of me: you must be shattered after your long flight. Let's talk again in the morning, shall we?"

"I've got nowhere to stay," I mumbled.

I noticed more than a twinkle in her eye as she stood up and said. "You can sleep in my bed tonight."

My body felt weak as she led me by the hand down a corridor that led towards her bedroom. At the door she paused and I was close enough to smell a rapturous trace of perfume upon her hair.

"Throw me my nightie will you?"

I brushed past her and gazed in wonder at her wickerwork bed complete with white duck down. The lighting was soft and blue, like the nightie I plucked from her pillow to give her.

"Till tomorrow then. Kalinichta."

She then walked away, without a backward glance.

The early morning sun poured through her lounge window like cream into a fruit bowl. I stood in the archway and pinched myself. If this was really a dream I did not want to be woken up. My next thought was to accept my fate and then to bathe in this delicious warmth.

"I'm making breakfast, do you want to eat British style or Greek?" she said.

I followed the direction of her voice through yet another archway and emerged into an old English designed kitchen of pastel blue, light oak and stainless steel. I caught her hovering over a coffee percolator.

"What you're making smells fine with me."

With a swirl of her clinging negligee she turned and faced me. "It is only simple coffee with tsoureki," she said flashing more than a smile.

"I like simple pleasures," I said softly.

As we sat down to eat at her kitchen table, I couldn't help but reflect that this wasn't the Stella I knew at all. "Do you have a twin?"

With her mouth full of sweet bread she mumbled "No! Why?"

I merely shrugged and looked puzzled at her.

Later, when she had dressed in another casual little number, we reclined once more on her sofa. My gaze fell through the window and soared up into blue skies and distant undulating white-topped mountains.

"If this isn't Heaven where are we?" I asked still munching on my tsoureki. It was the last offered piece.

She looked amused. "You're north of Athens, in a place called Marousi. Do you like it here?"

"Very much," I murmured gazing up into her twinkling eyes. "Have you lived here all your life?"

"No, I lived in Surrey before coming here." Her legs swept up onto the sofa and in the process her toes accidentally rubbed my right thigh. There was a questioning look now. "You could start by telling me a little about yourself. You don't have to say much – just a little to get me interested."

My mouth became as dry as the Sahara. "Is that a good toe-hold, to start with?" I asked slowly, whilst gently caressing her foot.

"Perfect," she murmured.

I became captivated by her black dress that curved in all the dangerous places. "You love denim, don't you?" I said at last.

She laughed. "Yes I do. Answer my question will you. I'm curious to know your name," and withdrawing her foot from my grasp retorted. "I'm also immune to flattery."

I sighed and adjusted my glasses. "My name is Ross."

My remark made her jolt and I became aware of some anxiety deep within. "Just Ross; how English," she said.

"You said that the last time we met."

"Is this some sort of game?"

I shrugged. "How I wish!" I took a deep breath. "Would you believe me if I said that last night I was in York, which is in England and in as many minutes as I am explaining this to you – I have ended up here in Athens...?"

My words were drowned from the convulsed laughter of Stella. "You're funny," she said quietly and then leant across and lightly kissed me. "Perhaps I've met you in my dreams."

We gazed at one another now, hands caressing hands.

"Does the phrase: 'I've come here to retire' mean anything to you?" I said at last.

She threw me a puzzled look. "You're not that old surely?"

"Gallagher gave me that as our password. Didn't you know?"

Stella shook her head slowly. "I've had a word with your boss this morning. He doesn't seem a happy man."

"I bet he had something to say about me being over here?"

"Yes he did. He claims no such instruction, other than track down your friend Austerfield in York. However his last instruction -after the sprinkle of colourful metaphors had subsided- was for me to place you firmly under my wing." She stroked her toe up and down my thigh. "If that's alright with you?"

I slid along the sofa until I could lie next to her. My voice felt husky. "I'll try to be as good as gold under anything you care to place me under".

She smiled and then kissed me again, this time more fiercely. Finally her hands cupped my face and she drew a short breath. "I really do feel as if I've known you all my life. We have met before, but it's all so strange; in another life somehow." Her fingers trickled through my hair as she looked deep within my eyes. "Why are you here?"

"When it all makes sense to me, I'll try and explain it to you." I stifled a laugh then sat up and breathed in slowly. "Gallagher gave me the job of tracing a colleague of mine called David Austerfield. That's why. He also goes under the name of Dimitri." I felt her body go tense and she stood up. "Do you know him?" I queried startled at her sudden movement.

"Of course I know him – he only nearly got me killed last night because I was so foolish enough to trust him, that's all."

"I'm sorry I blundered into your stake-out."

She shrugged and held my hand. "Sorry to have exploded like that. The fact is," she paused and sat next to me again. "I was his Controlling Officer and when he failed to show up at one of our regular contacts, I sensed he was in trouble. We had a tip off last night that he was attempting to leave the country. Manchester airport failed to spot him – but I bet he is in England now. He is a slippery customer by all accounts and it seems obvious that he's cutting his own deal." She snuggled down next to me. "It would be a feather in your leader's cap if you could help me find him."

"I wouldn't know where to look in this country."

Her eyes opened wide. "Surely you mean back in England now?"

"I have an instinct that he is back here; I am certain of that." I gave her nose a playful tweak as I kissed it. "My other boss called Michael Tombs also has the..."

She sat bolt upright. "Good grief! He's my boss too. Actually he is my Control here on Earth. If you know him too...?" her voice held curiosity. "You must be recruited in 'Top Management'." She looked intently at me. "But you *are* Earthborn?"

I felt a shiver run down my spine; should I ask the obvious question? It dangled upon my lips but I decided against it. I gave a nervous laugh. "I was when I woke up this morning; but I'm not so sure now! Tombs altered my watch to create pretty colours; these are coloured dimensions called Time Loops that seem to send me all over the place."

Her face fell. "Of course; I knew I had seen that somewhere else. You are lucky. Ben and I are trapped forever within these loops and everything we do appears to create others."

Here was my chance; my pulse raced. "I take it you're not from around here then?"

She cupped my face within her hands. "We come from a planet called Tengaluma. Does that scare you?"

"My mind whirled. "That sounds as if it is further than Surrey!"

I saw a flicker of amusement return to her face. "Yes it is a bit further than that: try for six hundred light years in the constellation of Aries. Your astronomers have designated my star coldly as HIP 9569, yet I shed tears each time I look up at it in the night sky."

My arms held her in a tight embrace. "You will go home and soon if I have anything to do with it. I will not let you down."

Her cheeks became ribbons of wetness. "Ben and I were chosen for this mission because our race and technology is almost identical to your own. You could say that we are perfect spies because of that fact. I was coerced by an evil species called the Gropie into bringing a viral quantum bomb to Earth. At least that is what *I* want to prove. I managed to crash land the transport vehicle but your own terrorists decided to salvage the wreckage for their own ends. Ironic don't you think: greed and destruction seem to have no planetary boundaries?"

"I don't know what to think anymore," I lamented.

She moved away and wiped her eyes in the process. "This self pity just will not do; let us focus our minds upon the problem in hand. There must be something; some clue we have overlooked."

"Does Rigel mean anything to you?"

She sat down rather abruptly. "What?" She raised an enquiring eyebrow. "From the Earth position in space it is the right hand star in Orion. Other than that, no it doesn't. Why?"

I threw her an admiring look before replying. "The word Rigel was used in Auster's telephone conversation with his Greek contact."

"Now that you mention it, I've seen that name somewhere. In a snapshot I think."

Stella climbed off the sofa and returned eventually with a wad of photos and sat next to me. "These are the last surveillance shots of Dimitri before he vanished."

I looked in dismay at her, and the Eiffel Tower stack. There was nothing wrong with her memory, but it took a few hours to find what we were looking for.

"Wasn't it all so simple," she said at last.

I nodded. "Now we can go and surprise him."

"Arrest him, you mean?" replied Stella.

Our destination was the Port of Piraeus and within the "safe house" of the yacht named Rigel we discovered a leather bound book with its spine ripped open. It was clutched within the hands of a dead man.

CHAPTER FORTY THREE

A Ripping Tale

At Time Loop Blue

00:03:45:00

We were hurling our way into Athens towards a nightclub called the Moulin Rouge. Stella's driving could be summed up in one word.

"WOW!"

However, my constricted throat muscles and eyes bulging from their sockets muted the enthusiasm in which my mouth had uttered it. In short I was petrified. Stella however positively gleamed with pleasure at this dance with death as her nimble hands manipulated that steering wheel like a racing driver. Abruptly the car swung sharply left which piled on the 'G' forces. I gasped.

"Slow down will you. I can only cope with one dead body per day."

She casually turned her head towards me and spoke as if this was an afternoon snooze in deck chairs.

"The dead body is Manolis. What makes you think Dimitri might have been taken to 84 Imittou Street?" Instantly her attention was switched to the road ahead as she swerved around a particularly battered lorry that belched smoke and abuse.

"Intuition," I shouted above the whining din of the engine.

"I'll go with that," she said turning again. "Incidentally – Ben thinks you're ace!"

I gazed at the innocent yellow book in my lap. "I'm impressed how a simple book cover can be used to smuggle contraband."

She nodded. "Since that cabin cruiser Rigel was in joint names of Dimitri and Manolis, we can assume either the real trigger is on its way to England or they were disturbed and Anya has it now."

"We'll soon find that out," I said adding, "A ripped book can speak volumes."

A momentary puzzled glance was expressed before the gear change which caused an abrupt surge of the car. There were more screeching horns as we jumped a red light. The rev needle obliged with the same matching colour and then further 'G' forces encased my ear within the seat mounting. We abruptly swung across a line of traffic, narrowly missing a white Yugo. The look of terror from the bearded occupant would haunt me forever.

"How could I have missed him?"

"God knows," I retorted, "I think he must have braked, instead of you."

She threw me another puzzled glance. "I was referring to Austerfield."

I looked down into the comfort of my lap before replying. "Perhaps he had been tailed to the Rigel, there was quite a scuffle by the way the bed clothes were strewn around the floor."

My voice was drowned by a horn that screamed mercy. She looked across at me. "Thank God for that observant waiter."

"I wish that rat Auster was laying dead instead of Manolis," I screamed.

"Really not much difference between them," replied Stella changing gear, which screeched in agony of the moment.

"Which brings me back to this parcel? Can that crystal ball of yours explain what may have happened?"

I couldn't answer because my body nearly leapt through the windscreen as she braked.

We had arrived.

Once parked outside the nightclub, Stella sought out three men who sat around a green metal table supping lagers. At our approach, they stood up to greet us.

My face beamed at seeing old friends again. "Hello Artemis, Pericles," I said as my hand gripped theirs in turn.

They gave a puzzled look towards Stella who clearly surprised, merely shrugged.

Artemis turned and gave a puzzled frown. "Have we met before?"

I nodded. "Yes we have, but you won't remember; it's a very long story."

He looked mystified and would have answered but Stella cut in.

"Has anything happened here recently?"

It was Pericles who responded. "About ten minutes ago two men and a woman have entered the building opposite us."

At this I began to experience severe anxiety: something was amiss, but I couldn't place it. "Did you recognise one as Dimitri?" I said.

They nodded in unison.

"We have got to get over there," I commanded.

"Don't be silly – this isn't time for heroics. You'll get us all killed."

I turned to Stella. "There's five of us and only two of them; the other is definitely our hostage. Trust me, I know this."

Reluctantly they accompanied me as I crossed the road, climbed the stairs and entered the apartment of 84 Imittou Street. Even before the door opened I smelt the stench of death that hung in the air like a battlefield.

I gazed into the startled face of Anya, who had a gun pointed uncomfortably at Auster; the barrel trickled smoke. Yannis wore a sadistic grin, and swivelled round to face us. Stella, breathing down my neck, was the only one of the cavalry with a clear shot, if she knew which one to pick.

It was a silent equation that summed up that room of death. Anya, Yannis and Stella had their eyes transfixed upon Austerfield, who was slumped in a chair. Anya slowly turned; her gun then pointed straight at us; I retched violently.

The world freeze framed and it felt as if I had been slotted inside a still-life watercolour. One that was full of red polka dots.

00:00:00

I felt no more than a tingling sensation this time.

Time Loop Purple -Green

00:00:00:10

Abruptly the room faded to be replaced by one devoid of occupants or furniture. When I saw Michael, my mind couldn't take any more. He just slid through the far wall walked towards me and guided me back the way he had come.

I smelt burnt cordite and then swirling blackness.

CHAPTER FORTY FOUR

Evaluation

Time Loop Purple

"Are you rested?"

CHAPTER FORTY FIVE

Last Bottle

At Time Loop Blue

02:03:00:00

My mind buzzed with a myriad jigsaw pieces. I strolled over to my fridge and released it of one bottle of unopened whisky. For some considerable time I stared at my temptress. Was this finally it then? There was a pause, albeit slight variations upon the usual rampant dragging the top off, before pouring a healthy measure into a shot glass. I gazed at its amber colour, marvelled at the smell and clarity of it all and was not surprised as the familiar compulsion returned. My mouth hesitated at the rim. Michael once said: "The confused mind stumbles?"

What was I to do now?

That question had a multitude of answers: the simplest was to down this glass, then the next and the next, until sweet oblivion.

Or was it the telephone call to London and the appointment with the cold face of Gallagher as I admitted defeat and then would come the expected measure of sympathy and the: 'you did your best old son' routine. Far worse would be the grilling by the enigmatic Tombs. I gazed up at the ceiling. "How can I find Auster? He's dead!" I let out a defeated breath. "And now you have put me back here – you unfeeling sod!"

The whirr of the fridge reminded me that I had forgotten to shut the door. I placed the glass inside the fridge, closed it and walked back into the living room. My mind raced as I stalked the floor like a caged animal.

I thought back to the Transit Station floating far out in space and the insatiable curiosity of Michael. He seemed confident that I had finally grasped how his alien mind functioned within his various Time Loops. Was that it: a meaningless, fruitless exercise? Had the experiment now concluded; the Earth sacrificed? These were questions that held no meaning to human beings captured within their secular lives. I screamed up at the ceiling. "We aren't capable of thinking fourth dimensionally are we Michael?"

With a jolt, I remembered something very important. I retraced my steps towards the fridge, retrieved my whisky glass, and drained it in one. My gaze became transfixed for some time on that beguiling bottle as I fought her sweet temptation.

Should I or shouldn't I? Another one couldn't hurt? Would it?

Three swift refills later, a feeling of self-loathing overwhelmed me. Abruptly I slammed the fridge door before re-entering the living room, the now empty glass still cemented in my hand. The world was about to end yet all my emotions remained self centred on that glass. I shut one eye which made walking easier and made my way across the room towards the table that contained my wooden hand carved chess set. The pieces that Ben had set up for me so many months ago stood in lonely vigil. Nothing had been altered. I placed my glass centre stage and then mentally followed those two moves that he had made that day.

First move: White Pawn to King-Bishop3, Black Pawn to King 4. Second move: White Pawn to King Knight4, before finally placing empty Whisky – Black Queen to Rook 5. It was the fastest checkmate possible: a 'Fools Mate'. I felt a great deal of sympathy for that White King.

"There but for fortune," I muttered, "there but for fortune." As if in sympathy I heard the chimes droning their hour. Why had Ben left the board like this? Was it a deep meaning, which I had failed to pick up on? As I stood there gazing at those chess pieces it finally dawned on me that it could not have been Ben at all. This was the trade mark of the cunning devious mind of Michael Tombs. The 'Fools Mate' was perhaps a solution and Schrödinger had either been solved or perhaps cheated? It was within this mindset that the phone rang. I was surprised to hear Stella; her voice assertive, commanding. Could I meet her in town within the hour?

"Where?" I enquired.

"You choose," came back the reply.

There was an air of change at Rik's. He looked as if he had just stepped out of a fashion boutique. All three – piece and clean shaven he looked suspiciously abnormal. If I had taken the trouble to have looked down I bet his shoes would have blinded me with their polish. Over the bar was a television and he was busy watching the tennis. "Might bring in the customers," was his weak excuse.

"You hate television – or sport," I remarked as a roar issued from the speakers.

He threw me a lame look. "It passes the time."

"It won't last."

He leant over to whisper, "there's a lady over there who was asking after you." I glanced around the empty bar and almost missed Stella who was tucked away in a dark corner.

I gave him a sly wink. "You are dying to know aren't you?"

"She's a stunner by no mistake!" He began polishing the bar with a duster. "I knew something was brewing when I saw you walk in wearing a clean shirt and tie." He leant closer. "You – wear a tie! You must be very careful with her; treat her like porcelain."

"You stick to your tennis," I suggested as I made my way over towards Stella's table.

He grunted. "You watch yourself. She's too good for you!"

Close up, my senses became aware of her light but intoxicating perfume. The style of her purple chiffon dress was simple but devastating as it moulded to her like cling film. She stood up and leant over to whisper her greeting; I felt her taut nipples rub against my chest and suddenly the world seemed alright again.

I felt myself blushing. "What brings you to England?" I asked.

She looked at me with reserved friendliness. "Let's drink; let's eat. And then we'll talk some more."

I condescended, with a nod and a smile. "It's just what I was going to say."

My remark was totally ignored as she scrutinised the menu. Her next request was for an unusual late harvest wine that Rik had to descend into the cellars to fetch; I was confident that he had acquired it. Rik for all his pretence at 'being one of the boys' knew his wines like a true connoisseur.

"Your very good health Ross," she said as she took the first sip. Let's eat now shall we?"

From time to time over dinner, I kept looking across at her as I made polite conversation. Her vibrant hair seemed to mirror the glow within her dark blue eyes. Occasionally however I caught the hawk within, watching, analysing, and calculating. Just as quickly however, she would gaze candidly with an air of ironical disinterest like an Egyptian princess.

Afterwards Rik excelled himself again by delivering two coffee creations. She seemed so appreciative about the evening that she kept emphasising each virtue by lightly touching my hand with hers, whilst my heart played the Minute Waltz.

She leant towards me, but this time I lost control of my emotions: I kissed her hard and passionately. Her body writhed within my arms and I was prepared to release her and apologise for my behaviour, but then she grabbed my head with both hands and thrust me down upon her soft yielding throat. As my hands trickled through her hair, I gave in to this wild sensuality of the moment and groaned with deep desire. From deep within, she gave a husky moan like that of a trapped animal about to be freed and I, the only key.

I retraced my steps from Nirvana upon hearing a polite cough. Rik was standing over me. "It's past eleven and I do have a home to go to," he said.

"I'm sorry for keeping you," I said humbly.

The look he gave was wistful, almost sad. "I too have my memories," he murmured as we left.

As we walked through the door and into the ashen night, Stella looked hard at me. "Were you paying attention to what I was telling you during the meal?"

"Yes of course I was listening – every word!"

Her hand lightly batted my head. "Good, because your boss decided that you should accompany me upon my next assignment. Frankly I was dead against it, because you are not a fully trained Field Officer, are you?"

Crestfallen I said. "No I am not."

From deep within I could see she was analysing the odds of success to failure. I firmly grasped her hand. "Together we will succeed in this mission."

"Will you follow my orders without question?" she said at last.

"I'm all yours." I murmured.

The tension lifted from her face. "Good. Then let's go back to your place!"

The lights and music were low and seductive; an incense stick burned. Slowly I edged over the sofa towards her. Delicately raising her foot, she pushed me back towards the other end of the sofa. "Forget it Romeo, we've got work to do."

"It's past midnight?"

She gazed across in a tired sort of way but managed a wan smile. "With Austerfield dead, Gallagher has confirmed my worst fears: the Viral Q' bomb has been planted somewhere in York. It could go off at any time!"

I sat bolt upright. "In York do you say?"

Stella threw me a wild look. "It was obvious really, what with Anya, Malik, Smythe and Austerfield – all residing within this city. She gazed around the room hoping to find solace. "You must know something about your friend's contacts here in York?" She looked stern. "I'll put this very bluntly. Did you know anything about his smuggling rackets?"

My eyebrows raised and I paused before replying. Even now my pride interfered with logic. "I really didn't know what criminal stuff he was up to. You must understand that."

She got up and turned the music off. Her voice held no compromise. "You must know some names?"

"Well yes. There was a man called Robertson."

"Robertson! Ben has mentioned him on quite a few occasions. What do you know about him?"

I gazed across at her startled face. "The only thing I can tell you is that he is a member of Triethe Grand Lodge." It suddenly felt I had been struck by lightning. "Of course – I'm forgetting the letter!" My hand delved into the depths of my trouser pocket. "Shortly after I had visited Robertson, his wife came to see me and gave me this." I took out the folded paper and handed it to her. "There is no writing at all. You will find it's a blank piece of paper."

She scrutinised it, then carefully licked one edge. "Where's your kitchen?"

Rather mystified I led her there and watched as she switched on my rather battered toaster, fed the paper amongst the glowing wires and gazed with an air of expectancy. "It is invisible ink. You would be amazed how many ways you can make it." She winked. "You can use either lemon juice or urine. If you're really adventurous you can..."

"I make my toast in that!"

Her mouth abruptly pecked mine. "Say Abracadabra?" She teased. "Go on say it."

"Abracadabra, "I lamented to her turned back peering into the glowing elements.

"Ah! There we are."

Within her hands my previous blank piece of paper, had now brown spidery writing upon it.

'Godfried Edrich Head of Triethe Inner Circle'

She looked impressed. "T.I.C. Of course! Before the smugglers trail went cold in Athens, Twelve had raided a warehouse they suspected was used by them. It was full of cocoa beans."

"Godfreid Edrich is the Managing Director of Seehbolm's chocolate factory," I suggested.

"A good hiding place to make a bomb."

I shivered. "A few years ago Godfried turned from a frequent visitor to his factory and into a total recluse up in his top floor boardroom."

"We've got to inform London." I watched her pick up my phone and punch numbers; there was a pause. "London Desk? Put this call through to Major Gallagher. Yes I'm aware of the time: this is urgent."

As her voice droned on and on, I must have dozed off.

I awoke much later, to find her breath, soft and warm on my face and her fingers lightly caressing my hair. The dusky warmth in her eyes had returned.

"Which way to the bedroom?" she whispered.

In the early morning light, I awoke warm and snuggled within her arms, but that didn't last long because my earlier fears returned. Ground Zero was merely a few miles away.

It was then that I heard the sound of a blackbird sharp and clear upon the air. Was it prelude to Armageddon? I became lulled to sleep by its innocent melody.

CHAPTER FORTY SIX

Phantom Kiss

Time Loop Blue

00:10:11:00

I checked my shirt for creases, straightened my tie and prepared for a normal working day that Ben had fixed up for us.

"Is Ben convinced that this is the right chocolate factory?"

"He's convinced, so shut up and zip up."

Stella had equipped me with that little bit extra: strapped around my left inner thigh was a P7 handgun and the only way to reach it was via my fly!

I didn't mind the way she lovingly attached this instrument of death, but when she threw me an extra 8 clip, I coughed and realised she meant business! Her words to me were simple: "That gun, can be drawn, cocked and fired in one easy operation: and that could mean the difference between life and death."

For the third time that morning I inspected myself for tell-tale bumps of the 9mm kind. In the mirror looking back at me, all recently cleaned teeth and white coat was Mr Scientist.

"Was it all for that woman?"

"Huh?"

"I do know that before your divorce you had won many trophies at your gun club. Then suddenly you left. Why?"

I turned around and caught a glimpse of pink thigh peeping above black lace stocking and a gun holster, prelude to a hastily fastened coat.

"I merely retired," I growled.

Stella peered over horn rimmed glasses, blew me a mock kiss and then began to tie up her hair. "Personnel are expecting two Quality Assurance inspectors from their Harrogate factory this morning. Are you ready and up to the calibre they expect?"

My reply was a nod and a phantom kiss.

Mr Faulkes, the senior Quality Assurance inspector, had his eyes full of computer when we walked through the door of his office. All khaki shirt, brogues and thinning black hair, I caught him muttering under his breath.

"Having trouble with your spread sheets?" I asked cheerfully, trying to force a smile upon his dower expression. He looked up from his keyboard and peered at me through glasses that looked more at home in the bottom of a whisky glass. His gruff Scottish accent was designed to intimidate. "Who are you?"

Our guide from Personnel, a wimp of a lad who looked as if he had just stepped out of a tailor's shop window, hastily brushed past me and stammered, "They're from Harrogate, George. Top notch."

George stood up, placed a frown upon a frown and gave his best reserved smile. "So you've come to help us solve the Easter egg problem, have you? Well for what it's worth I think you're a damned imposition."

I looked weakly at him and turned towards Stella. The frozen stare she gave made me realise he'd better watch his step.

He turned to Taylor Dummy. "Will yea take 'em up to Mélange Paul?"

Without further ado, he turned his back on us and returned to his computer screen. I caught him picking up the phone however as Paul ushered Stella and myself through the door; his glance towards me held a haughty sneer. As Paul led us down the corridor he seemed clearly embarrassed.

"Is he like that with everyone, or did we catch him on a bad day?"

Paul threw me a fleeting glance. "It's his way I'm afraid. You'll get used to it."

I noticed Stella was deep in thought so I merely shrugged and allowed the silence to convey our thoughts. We appeared to wend our way along sub terrain corridors, up endless stairs and past countless conveyor belts until finally after a rickety ascent in a lift, we arrived.

George strummed his fingers on his desk top. "Yes I know its Personnel; I've just dialled that ruddy number! Now get me Cyril." There was a slight pause, a cackle in the earpiece and then with a tone, laced with sarcasm George replied. "My friend. You simply *will* not do. Cyril is still Head of Security *isn't* he? Yes, yes, that's right, do I have to repeat myself." He pulled the phone away from his ear, looked in disgust at it before returning it back. "I'm not interested in excuses: pull him away from his dinner if you must. I want to speak to *him* not the oily rag!" There was another pause whilst the request was dealt with.

A few minutes later and in one convulsion he shot forward like a guard dog straining on its leash. "Ah there you are. Do I have to repeat myself twice? It's George, from York." He held the phone away again, before replying with: "I'm so pleased you've remembered me now. About those two Q.A., people you've sent over today. I want to know how qualified they are in dealing with my problem with the Easter eggs. I didn't ask for assistance so who sanctioned it?" He listened intently interjecting with the occasional "Oh?" and "really", before his face suddenly held an air of cocky triumph. "What do you mean you don't know anything about them?" A malignant gleam appeared within his eyes as he listened to the man's plaintive requests to let him look into it. "I definitely will not leave it within your incapable hands. I know exactly what to do, even if you don't."

After he had slammed down the phone, George Faulkes sat in his armchair and carefully lit his pipe. In a confectionery factory it was totally against the rules – the very reason why he did it -but this time he would enjoy being found out. He lazily watched the smoke trailing from his pipe and seemed to smile when it disappeared with a flourish as he exhaled.

What was it that so excited him? From deep inside, memories were unleashed of dormitory torments as a new boy. A 'fag' they called him. Of course as he grew older, he savoured the time when it would be his turn to 'initiate' new boys into the school.

It was an enjoyment to savour, as this was now; Cyril's head would roll before this day was out.

Paul left us in a small office with Gordon, the Mélange team leader, and then gave a hasty retreat. All white cap and coat, he was a well rounded jolly man whose laughter lines seemed to go on forever. His face shone with pride as he shook our hands and said: "Gordo's the name. It's a reet craftsman's job up here, bah no mistake."

What seemed like an afterthought he motioned us towards a white metal framed window. "If you look carefully, you can just see the 'White Horse' of Kilburn."

"I can't see it," declared Stella, frantically scanning the horizon.

Gordo bent down so that he was eye level with her. "Follow the skyline down until it meets the hill that looks like a table top."

Her face flooded with wonder. "Oh! I can see it now," she exclaimed.

"First day here then?"

She laughed. "Yes. It is"

Gordo scrutinised me. "Your face seems familiar. I remember you waving a video camera in front of my face last year, if I'm not mistaken?"

I laughed. "You have a good memory. Yes you're right. Unfortunately I was made redundant, but later managed to get a job at Harrogate."

His face shone in admiration. "Cor. Sacked at one place then taken on at another. I call that reet smart!"

I shrugged. "Yes, I suppose it is."

We followed him over to a bank of three whirring gigantic stainless steel spheres and watched him as he opened an inspection hatch. He indicated us to see inside and I gazed in awe at seeing a brown viscous swirling mass being agitated by huge metal paddles.

Gordo puffed out his chest as he said: "Mélange is the process by which all the main ingredients are carefully stirred until chocolate is finally produced. It's a French word for stirring, I think. "

"So what's wrong with the Easter eggs?" I enquired.

"Our Quality Assurance guys are finding the eggs are starting to 'bloom' in storage."

"That's strange. What are the temperature settings in the storage room?"

"Seven degrees."

"That's normal storage conditions," I said airing my knowledge towards a now open mouthed Stella. He walked over towards a sliding door expecting us to follow, but Stella grabbed my arm. She whispered in my ear. "What's 'bloom'?"

"It's when the cocoa butter has crystallised out of the chocolate." I hissed. "It looks like a grainy white smear across the chocolate."

"What causes it?"

"There are many reasons, but the obvious is extreme cold."

"Storage Room is top floor," he said. "I'll take you there."

The room was strangely musty and held that haunted feel. Wooden boxes greeted you everywhere you looked.

Gordo walked quickly over to a heavy wooden door holding a crowbar. He turned to give a mystified look. "The lock is frozen solid," he said levering it with the tool.

I helped him heave open the stubborn sliding doors, we went through and closed them behind us. He dropped the bar casually upon the floor. The temperature inside was noticeably cooler. Stella shivered convulsively. "Oh! It's cold."

Gordo frowned. "Yes. I can't understand it." There was a look of bewilderment as he walked over to the far wall and scrutinised a thermometer. "Most odd," he said.

"Why?"

"It reads minus seven, that can't be right."

I glanced around the room and saw that it was stacked to waist height with wooden crates and in each was layer upon layer of Easter eggs. In the far left hand corner, laying quiet as a mouse, was a huge stainless steel drum which was different to those we had just observed in motion. It looked out of place with its gleaming metal amongst the age worn crates.

Gordo poked his hand inside the tray nearest to us and extracted an egg and handed it over to me. Even with my untrained eye, I could see something was wrong with the chocolate.

"You certainly do have a problem here," I said "Look how the chocolate surface is gritty and with those white streaks running across it?"

"So that's 'bloom', how peculiar," Stella remarked as she stroked the chocolate surface with her fingernail.

My gaze returned towards the huge steel ball. "Is there any reason why that is here?" I said walking over towards it.

"I assumed it must be something to do with you lot."

"Why do you say that?"

"A few months ago I saw a couple of 'white coats' supervise its arrival here. The delivery man was David Austerfield. I must admit, I'm mystified as to why it's here in the 'cool room'." His face looked genuinely puzzled

They walked over towards me and Stella placed a hand upon the brightly polished surface. She recoiled swiftly. "Oh! My hand nearly got stuck to it."

I could see in Gordo's face the look of the perplexed as he too attempted the experiment. "My God, that's reet cold that is."

Stella was now examining the drum's closed inspection hatch. Abruptly she threw me a worried look.

I bent down and retrieved the crowbar. My face was quite impassive but I trembled. "We may have found what we've come here for."

"Have you cured the Easter egg problem then?"

My hands shook. "Not quite. We've found our VQ bomb!"

"Did I hear you right?" he exclaimed, as he inhaled to bursting point. "A bomb! What bomb – are you joking?"

"No," I quietly replied to his dazed face.

"This is highly irregular. I'm going to have a firm talk with foreman about this."

He left before I could catch his arm, Stella shrugged. "Let him go," she said softly. "Let him go."

I gazed into her anxious face a moment or two and didn't speak.

"You knew it was here, didn't you?"

"With David Austerfield as the delivery man, who needs a crystal ball?" I declared.

She looked deadpan. "What do we do now?"

"Pray," I whispered.

CHAPTER FORTY SEVEN

Eternity Beckons

Time Loop Blue

00:02:12:00

His face was like a Borneo shrunken head. Only the glowing demonic eyes registered life. The gaze barely acknowledged the view from the window which was of a distant hazy landscape. Peeping through this shimmering veil was the White Horse.

That was his entire experience: this room; this view; this moment. The gaze was held whilst the phone rang and rang and then almost with petulance he turned his back upon the world outside. Now abruptly he re-entered his life as the Company Director with its bland Company room and large gold framed pictures; the Company desk, so huge dark and polished you could swim in it, and the Company chair, all red sumptuous leather and an aroma to match. To his right slumped back in a chair, was a blackened shrivelled corpse.

Amongst that sea of the gigantean, abruptly shrilled a miniscule white phone, stark and central upon the table; it was grasped firmly.

"Yes, what is it?"

There was no flicker of emotion as he listened; his reply was terse. "No. Not the police. I'll deal with this."

The handset was carefully replaced and now his face became pensive, and calculating. Reaching down to open the drawer at his right hand side, he pulled out a yellow leather book from within and placed it upon the table. Its spine had been ripped open. He next produced a square silver clock like device and by pushing the dial face induced a red display of 00:02:12:00.

Slowly almost with a resigned composure he leant back in the armchair and contemplated his next move; he rang a number, spoke energetically down the phone and waited; his entire world focused now on the clock face and then on the book upon the table.

Even when he heard the commotion outside the door, his gaze never left that leather bound volume.

She helped me jemmy off the inspection hatch and then stood in awe at the device within. It was bathed in rippling dense blue smoke. To my uneducated eye it appeared like a harmless looking donut glass ring, which gave slow pulses of purple colour. Perched in the middle and suspended with invisible wires was a pencil shaped object. Surrounding the donut were a mass of wires and pink fluorescent tubes.

"I've only seen the blueprints, never the real thing." She murmured busily examining inside. "See those tubes?" She tapped her finger nail upon the right hand tube, "they're full of liquid Hydrogen."

I shivered at the intense icy smoke as it wafted over my bare face and hands. "Why does it need to be so cold?"

"It is to maintain the super intense magnetic flux which is generated by field coils within those tubes. And the pulsing donut is the timer and that," she pointed to the pencil shape, "is the Red Mercury device."

"So that is where it sits. How does it work?" I enquired.

"The device unleashes quantum energy by a viral multiplicity effect: very much like the early universe when the Weak and Strong forces were in coexistence."

"And in simple speak?"

"It will wipe out all life on Earth when it explodes."

"Ah! You mean the deluxe model. Does it come in other colours?"

Considering the absurdity of the remark and the situation, Stella threw me an attempted smile before she carried on with her inspection. "Were in luck," she said at last. "The Trigger hasn't been activated yet."

"Refresh my memory again?"

"The Red Mercury Trigger needs a timer to start its countdown sequence." She pointed to the donut. "When that colour changes to red then it's activated. Then after that – BOOM!"

"How comforting." I remarked drily. "Of course it might be the dummy trigger."

She held an air of contempt. "You still hold a lot of faith in your friend Austerfield."

We had become too immersed in trying to sabotage the weapon to realise that we were not alone.

A familiar sledgehammer perfume set my nerves on edge.

A female voice snarled. "Come away from there and turn around slowly."

In the doorway were Anya, Malik and Yannis, waggling revolvers at us. Abruptly, behind them were George, Taylor Dummy and a cowering Gordo. It was only Anya who had bothered to dress up for the occasion with a little number of black velvet. They slowly entered the room.

George wagged his finger. "Ya didna think yu'd gerraray wi' it di'ye?"

"You daft fool," I cried. "This is a bomb and we are trying to defuse it!"

"And I'm Rob Roy," he scoffed laughing in my face.

The whole room abruptly vibrated and looking down I saw to my horror that the device had now turned to glowing red.

"The bomb is on countdown," I screamed at Stella.

Stella glanced briefly at me and pleadingly at Gordo but even his smile had faded now. He did however grab George's arm and admitted: "These aren't the normal security guards are they?" His gaze next fell upon Anya. "And she's foreign."

Peering through his thick lens George realised he was right. "Who are you?" he said. "And why you carrying guns?"

"None of your concern," sneered Anya.

The first whisper of fear stirred in George's mind and he slowly began to edge away. Malik's revolver barked once and he collapsed to his knees mouthing a silent protest and then lay spread-eagled, lifeless upon the floor.

Gordo's mouth opened and closed like a gasping goldfish, a fact that Anya acknowledged with a sadistic smile.

"Having fun are we?" She shrieked with hysterical pleasure, when Gordo merely blubbered incoherently.

All their attention was drawn towards him and I realised then that this was my moment. My hand quickly and very awkwardly unzipped my fly. I grasped hold of the P7 automatic.

Stella gave me a sideways glance and then edged towards the nearest crate. Unexpectedly Gordo and Taylor Dummy tried to make a break for it, but Anya released a high pitched shrill, and two shots barked out and I heard an unearthly scream that became choked as two bodies crumpled to the floor.

I pulled out my gun and aimed it at Anya. The gun spat flame but it was Malik's blood that spattered upon the floor. He turned to give me a scared look, his gun uselessly firing into the air before he fell like a sack of potatoes. I noticed that Anya had now cowered behind Yannis, so I began to aim at him but Stella violently grabbed my arm and dragged me behind the crate as a staccato of bullets filled the room with echoed violence.

My mind fleetly registered Stella's gun recoil and Yannis jerked backwards clutching his arm, his gun bouncing across the floor towards us. I hurled another couple of shots towards Anya but only succeeded in hitting the wooden door. The air was thick with cordite.

"You're out of practice I see," remarked Stella icily. I turned towards her and saw that she was trembling.

Silence, when it came, brought with it a coiled tension. We waited, daring not to speak; milking the room for any clues of how to escape.

Anya's voice filled the room. "Your friends are still breathing. Throw down your weapons or else I will kill them."

We peered around the drum and saw her lifting Gordo's head up. He was moaning and obviously alive. George looked decisively dead; Taylor Dummy groaned.

My lips trembled. "What now?"

Stella looked down and gazed at my crotch. Her reply was monotone. "For one thing, do up your fly: let's try for a dignified surrender!"

With our hands raised above our heads, we slowly walked into that naked room.

Anya led us at gunpoint along a myriad of winding corridors until finally we appeared to be approaching a dead end. We waited patiently for some moments staring at this blank wall ahead. Anya looked briefly indecisive. I turned slowly towards Stella; by her expression I knew we shared one mind: grab the gun whilst there was this short interlude.

Inexplicably our attention was drawn towards a whirring noise and then at the wall. Slowly it swung back to release a shaft of golden light which revealed a short corridor leading to a room beyond; we were pushed through and into that room.

Once inside, I became focussed upon the back of a huge red leather chair which seemingly was attached to a bulbous dark purple head. It turned and peered around the chair back. I looked into cold red eyes; the face if you could call it that, was more the shape of a festering potato. Huge thick rubber lips spread into a sickly grin.

"Ah! There you are. I was so looking forward to meeting you both. Forgive me if I don't get up."

"The Gropie – I thought you were dead!" gasped Stella as Anya roughly pushed us forward and tied us up. With a hypnotised stare she left us to our fate.

My stomach heaved as I caught the smell of rancid cat pee. I noticed Stella gasp at the sight of a yellow leather bound book upon the desk. We both jolted at seeing the mummified corpse which sat crumpled up on a chair at the far end of the table.

"My name's Godfried Edrich. Welcome, please do come in." He followed our gaze. "Meet the human Godfried Edrich who sadly has now outlived his usefulness."

I started to tremble and fought hard to stay in control. "Don't you know there's a bomb about to explode back there?"

He grunted. "Yes I do, exciting isn't it?"

Stella's interest still lay upon the desk. I watched as she strained her neck and then mirrored her posture. Of course! What else could it be but that yellow leather bound volume?

Godfried looked at her and then across at me before resting a curious gaze back towards Stella. "I see we must enjoy the same taste in books?"

"What is it you want?" she snapped.

The rubber lips dribbled green pus. "I want this planet," he snarled.

The fact that we had been strung up like a bunch of bananas on his heavy duty coat stand nailed to the wall, didn't fail to amuse Godfried as he guffawed in mirth at our attempted struggles to keep upright; our feet barely touching the floor.

He took the book and opened the spine to reveal a secret compartment. "Clever place to conceal a weapon."

"What do you hope to gain by all this destruction?" I cried.

His lips opened wide enough to swallow the table. "Destruction – my dear man, you are deluded."

"You maniac: there's a Virus Q bomb about to explode!"

He pointed a finger towards me, like a teacher scolding a pupil. "Triethe is an organisation that fertilises, encourages, and then prunes deadwood from ailing cultures." He preened himself. "Earth will soon become devoid of all life – then it will be reborn and sold off into a viable lucrative market. We've done it before on other worlds like yours that are tottering on self oblivion. We help them commit suicide and then find interested buyers."

I gave him my smile reserved for failed job interviews. "You will liquidate all life forms on this planet – purely for profit!" My body ached as I tried to free myself. "You won't get away with it – TRINITY are on to you."

"You lack vision; what a pity."

"Of course!" I exclaimed. "You think TRINITY won't find out or investigate because they will assume that a global nuclear war has broken out."

"Bravo for you for being so clever whilst being so late to do anything about it." He reached across the table and took hold of the digital clock. He reset it for 20 minutes.

Stella gave a haughty laugh. "They will not be fooled this time..." Her voice tailed off.

"I do so would like to carry on with these little chats, however I have a teleport beam to catch and I must not miss it."

When he activated the clock, the glowing red pulse quickened and increased in brilliance. I could just hear the gentle monotonous tick.

His next move was to stare at us; his breath stank of rancid meat as he spoke. "I've given you the means to watch your inquisitive lives ebb away. Enjoy it while you can!"

He picked up the phone and urgently tapped numbers. "There you are Anya. I have decided to move forward our operations. My helicopter will arrive in five minutes time on the Rose Lawn. Have your pleasure with our hostages, but do not fail to be there!"

Abruptly his entire body became encased in swirling light and vanished.

Stella screamed hysterically. "I thought Transit had been closed down – how could he escape like that?"

CHAPTER FORTY EIGHT

Flushed Tomato

Time Loop Blue

00:00:20:00

Anya prowled around the room, her face flushed like an oven-cooked tomato. There was a gun in one hand and a tumbler full of water in the other. She then leant towards my face, and caressed my chin almost lovingly with the back of her gun. Abruptly then, she raised it as if to strike. For a moment I noticed the manic gleam; felt her garlic breath, short and sharp upon my face, but then she backed away quietly laughing to herself and opened her mouth as if to speak: I didn't need to be the genius to know what was on her mind.

"You're not so clever, now are you little man?"

I didn't say anything. What could one say being trussed up like a turkey at Christmas and gazing at the wrong end of a gun? There was a frisson of excitement in her voice. "What is to be done with you?" she said taking a sip of water.

Be damned, I was going to speak my mind. "Can't you see that he has left you in the lurch?" I watched her mood change as she digested what I had said. Carefully she placed her tumbler upon the window ledge and looked at me in puzzlement. Action was called for. "Don't think for one moment you're not expendable too. After all, he's eliminated everyone who could possibly link him with his Organisation. Are you next?"

In one bound she flew over to me and I howled in pain as her gun connected with my jawbone. I flinched which caused the already groaning coat rack to give way. We crashed in a heap on the floor. Her manic eyes bore into me.

"How dare you," she screamed

Stella struggled to move around so that she too faced Anya. "He's right and you know it. He is hell bent on worldwide destruction – what part of oblivion don't you understand?"

She raised her hand as if to strike. "Shut up you stupid cow; his main aim is to bring world leaders to their knees and then to a lucrative ransom table."

Stella scoffed. "You know about that dummy Trigger, don't you? Perhaps the real one is already in place?"

I saw a flicker of doubt in her mind and slowly she lost that manic expression.

"Listen to her woman. That shrivelled corpse is your answer. There's only one thing you can't do: and that's run away from a Viral Q device that has the capacity of many hydrogen bombs going off all at once!"

Her eyes held caution. "A Viral Q what?"

"A nuclear bomb!" I screamed.

A helicopter noise far off precipitated a reaction from her: she sprang up to gaze through the window. The throb of the rotor blades increased in volume. She then cursed in our direction and raced towards the door. Intuitively we both rolled for cover underneath the table, dragging the stand with us. Mercifully the ropes felt slacker and I wriggled to free one arm.

She turned and raised her gun. "Now you die!" I heard a shot and a chunk of wood from the right table leg whizzed past my ear. The door swished shut; a lock clicked. Quickly in case she returned, I released myself and Stella from the ropes. She leapt towards the window. "Come here and look. The helicopter is early so perhaps the Gropie wanted her to escape after all."

"Do we have time to disarm the bomb?"

"No we do not." Her face fell. "Sorry."

Far below we saw the coloured dot of Anya running towards the parked helicopter and climb inside. As the craft climbed upwards it drew level with us, I noticed that the pilot seemed to turn and look in our direction.

Abruptly the craft exploded like a rocket on Bonfire Night; a prelude to an intense shake and growl from within the building. A blinding flash of sheet lightning streaked across the sky and then the entire world appeared to roll up like a venetian blind.

"This is it!" cried Stella grasping me tightly.

Inside the shaking room the tumbler of water on the window ledge toppled over splashing my wrist watch with liquid. A sudden electric shock to my wrist brought back a distant memory.

"Oh no!" I exclaimed. "Not now."

CHAPTER FORTY NINE

Goodbye Sucker

Time Loop Purple – Blue

00:00:05:00

The room had become still life. My attention was drawn towards the table and that silent clock with its second hand frozen between one and zero seconds. Stella held the look of the Mona Lisa.

Life – or death?

Was I experiencing the plight of Schrödinger's cat? Life and death within total balance? Strange thoughts wandered through my mind as if they had been given a licence to roam there. I re-lived my time that had been spent tumbling through the various dimensions chasing after Auster which had ended in his death. It was so surreal, but then Stella shone through as vibrant as a rainbow.

Then I saw white gloves, some with strange motifs, some without.

Perhaps Robertson wore his at his concerts, but Auster?

He hated music. He loathed it. He didn't always though?

I recalled how his face was as bright as a button playing violin on my sofa. I also remembered seeing his white gloves.

That violin was another link to the past when we both were in a pantomime.

A pulse of blue light from within my watch rapidly caught my attention. I noticed a 3D image materialise there. It was of my old school and so I gazed mesmerised at it. Perhaps it worked like that enigmatic shoe box I had seen whilst on Transit. I concentrated intensely upon that displayed image.

Abruptly the flash changed into intense purple and enigmatically I was sucked into my watch.

CHAPTER FIFTY

Queen Whisky

Time Loop Purple – Blue

00:00:20:00

I looked out across the footlights and trembled. At the other side of that light barrier were hundreds of dewy-eyed parents eagerly expecting a pound Stirling performance from a two shilling and sixpence entrance fee.

They saw a seventeen year old boy dressed as a cat. From the wings I trembled knowing the fear he felt inside: that boy was me! At least I couldn't see the audience because of the footlight glare. Like a phantom, I stood alongside myself and it was unnerving to be able to offer no form of help or guidance. My performance was not RADA material, but I watched enthralled as my younger self pranced and meowed around the stage.

Finally, out of breath and with knees knocking to the beat of the piano (played by Mr Gordon -nicknamed Flash) we stopped and gazed transfixed into the glare; there was a defiant wriggle of my tail.

To my left, trying to wave me off with his script was Mr (Gobbo) Stroud, Head of Drama.

We obliged willingly.

His script and my head connected. We both flinched and cowered. Gobbo's face peered close up; eyeball to eyeball. "I know this is first night, but please try and remember your lines? Try not to act the idiot!"

He proceeded to droll on and on. I watched helpless as my crestfallen younger form slunk away to the safety of the Wings. Next to each other now, we both nodded almost with shared thoughts: his nickname of 'Gobbo' was apt.

Tonight however even 'Gobbo' appeared magical. This was the ultimate experience and a glance in a wall mirror prop confirmed it: I possessed no reflection!

I had somehow managed to propel myself back in time and now was re-living my school days. What could I do with all my attained knowledge and experience, on tap? If only I could climb back inside my seventeen year old body? I turned and gave my younger self an envious stare.

Abruptly there was high pitched laughter from behind. I twisted around and became confronted with three girls aged about seventeen who were dressed in black tights and baby doll nighties. From the words written in black upon their backs, I realised that they were:

Hey.

Diddle – One.

Diddle – Two

I stood spellbound as Diddle – Two came across and pulled at my tail. "Hi sexy," she sniggered and to the obvious delight of her mates, stroked my furry bottom.

This frivolity was cut short by the urgent voice of Gobbo, his script waving like a swan on take-off. "You're on next. Go on now and hurry!" His stage whisper appeared to echo around the building.

I observed Flash hastily flick to another page of music and to the haunting clonk, clonk, and clonk of the piano, the girls skipped, and hopped onto the stage and meandered towards the set that consisted of three brass beds. They climbed into them. The bedroom furniture and windows were painted upon the surrounding walls. Van Gogh might have appreciated the style.

My attention wandered into the ethereal shadows of the audience and then my heart stopped at the sudden realisation of it all. Amongst those faces, good humoured and glad of the night away from the telly were mum and dad. They had died many years ago – yet here in this time period they would be young and vibrant. Emotions raw and instant welled up inside me and my face flooded with tears.

I detected movement stage right. Peering through the footlights was a very terrified Austerfield. He was dressed as a fiddle and clutched within his white-gloved hands was a violin. The stage dimmed and as blue light spilled over the brass beds, a yellow spotlight highlighted centre stage.

Gobbo was waving again. The music struck up, and we were on.

"A feel a reet wassock," wailed Auster, as we entered the spotlight.

I noticed that around his wrists were glittering watches and I guessed they must go right up to his armpits.

My younger self chastised him. "You'll get expelled if you try and off-load that lot in here, button up your shirt sleeves, you daft idiot and start playing."

As Auster carefully lifted up his violin, I cringed and prayed for a miracle. The bow hovered and there was some sort of contact. The instrument screeched and howled in torment; it all seemed in slow motion. After only a few minutes, a rapidly disgruntled audience had had enough. Slow hand claps followed. Frozen to the spot, we gazed beyond the footlights, and pleaded for mercy from a now hostile 'cat-calling' audience.

Suddenly a man leapt from his seat and entered the central aisle. He paused momentarily and glared up at us. Auster stopped playing; tears rolled down his face. "That's my father," he sobbed. We both shivered as he stormed out towards the exit.

I knew this was a pivotal moment, yet I felt so uncertain and confused about what to do next. Time however – even at this TL, was not on my side. I remember Tomb's urgency regarding fragmented Purple states – how long had I got before it evaporated taking me with it? Fear welled up inside, but my instinct was to counter this with analytical reasoning. Could I move objects like Tombs had done in Purple TLs? I pushed at my younger self but my hand went right through his body.

"Do something!" I bellowed in my younger ear knowing how futile these actions would be. However something registered because he turned with a look of surprise.

"Auster," screamed my younger self grabbing at his arm and shaking it. A shirt button flew off. "For God's sake *do* something."

Abruptly I felt a mild electric jolt and the entire stage appeared to stretch and twist like rubber. A Gaussian blur began to sweep over the audience accompanied with an intense wind like roar. Nausea overcame me and I nearly collapsed. Everything then stopped like a jammed film reel in a projector as an unearthly stillness permeated the school hall.

00:00:00:00

Time Loop Purple-Green

00:00:05:00

Looking down at my watch bezel I saw that it had settled into a steady rhythm of TL Green with a Purple outer ring. I stood in amazement as the whole room snapped back into focus. Wasting no time I decided on another course of action. My ghostly body shoved against Austerfield and this time I felt some resistance. This proved too violent a push however and for one dreadful moment I thought he would fall off stage; more shirt buttons popped off. His face became scarlet with rage as he regained his balance.

"Ross. You swine! You'll feel my violin over your head for this."

What stopped him in his tracks as he raised the instrument was the gasp from the front row as his exposed arm revealed numerous watches that glittered up to his wrist.

"Oh gawd!" he blurted out which caused a murmur of disapproval from the front row.

"Improvise you daft pudding!" I heard my young self say. "You're good at jokes; tell them one."

An expectant silence slowly permeated around the hall; all eyes appeared focussed and clearly enthralled.

"Well OK," he said, waving his violin frantically and squaring up to his now attentive audience. "Since I'm on the fiddle.... Anyone want to buy a watch?" He raised one arm and then slowly repeated with the other. "And this side is very much second hand."

From the front came a titter that cascaded into a ripple of laughter around the theatre. He waited for a moment and then said: "They are going cheap, or cheep but they can make other noises as well!"

Auster then began an impromptu gag routine that suddenly caused the entire audience to fall recklessly about in raucous mirth. I too felt overawed as tears welled up in my eyes.

This intensity of laughter only stopped when Gobbo poked his puzzled head from the side wing, weighed up the situation and began to clap in admiration which precipitated an enthusiastic response from everyone. Standing at the back was Auster's father who finally held his hands high and clapped with vigour. Auster jumped off the stage and ran towards him.

As the curtain fell, a white hooded figure came through the opening and stood alongside me. I felt my hand being squeezed. I turned.

"Well done," Tombs said his face full of admiration. "Queen Whisky takes the King – how inspirational!"

It was the last thing I remembered before the room swirled up and sucked me into her bosom.

CHAPTER FIFTY ONE

A Flight Pleasure

Time Loop Green

00:02:35:00

The Teleport this time took my breath away as I was unceremoniously dumped within a busy dusty street. I smelt sea salt and barbeque on the sultry breeze; it was dusk.

For a brief moment I paused to assess my surroundings. What had Tombs planned for me now? In front of me there was a sign that read 'Appaloosa Taverna'. With its wooden frontage and thatched roof I guessed I was back in a coastal sea port near Piraeus Greece. The obvious clue was Ouzo bottles adorning the outside tables and Greek waiters gossiping to each other.

Out of the corner of my eye I spotted the white suited Auster with his long confident strides; I fell into step discretely behind. This was no chance thing: Tombs was behind this encounter and I was back inside his laboratory maze once more.

The *click click click* of his boots seemed to resonate along the promenade. He paused momentarily to gaze across the bobbing ships anchored in the harbour. They looked more like cocktail sticks in an enormous drink. His next move was towards a cabin cruiser that was sleek and long, built for tremendous speed; closer inspection revealed its name: The Rigel. Casually he walked up the gangplank unlocked the cabin hatch and went inside. Casting caution aside I crept up towards the hatch. I heard male voices. The narrative was mostly Greek but occasionally Auster's English expletives resonated. Looking through the window; my heart froze.

Inside there were two men facing a third man whose back was against the cabin door. I recognised Auster but not his colleague; the third man was that villain Yannis waving his arms wildly. Suddenly a dark coloured automatic appeared in his right hand; it pointed at Auster; his thumb flicked off the safety lock. My heart skipped a beat.

My instincts kicked in before self preservation entered my head. I shoulder butted the door for all it was worth and felt stiff resistance which abruptly melted away as the door gave way; I collided with Yannis. There was a 'crack' of pistol fire mixed with splintering of wood; Auster kicked away the gun from the now supine assassin. I followed through with a well aimed fist to his face. We both looked down upon a now unconscious body.

Auster barked. "Manolis get some rope to tie up our guest."

"I hope you don't mean me?" I said taking a deep breath and nursing my bruised right hand.

Auster gave me a look of deep admiration. "From now on you are going to be called Mr Magic for that stunt you just pulled; talk about the cavalry coming over the hill in the nick of time. Phew!" Abruptly he fainted. Manolis grabbed him and laid him down upon an adjacent bunk. Above his head I noticed a row of books and right in the middle was a yellow leather bound volume. Whilst their attention was distracted I extracted it from the shelf.

"Not so fast," snarled Manolis as abruptly a gun barrel nuzzled against my neck.

Auster lifted his head and lightly brushed the gun away. "He's one of our men – so let him be," he looked directly at me. "Although I would like an explanation as to why you have fancied that particular book?"

I gazed back at them both and mentally saw my chessboard. My hand hovered over each piece and placed White Pawn to King-Bishop3, Black Pawn to King 4. Second move: White Pawn to King Knight4, before finally placing empty Whisky – Black Queen to Rook 5. The next thought that popped into my mind was the image of Austerfield reclined upon my sofa in rapture playing the violin.

"Our mutual business colleague Mr. Michael Tombs requires this rather urgently," I demanded.

Auster gave me a thoughtful look. "I too know a little about his private little mission! But..." He proudly punched his chest, "you and I will personally take it to Michael. There is my helicopter outside and a little jaunt to England will do just that."

I gazed down upon my watch pulsating with its green display. "There's a faster way of travel," I said firmly but then hesitated at twisting the bezel. A smile invaded my entire face. Of course; I had all the time in the world!

"It would be a pleasure to fly with you," I announced proudly.

CHAPTER FIFTY TWO

The Prime Minister Awaits

Time Loop Green

00:00:05:00

My mind took some time to re adjust: like waking from heavy sleep. Perhaps it was the sight of my neighbours' startled looks as a helicopter lifted from our quiet cul-de-sac and into the blood soaked twilight. Or perhaps it was seeing Auster's sublime face playing the violin, but suddenly reality kicked in and I was standing like a zombie facing my chess set. I heard a polite cough from behind and then Michael stood adjacent to me; from within his flowing robes he produced the Red Mercury device.

"Observe: 'The Fools Mate'!"

"What!" I cried.

His voice held urgency. "I have finally got what I required. However our colleagues are still in danger."

I felt the colour drain from my face and a black cloud swirled before my eyes as my body gave way.

When it cleared I felt guiding hands lift me onto to the settee. "You appear distressed; let me assist?"

My shoes were removed and replaced by slippers. "Thank you," I murmured and then tried to raise myself up. I gripped him by the arm. "Why do you still treat me like a caged rat running around a laboratory maze?"

He gave me a direct stare. "Have you still no insight? I have observed three species within EarthZoo and only the Tengalese appear to have evolved into a well balanced civilisation." He sighed deeply. "Why then should I treat you any more different than a lab rat when Earth and the Gropie species have clearly shown no evolutionary progress in the slightest?"

"I've failed to save Earth then – I'm so sorry."

The whisky bottle was placed in my hand; a whisper of a smile invaded his face. "That statement is illogical; success is failure turned upon its head. However this is not a safe place to stay for too long because the Earth is still locked within fragmented Time Loops and could disintegrate at any time."

My jaw dropped. "You mean...?"

"It would be more prudent to discuss this matter in a place of safety."

00:00:00:00

Time Loop Purple

I am floating in a weightless slumber between Heaven and Earth?

I hear fleeting human whispers that intertwines with the play of the sea.

Ebbing and flowing; then a drifting silence.

I am at peace; I am.

Oneness.

"Are you rested?"

That voice invades my mind like a light switch being turned on. I open my eyes to find I am slumped within the alcove.

Across to my right there is Michael relaxing in his usual place close to the window; I smell fresh lavender.

"Observe your success."

"Success – I have failed?"

He moves over towards the strange box, adjusts the dial and returns. "You cannot ever fail me Ross. Success is failure turned upon its head."

"How can this be?"

"Here is your answer. Observe your planet Earth."

I gaze enthralled as the black void ripples and slowly a new image appears. We suspend like a spacecraft in a close parking orbit. It is bright blue and fluffy and I want desperately to reach out and hug it; abruptly it becomes bland and grey, totally devoid of life. Involuntary I gasp out loud.

He raises his hand. "Your personal contact with me still leaves you exhausted. Perhaps you must rest awhile?"

"I am feeling fine – just a little dizzy – but please continue."

"As you can observe; Earth is in two states now. However with your help I can now stabilise the Time Loops."

"Don't tell me: let me guess- Schrödinger's problem; the cat was never in or out of the box?"

He looks approvingly. "Very good; you do show promise – but I expect nothing less from you now." He raises a finger. "Your surmise is correct. However there is more that you can deduce?" he holds up the leather bound book. "So – *please* do continue."

"I wish I could!"

I notice a stifled laugh at my bewilderment. "Ha! And still you do not comprehend." From within the folds of his garment he reveals a letter. He puts it into my hands. "Taken from your mantelpiece; please open it."

Mystified I do his bidding. "Why! It is the letter from Auster." I release a huge sigh of relief. "I have been invited to his wedding anniversary and..." I scrutinise the oblong card. "These are two flight tickets to Athens. I am so glad that finally he remarried."

I observe a fleeting look of admiration. "Forgive my emotion, but it is a relief to know now that this mission is finally over."He momentarily pauses and I observe tears hover in balance within his eyes; he turns away. "However you are quite wrong with that assumption of a remarriage. In this Time Loop – TL Green, his wife did not die needlessly. Here they both lead fulfilled happy lives." He faces me square on. "And it's all down to you."

I shake my head in disbelief. "What have I done – my main concern was saving the Earth." I could see he was clearly moved because he sighs and turns away again.

"Again you are very wrong. Your action has touched others – and they have done likewise. Good creates more good."

"Surely we are at stalemate: the Gropie has won and destroyed the Earth; your TRINITY team Ben and Stella are doomed forever. What more is there to say?"

He quickly turns to face me; there is a concealed laugh. "No, you are quite wrong! Both Stella and Austerfield fulfil their missions successfully. Your work too is done due to your intervention in Greece. In my hands is the solution which prevents any catastrophe you have described ever happening. The Gropie cannot escape because of the confinement within EarthZoo TL Blue which is more secure than any prison. The Gropeni species have failed their probationary period and therefore are expelled from the Forum Community. However I am disappointed with you for not understanding the task set for you." He pauses and I detect the return of the 'vet and pet dog' relationship. In my mind's eye I relive the 'Fool's Mate. Watching the pieces move around the chessboard I feel a sliver of ice trickle down my spine. "This is all some form of test – isn't it?"

He points outside and I follow his gaze and become bedazzled by the view as once more we become suspended amongst galaxies. "Each speck of cosmic dust is an evolutionary process. You are witness to birth, death and rebirth."

"But....?" My voice tails off as I become lost within the infinite of space and the meaning to his words. Abruptly there is a mind connection to which my whole being succumbs. I suddenly feel ridiculously elated by it all. Time – space; all simplistic concepts of..."

He grasps my arm firmly. "Enough! What I say now will one day make sense. You have revealed that your Earth species *have* shown great promise however slow they will take to evolve. The possession of your trinket technology is no precursor to wisdom however. He turns to gaze out of the window. "Our Galactic Community will make official contact with your politicians in a few years from now – if your species continues in their upward evolutionary path..." He displays a brief glance of affection. "And I have chosen you to become our official liaison between them."

I look surprised at him. "Why choose me?"

"Life is not how high you can climb or length of stride. It is all about how well you can survive. Your proof of that has given purpose to your life: *this* was your destiny all along!"

"We are not all terrorists and extortionists – there are good people on Earth too."

Michael Tombs gives a knowing smile. "It took me time to evaluate your species correctly; self interested terrorism still plagues your planet however." He appears embarrassed and turns to look outside. "However I have grown to love your planet with all its diversity."

"Will I ever see Stella again?"

He swiftly turns. "That diary of yours will become useful." He walks over towards the table and adjusts the control.

"Observe," he commands.

We are now at street level and looking at an open black coloured door flanked by two policemen. Inside to my right is an unusual black wooden box. Open sided it contains a seat. I then perceive long corridors and a sweeping staircase whose walls contain pictures. To my surprise I recognise some as past Prime Ministers. Abruptly this vision vanishes to be replaced with the now familiar galactic view.

He walks back to look intently at me, his voice urgent. "Presently I will make it possible for you to visit that location..."

I involuntary gasp. "But that's No10 Downing Street!"

He briefly nods. "Whilst there the Prime Minister of that time period will make contact with you; for him it will appear as a chance encounter; to you it is not. It is crucial that you say these words to him verbatim. He leans over and whispers in my ear.

I move away astounded. "You want me to say that: – 'I am writing a book about the future. And from its pages the children of tomorrow will thank you for saving them from...'"

"No! That is not right! The children of tomorrow *thank you* – present tense if you please. Aboard this Transit Station we abide in the *'forever present'*." I see reproach upon his face. "Time space rules do not apply here. As you speak to him, the future will become the present." He pauses. "And you must end with..." He whispers again in my ear.

"What does it all mean?"

"You cannot ask that: the Prime Minister is my concern not yours! But I insist you repeat verbatim once more what I have told you. Eventually you will play your part in that mission."

I did his bidding and finally add. "Yes I have it all memorised now." Even more mystified than before I ask apprehensively. "Does that mean – what I think it means?"

At my questioning look he took a deep intake of breath and his face becomes thoughtful. "Oh yes, and much more! Mankind must evolve into a more civilised species which our Galactic Community can interact with. You have briefly experienced enlightenment. When your species does likewise there is hope." He stands and holds out a hand to me to follow him. "When I revolve this wheel..." He makes his way over towards the strange box. "You will be returned." As if on impulse he takes the yellow volume and points to the secret compartment. I gasp at its contents. He looks steadfast at me; his features expressionless. "And finally to your last – and poignant question: Will you ever see Stella again?"

I watch mystified as his body liquefies into a solid flowing pillar of white light.

"Well, what do you think?"

CHAPTER FIFTY THREE

Air Tickets

Doorsteps come in all shapes and sizes and York's Micklegate has its fair share. My favourite one is half way up or halfway down this street depending on your viewpoint. After a good or a bad night out, it's my final resting place.

Tonight or perhaps more accurately 2am early morning was however a deviation to this rule. This doorstep felt familiar yet it was further up the street. Although cold and wet (it had been raining) vital things were missing. I should be totally drunk as normal at this time and the inclination of the cobbled road (it's on a hill) should be swaying pleasantly so that I have to hang on to the doorway. Now however I have never felt so level headed; practically buzzing. The last time I felt like this was after my divorce five years ago! It was to be short lived of course with mother dying and then losing my job, all within two months of each other.

I realised now that this was no excuse to go to pieces and turn into an alcoholic. I had hit rock bottom and then discovered a basement attached to it.

Fragmented thoughts filled my mind. My previous recollection was last night in my living room. There was a gap between that memory and now but this morning painful thoughts had taken on a fresh perspective and had become soft focussed and manageable. I had become a new dynamic person squatting within this No 84 mouse grey painted doorway; there was a purpose in my life: if only I could remember it!

Plainly focused within my left hand was an empty whisky bottle. I marvelled at feeling its texture. The equation – alcohol plus mouth- should equal oblivion? Another missing point was my clothes: they were as dry as parchment yet outside my doorway the rain was pelting down. The final thing that spooked me was on my feet. I was wearing carpet slippers. Now I know that occasionally I am forgetful but tonight coupled with all the other irregularities, that took the final straw. I began to shake and it wasn't with the cold. Something nuzzled against my left thigh. Looking up at me with shiny red eyes was a rat the size of a small cat. We gazed at each other with curiosity and silence. The rat had wet black fur, slender delicate paws and shimmering whiskers. It began to wash itself vigorously. "Don't forget behind your ears," I silently mouthed.

Down the far end of the street the echo of footsteps, sharp on the dawn air began to hold dominion. Fearing that it might be the police, I cowered within the doorway. A figure abruptly appeared. All black glasses, white overcoat and black hair he scrutinised me closely.

"There you are – how are you feeling?"

"I am fine thank you – just taking a rest." I scrutinised him closely. "Do I know you?"

He turned as if to go. "Don't worry; it will take some time to adjust to your new surroundings."

He took off up the street and I watched transfixed at this retreating form. The rat too then scurried off into the rapidly advancing dish water sun.

I stood up to go home. An abrupt thought trickled into my mind. I am in love with Stella, if only I could find out where or more importantly, who she is? And then poking out of my coat pocket were two flight tickets. Upon my wrist was a genuine Rolex; I felt the bee's knees!

My gaze finally fell upon the bottle and then in the direction of Black Glasses.

"What do you want me to do now?" I cried.